That Nantucket Summer

That Nantucket Summer

Doreen Burliss

Copyright © 2023 Doreen Burliss

All rights reserved. No part of this book may be reproduced in any form or by any electronic or mechanical means, including information storage and retrieval systems, without permission in writing from the publisher, except by reviewers, who may quote brief passages in a review.

Paperback: 979-8-9861095-2-7
Ebook: 979-8-9861095-3-4

Library of Congress Control Number: 2023908046
Printed in Boston, MA

That Nantucket Summer is a work of fiction. The names, characters, businesses, places, events, locales, and incidents are either products of my imagination or used in a fictitious manner. Any resemblance to actual persons, living or dead, or actual events are coincidental.

For Nantucket,
you had me at "Yesterday's Island"

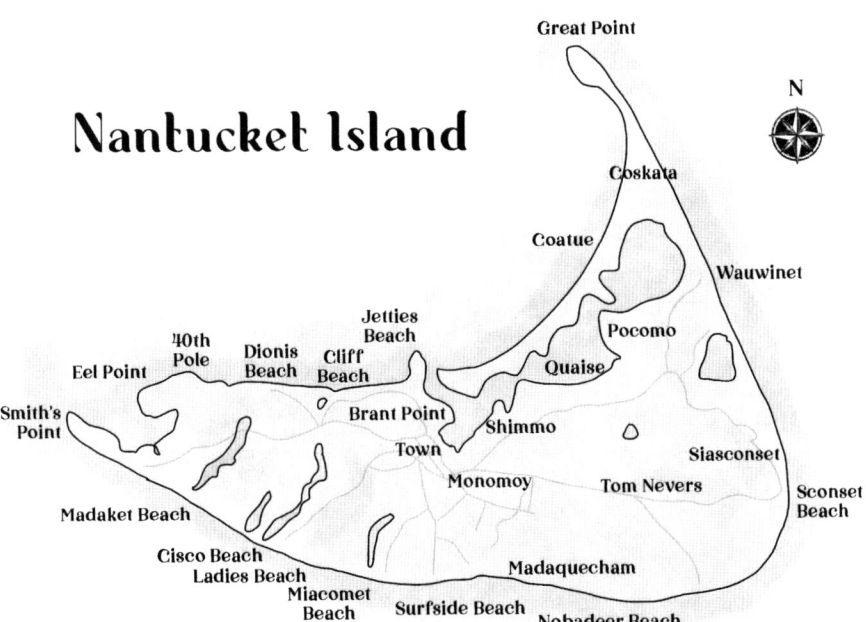

Chapter One

NIC STOOD ROOTED ON watery legs in the walk-in closet holding a fat roll of plastic bags, about to turn decades of her dad's precisely collected and strictly organized wardrobe into piles for the Salvation Army. *I can do this,* she said to all the silent versions of her father, fingering the flannels on down the line, *what we keep means more than what we let go.*

She wondered how much of this ache she'd predicted and how much of it was a black surprise. The quiet pounded. She grabbed her phone and chose an indie rock playlist. The last thing she needed filling the space was the nostalgia of Seals & Crofts or Jim Croce from childhood car rides, with her parents up front keeping them safe and headed in the right direction. She set her phone on the shelf of hats — *so many hats* — and turned to face the measured rows of wooden hangers displaying a lifetime of phases and moods, the cast of characters her dad allowed himself.

Before she removed the first shirt from its hanger, she tried to make sense of her dad's order: dress shirts, casual shirts, plaids, flannels, and then the parade of chambrays. When had he started ordering from Stio? And Carbon2Cobalt? *So cute*! And then there were the things from the decades with her mom — it was losing her all over again. Tears welled and her throat throbbed. Nic would never see him wearing any of these things again. She would never see him again.

And no one would ever regard her with the same sense of awe as her father.

It was unseasonably warm for late May and the central air goose-bumped her bare arms so she slid a worn L.L. Bean flannel from her mom's era off its hanger and onto her body. A hug from another lifetime. She carefully unbuttoned the top button of the first shirt and folded it crisply before laying it at the bottom of the giant clear plastic bag. The ones she had no memory of him in were easier, some pressed, just back from the cleaners. But the ones that still smelled like him undid her. She hugged them, breathed them in, and whispered, *I love you, Dad* with each gentle fold.

The tender ballast of all the years landed at once. Both parents gone now. With her heart tripping over its next beat, she felt childlike, a kite cut from its spool.

She kept his suits from the courtroom days in their garment bags, folded ties in half, and his khakis in thirds. When in the wild world did he get *skinny jeans*? Oh, sweet Jesus, those had to be a gift from Tina, her father's first girlfriend after her mother died, trying to young him up, get him closer to her ridiculous age.

Gino Tucci had been too charming for his own good.

This was too good not to document in *Snapchat* to her siblings and grown children; "can you picture Papa in these?" she captioned it.

Laughing felt so deeply good.

Oh, the way his shoes still held the form of his feet...that familiar size and strength. The command he reigned in his size fourteens. Nic thought of all the places those shoes had taken him with her mother and siblings, the miles covered, the mountains climbed — with each child getting a turn on his back over the years — the sports fields run as a notable athlete, the country roads traipsed in Great Britain during her semester abroad, the city streets of France, Spain, and finally Italy. And how those steps always brought him back home, the place he treasured above all, his own back yard. Where he planted, weeded, watered, mowed, raked, and built things, cultivating a life for his family.

How does anyone bear when it ends? The disassembling?

Nic wouldn't be able to finish this herculean task in a day. Would it have been better or worse having her brother there to help? There'd been a flood of tears already between them. And their sister, Mia, too, but Mia had returned home to the west coast directly from the cemetery. She wanted out ASAP — only death, she'd declared, ever brought her back to the east coast. She'd done what she could but was more about the sprint than the endurance. She didn't really get it — *imagining* doing a thing bore little resemblance to being heart-deep in it.

Nic hefted what she'd been able to bag so far into her truck, wishing the bags weren't so transparent — wasn't that the tie Dad wore to her brother's wedding looking out at her? That's definitely the cozy shirt she'd gotten him last Christmas, because he was always so cold then, with snaps because buttons got to be too tricky. An avalanche of sorrow.

The hundreds of daffodil bulbs he'd planted that edged the stone wall and the front flower beds, a riot of yellow, were papery now and slouching. He'd always called them jonquils. Every year they rose up out of the cold hard ground, multiplying, defying the odds and savvy critters — what a gift to leave behind. She tried to be happy about that instead of so damn sad, but she wasn't there yet.

A painstaking process, cleaning out the house preparing it for sale, and she and her brother were under enormous pressure to do it fast to make the most of the fickle real estate market. It seemed an impossible, colossal task. But people did it all the time. One thing at a time, one day, one room, one closet, yielding towers of boxes of photos, keepsakes, cards and letters. And it all had to be completed before her trip to Nantucket.

Nicolina took the small successes as they came. Each drawer, shelf, and hook that had been relieved of her dad's clothes and shoes.

There came to be an echo to the place, creating a distance that tried to push her heart out of it. Being there alone, without her brother or dog, broke her in new ways.

But after that first trip back to the house with Snoopy after her dad died, when Snoop sprinted to his room to find him, black ears flying, white paws up on the bed, looking everywhere for him — she came undone all over again. Snoopy and her dad had been fast friends. Less than a month earlier, they'd watched "Call of the Wild" together, her dad's pick, on the leather couch. Sharing popcorn. Snoopy's first movie, Dad's first animal on the furniture.

She brought up the empty trash barrels giving honest consideration to her sister's suggestion to leave a case of beer for the waste management guys when this was over — they'd been pushing the envelope in a big way trying to avoid having a dumpster on the property. Washing up before hitting the road she tried not to spend too long on her reflection. There was a drooping. She pulled her shoulders back, reversed the curve of her posture. Her long hair hung limp and her roots were showing. Maybe it was time for a few layers. Nothing too Farrah Fawcett but just something to soften the lines. Her eyes were her best feature, a pistachio-green, a radiance that belied her grief. She felt lucky to still have a favorite thing about herself in her forties.

Behind her in the mirror the laundry door stood open and she noticed that her dad had hung a few things to dry. Every damn little thing pierced her. She pictured the care he'd taken hanging them, could hear his measured breathing — deep breath in, then out. They'd known his rare heart disease would take him down — but it gathered a cruel precipitous speed toward the end. She pictured him arranging those Dockers carefully to air dry for when he wore them next, the effort it must have cost to pinch the clips and press creases with the merciless betrayal of his usual brawn.

Enough! Evelyn, her oldest, was working an early shift and Nic needed to get home to Snoopy — he had a thing for her paperbacks and the occasional hardcover. Her son, Ben, was either still in bed or actually looking for a summer job — she really needed to make sure he knew that at age nineteen, and a rising college junior, working was not optional. Nic was glad for the hour drive back home to let thoughts come and go as they would.

Chapter Two

CADE — SHE LET THOUGHTS of him seep in like honey, a dessert she'd saved for after the harder things that needed thinking through. They'd been seeing each other for only four months but her feelings were already so much bigger than that blink of time. It had taken three years since her divorce to even consider dating and she was acutely aware of the armor that still girdled her heart.

Cade Swain was almost uncomfortably handsome; six feet, three inches tall, intimidatingly confident, with a disarming head-tilt when he smiled that drew her attention to his luscious, longish walnut-brown hair. When he looked at Nic, with the darkest blue eyes before being navy, she felt singularly remarkable. His laugh was huge, like a happy oak tree, broad and soaked in sun, and being in his company felt like a gift.

He went in and out of the most legit Australian accent on a whim, had solid juggling skills, saw the best qualities in everyone, and expected absolute loyalty from the people in his orbit — as he would offer nothing less. He was a civil engineer, bridges and tunnels were his jam, and the city of Boston kept his successful firm busy. He had an ex-wife, Reagan, Nic had never met. They'd been married for eleven years, divorced for three. They'd both rowed at Duke University but went their separate ways after graduation, reconnecting again in Boston where Reagan was in law school and Cade was climbing the ladder at CJB Group. Cade hadn't provided details but to Nic it sounded less about gooey romance and more a marriage of mutual drive and relentless ambition. And the years rolled by under their wheels. When they looked up to breathe, it turned out that Reagan could never find the right time to be pregnant, and that her career as a corporate litigator was her true love.

Nic and Cade were heading to Nantucket in two weeks for his cousin's wedding, which meant that they'd get to be there when spring turned into summer. June twenty-first was Nic's favorite day, summer solstice, the longest day, and the shortest night of the year. When she and her sister, Mia, were little, they'd put on fairy dresses and twirl with ribbon wands with their mom until dark, counting the fireflies that flashed on and off. It had always felt like the beginning of something — the fantasy of summer, enchanting, ethereal. It had seemed to Nic that her mom had always spun with her own secret dreams on those nights, like she wanted to keep that feeling in a jar like the fireflies.

Nic had visited Nantucket island once in college with friends, but they'd only had a day to bike around and see what they could see. Since then, Nantucket had become quite the destination location and she felt a jolt of excitement about being a guest at Cade's family's summer home there, and beyond intrigued that he shared the blood of one of the founding families — a true Swain descendant. But she was barely allowing thoughts in at the edges of such concentrated time with the whole family — her relationship with Cade still sparkling and tender. If things went wrong, she didn't want their gossamer bond to go with it.

As an English teacher at a private high school, Nic had the summer to read, write, and to fill her sketch pad with new drawings and ideas for her watercolor painting. She understood that along with Nantucket Island's rich history as once whaling capital of the world, it was also an artist's mecca, attracting photographers, painters, sculptors and writers alike. She couldn't wait to capture that special light *and* to get her hands on some literature about that half-imagined place called Nantucket. After so many semesters assigning *Moby Dick,* she would now have the opportunity to experience Melville's "small elbow of sand" for herself.

Chapter Three

REALTORS LIKE WOLVES LINED up at the door — finally her father's house was ready to be shown in its best, least-cluttered and de-personalized light. It would sell fast, they'd said, and be gone from her forever. On her last drive home from her dad's Nic pressed a tear away and looked over at the box of old letters sitting next to her that they'd found at the bottom of their mom's hope chest. She and Enzo hadn't had the luxury of time to sit with them, or any of the piles of catalogued years, to laugh and cry and say, *remember this*?

The drive back from her dad's Maine house was an hour most days, but summer traffic piled up at the least expected times. She'd talk herself out of worrying what Snoopy might be getting into and crank the only station that came in clear. It was always country. Carrie Underwood's "Two Black Cadillacs" came on and Nic burst out laughing. Her dad had had two relationships since her mother's passing, and thinking back to his recent service, it had given her a misplaced chuckle when she'd pictured more than one woman showing up — would they take turns laying a red rose down? Share a crimson smile and walk away?

Sorry Dad! So disrespectful. *Shit*.

She also begged the universe on a regular basis for Cade's firm's Back Bay bridge project to wrap up in time. She knew he had a solid project manager, but he could never fully relax thinking he should be on-site. The last thing she wanted was for him to have to leave the island to handle some crisis on the job. From what little he'd shared about his mother, it wouldn't be a recipe for success being left alone with her.

Contemplation circled as the miles sped past. Orphan, Nic thought, she was now an orphan. Did that even apply to grownups? (Did actual grownups say *grownups?*) Her parade of thoughts marched along to the country songs. She'd punched the radio off when Tim McGraw's "Live Like You Were Dyin'" came on. Please. She'd been through all this brutal loss before losing her mom nine years ago. Was she going to *love deeper*? *Speak sweeter*? She sure as hell wasn't going *any* number of seconds on a bull named Fu Manchu. Christ. *Sorry again, Dad*! Fuck it, he was gone. He couldn't hear her swear, burp or scold her for that third glass of wine anymore. Would she go off the rails now? Jesus.

Nic felt bipolar half the time, bouncing between the heaviness of losing her father and that summer's-around-the-corner high. And let us not forget guilt. Guilt for feeling even remotely joyful about anything. Tri-polar? Human beings were so tortured. Why couldn't they be as guilelessly euphoric twenty-four/seven like dogs?

Dogs…Snoopy. What would her velvety white and black forty-pound labradoodle be up to? She figured the groan of the garage door would tip him off and she took the stairs two at a time. She heard him careening to the door as per usual and was careful not to knock him out opening it. Kisses first, and stand-up hugs — that were technically, apparently, bad behavior. But that Nic loved more than any single thing. And, if anything, encouraged. *As if* she was going to go about setting things down on the counter first, as prescribed, before greeting him. What kind of heartless bullshit was that? She looked quickly around for a heap of shredded paper, annihilated reading glasses, dumped tote bags. *Nothing*?

"Who's mommy's *very* good boy?" she said accepting more kisses and high hugs before sitting heavily on the couch. Next to what could only be the soggy, illegible detritus of a jury duty summons and a five-dollar bill.

CanNOT be mad at him. Cannot. It was her own fault. Crate-training, blah, blah, blah. He became a puddle of rejection in the crate. She couldn't do it. Laying her head back, she closed her eyes while Snoopy spilled over her lap. In that foyer of sleep, where she felt open to any potential super-natural goings-on, she looked for her father. A sign, a bird, a whisper, *anything* to let her know he was still somewhere.

The clawing on her bare thighs as Snoopy launched off her lap to greet Ben put an end to that. "There's no food in this house," came his familiar refrain as he stood in front of the gaping refrigerator.

Salty comebacks jumped to her tongue but she bit them back. "We have eggs, there's oatmeal, probably some frozen waffles, what are you looking for?" she said before letting her eyes close again. Grief weighed a thousand pounds and was exhausting.

"I don't know," came his equally familiar response. She knew without even looking that he'd be checking the expiration dates of everything — pronouncing freezer burn on the waffles and naming the exact amount of time that had passed since the *best before* date on the eggs. Of course, she LOVED having the kids home from college for summer break, but it was going to cost her — her soundness *and* at the grocery store.

"Cut me some slack, Benj, and they sell groceries to anyone you know."

Before she got to ask about any job-updates, he was tapping back texts and out the door with a, "goin to Kelly's Roast Beef with Joey." Nic felt bad about being relieved.

She needed to stop feeling bad about stuff.

∞

Snoopy needed a long walk and so did Nic. She loved "unseasonably warm", you couldn't help but feel lighter in all ways in just shorts and a t-shirt. And she was one of those people who really did stop and smell the flowers, especially the lilacs that hedged neighbors' properties along the road. A potent blast back to every May of her life. And Snoopy wanted to sniff everything. It took a while to get a couple of miles in. *Your dog should be heeling at your left side on a short leash with slack, keeping stride with you and no stopping,* the breeder had told her. *What?* Okay, so maybe running with him was out, she'd become a walker. He was so damn adorable with all that pounce-sniffing and pretend-hunting, up to his ears in holes. It made him so happy, and she could tell by his jaunty trot how important he felt thinking he was on to something.

She let a happy anticipation sneak in about going to Nantucket. Cade's cousin was getting married at a fancy beach club and it promised to be a spectacular event. Nic couldn't wait to see what the fuss was all about. Her parents had always brought them to Maine beaches, never the south shore — she couldn't imagine them ever taking on Cape Cod traffic. And even though Nantucket was technically part of their home state of Massachusetts, it was a world away. It was a two-hour drive just to Hyannis — in the unlikely event of *no* traffic — and then another hour on a fast ferry. Nic liked the thought of it taking so much to get there, appreciated that feeling of being completely transported.

But how would it be staying in the family house with Cade's sister's family and his parents? That would be some serious togetherness. Nic knew precious little about Cade's family, figured it hadn't been necessary or even wise to know too much too soon. After surviving a marriage with a cheating husband, she was allowing herself a guarded optimism at best. But things were getting real, and fast. Wasn't that another accouterment of loss, exaggerated emotions? She supposed it either brought people together or pushed them apart. Yes, death definitely changed the way you saw things, how you felt them. Which reminded her, she really needed to remember to check in with her kids about losing their Papa, and her siblings — it was their loss too. People say they're fine, but that's almost never the whole story.

After their walk, Nic could have easily gotten sucked back into the couch for a nap, the depletion was absolute. You rose to every occasion because it was the only choice; funeral arrangements, the obituary, the need to give yourself over to other people's tears and memories — and thanking them. That was so important to do.

She had to start thinking about packing, what did people wear on Nantucket? It seemed to carry its own aura, have its own *members-only* mystery. That's how people spoke of it, wrote about it anyway. Should she be concerned that Cade had offered to watch Snoopy so she could go shopping?

At least, and through no special efforts of her own, Nic looked good in almost anything she put on, had gotten lucky with her swim in the gene pool. Her ex-husband had always gone on about her *smokin body* — but since he'd ended up spreading his Brad-ness around, any pride she'd taken in the way she looked was tainted. She'd rather read than exercise, eat steak tips instead of fish, pick pie instead of fruit, and would choose wine over water any day. But she wore clothes well, so there was that. But just what kind of clothes should she be wearing on this island of Nantucket?

This fitting-in nonsense, when did that end?

Would Cade turn into a different person there? Wear whale pants and sport coats, drink gin and tonics, have a higher laugh? How old was *old* money? And what did that mean exactly? And why was it better than new money? *Was* it better? Maybe she should stick to Maine...

Cade's parents had to be getting up there, eighties anyway — how were they both still thriving? She had to stop thinking like that, taking her orphan status so damn personally. John and Prudence Swain... Quakerish? WASPish? She also needed to stop with the judging. It was the fatigue talking, she told herself, that envy of everyone who still had parents. Jesus, was it wine-o'clock yet?

Ev texted saying she'd be working a double and Nic remembered Ben would be home late. Perfect, no dinner needed making. Wine and cheese it was. Nic decided it was as good a time as any to open the box of letters her brother had found in their mom's hope chest. She'd left it in the passenger seat of her car to be sure Snoopy couldn't snack on it. That's not quite fair, he never *ate* any of her things, just chewed them up then redecorated the house.

Great, down the stairs and out through the garage. Her back was aching from all the moving and the lifting — which had begun with the moving and lifting of her dear dad those last days, in his own home instead of a hospice house. Adrenaline tricks you, then leaves you wondering when that train ran you down.

Snoopy was very interested in the box that smelled of cedar from the hope chest. Nic removed the multiple elastics holding it together and they disintegrated one by one at her touch. She was met with a musty woody smell and was afraid to handle anything, it all looked so fragile. There were loose stacks of white envelopes and some bundled precisely with a thin red ribbon. Did her father do that? The letters all seemed to be from her dad to her mom, so that meant it was her mom who took such care; the saving, sorting and beribboning. Where were her mom's letters to him? Most likely he didn't save them. Men, she thought, tended to move mostly forward.

But Nic thought about it a minute, about the unexpected things she and her brother had found that he *did* save. Like the original, hand-graphed chore charts of their childhood and copies of each iteration thereafter — including the twenty-five cent raises and bonus chores for bonus bucks. Holding those in her hands, her dad's square all-caps printing, she was ten years old again — sullen at having to dust every rung of every chair, door jamb moldings, wainscoting, and the mullion bars of every window before making plans with her friends.

His military training glared from those pages. He'd been softer as a grandfather.

Without letters from her mother, would Nic get only one side of their epic story? She knew her parents had met in junior high school, could hear her mother telling her about the first time she ever saw Gino: *He was new in our school, and I saw him running by up the stairs and I said to myself, I'm going to marry that boy.* Nic had wanted to hear it over and over again.

A fairytale, the kind that belonged up on the big screen. Sofia Fiore, the quiet beauty at the prom in pearls and pale yellow tulle, with winsome Gino, class president and football captain, in his white tux jacket and black bowtie. It felt wrong being in that box at all, like reading someone's diary.

Why had the letters been locked away? It had taken Enzo weeks to find the key. Nic nodded off thinking of her parents as young teenagers...

She woke up at the sound of the side door latching closed, ever so carefully. Sweet Evelyn, so considerate, but once you're a mother, your whole body is an ear. Nicolina sat up, toppling the box of letters from her lap in the process. Snoopy was only too eager to help pick them up. "Drop it!" she scolded, "Snoopy, drop it *now*, you naughty boy." It appeared that before she'd drifted off, she'd untied the top bundle of letters, and now they were a strewn fan of small rectangles.

"What's all this, Mom?" Evy asked shrugging off her bag, pulling out her hair tie to set free her long milk-chocolate colored hair and crawled over to Snoopy. She had him at *who's so cute* and he dropped his prize. The letter was definitely worse for the wear, but Nick tucked it back in the box for tomorrow.

"How was work, Ev? Any celebrities leave you an outrageous tip?"

"What celebrities, how much wine have you had? Newburyport is awesome but it isn't exactly Beverly Hills — are you alright?"

"Ha, ha. Isn't it kick-off weekend for the waterfront concert series? The River Festival?"

"Um, no, that's next weekend but, okay, I get it now. Hey — remember that year just me and you went to the concert and then we went to Oregano's for dinner?" Evelyn said.

"Oh my God, of course — Kaleo was playing! We LOVED them. And Revivalists, that was awesome."

"Right — and then at Oregano's, we're sitting there waiting for our pizza and Zack Feinberg walks in!"

"I remember. And there I was looking to see if David Shaw was right behind him, ha! Wait, is Zack the one who signed your Vans? Revivalists guitar player?"

"Exactly. So yeah, I suppose a cool musician could wander in some day. That would be fun. But hey, Molly got the phone number of a pretty hot dude. I mean a little *sus* if ask me. He just wrote it on his bill, it's not like she asked for it. And then he was gone."

"Well, that's ridiculous — do people actually talk to each other anymore, I don't get it. No one knows what to do when they're face to face these days. Always this need to hide behind one kind of digital screen or another — and *this* guy — leaving his number and bolting —what even is that? Unacceptable."

Lying on her back with Snoopy curled up next to her, Evy stared at the vaulted ceiling of their family room, "I hear what you're saying, Mom, but it's just impossible to meet anyone these days. I mean, yeah, everyone talks about wanting to meet someone *organically*, but, seriously, how? Is anyone actually approaching people out in the world? Not really. I mean bars and the gym are the only places we go, concerts and music festivals, but are those actually conducive to meeting people? Ugh, and online dating sights — don't even get me started."

"Oh I know."

"Oh please. Look at you and Cade. You struck gold first time out, you know nothing!"

"Well, I had to talk to a lot of meatheads before I took a chance in person and ended up with a prince. And by talk of course I mean email and Facebook messages and all that. You know how it works, and so many phonies and illiterates, I did my time. And, no, I don't envy your generation, for a lot of reasons, but mostly this — trying to meet someone you're going to love so much you'll be willing to contribute to the demise of our environment by having a family with him and then tripling your carbon footprint!"

"Tripling your carbon footprint? What are you guys talking about?" Neither of them had heard Ben come home and were startled at his voice.

"Hey Benji, how's it goin, bro?" Ev said, "Mom's trying to commiserate with our generation about dating apps and that went straight to me meeting the man of my dreams, having kids, and the ultimate collapse of the climate, you know, the usual stuff."

"Okaayyy," Ben said, "do we have any ice cream?"

"Yass, that would be perfect, do we?" Ev said, divesting herself of the pup and heading to the freezer. *Stop it*, we have an untouched quart of Brigham's Coffee! Buckle up..."

Nic laughed, still kids after all, with their Hershey's chocolate sauce, whipped cream and sprinkles. It's the little things...

"Okay you guys, I'm going to bed. But wait, just to remind you that Cade and I are going to Nantucket in a couple weeks for that wedding, remember? And you'll be staying with your father."

"What? Ugh, I forgot about that, why can't we just stay here?" Ben said.

"Yeah honestly, Mom, we're completely capable of staying home alone."

"Not the point my dear children. I'm remembering my Portsmouth girls weekend away when you guys Snapchatted me by accident with a house full of kids, purple lights, and *not soda*!"

"Oh yeaaahh," Ev said with a smile spreading across her face and up into her hazel eyes, "that was epic, ha! Anyway — isn't it a little soon for you two to be spending a whole week with his *parents*?"

Curled on the couch with Snoopy filling the hollow her folded legs made, Nic considered her daughter's question, the one she'd been shoving to the back burner. Things had been moving fast with Cade, was that smart? She was so excited to see Nantucket that she hadn't actually pictured what the day-to-day and every night together would be like with his whole family. "Well thanks, I was trying not to think about that."

Evelyn came over with her mounded bowl of ice cream, kneeled beside the couch and hugged her mom. Of course Snoopy misunderstood it as an invitation for a lick or at least fetch and jumped off the couch to bring her his crusty hedgehog. "Oh Mommy, I didn't mean to freak you out, I'm sorry. It's gonna be super-fun, I mean a Nantucket wedding? *Dreamy*. Don't overthink it. You deserve to be so happy and I really like Cade. You never do anything for yourself, you've spent your whole adult life taking care of everyone else. It really is your turn."

"What if they don't like me, or I wear the wrong clothes, or I don't measure up to whatever scale they have? What if they're just your basic privileged, entitled white people?"

Evelyn looked confused. Checking things off on her fingers she said, "One: what, are you, twelve? And two: um, Mom? We're white."

"I know, but there are varying degrees of whiteness, don't you think? Oh this sounds all wrong...here I am imagining them as the people whose ancestors stole Nantucket Island right out from under the thousands of Native Wampanoag people already settled there."

"Wait — the *what* from the *who*? Not following."

"I should shut my mouth — a little information is a dangerous thing. From what little reading I've done about the island's history, the white man — English settlers — came to Nantucket in the mid 1600's and decided it was theirs instead, they'd purchased rights to it from some Earl who'd received it in a grant from the English Crown. How does all that work? Wampanoag tribes were already living there. Of course I need to do more research, but Cade's ancestors were among the first ten families considered to be the original *Proprietors* responsible for the English settlement of Nantucket!"

"Wow, that's pretty cool though, right?"

"It is, yes, let's leave it at that. I need to go to bed."

Chapter Four

NIC WAS A NEW woman after a solid night's sleep and charged for a new day. Since she needed new clothes for Nantucket, apparently, she decided on a Newburyport afternoon. Ev was working the early shift at Agave and Nic could totally be in the mood for Mexican. Evy wouldn't be able to join her of course, but sitting in her daughter's section would be almost as fun.

Nic's friend, Jen, had told her to try Native Sun or Amy Williams since she preferred more fitted than flowy. She was a compact five feet, four inches and felt lost in the Bohemian style of Ganesh that Jen pulled off like a Hollywood hippie. How she missed Francesca's on State Street since it closed a year ago — she and Ev used to find the cutest dresses and tops there.

She saved Jabberwocky Bookshop in the Tannery for last, that would be the best part. Nic often spent long hours there curled in a deep chair trying to limit her picks to three. She'd had the manager order her an older volume of early Nantucket history — it was in, and she wanted to see what else they might have.

A chicken avocado wrap and a margarita at a tiny table with a window where Evy waitressed was perfect. Day-drinking was a guilty pleasure. Evy popped over in between customers and Nic loved this voyeuristic opportunity of seeing her daughter's server persona — endlessly courteous, attentive, gracious. And it struck Nic in comparison with the Evy at home, how she'd often show the other side of her coin and give the people she loved the most the least margin for error.

The last stop of her Newburyport afternoon was sitting on a bench along the waterfront with her new book. The people and dog watching always got her, impossible to keep her eyes on the pages of *Mary Coffin Starbuck and the Early History of Nantucket.*

It hadn't been easy for Dave at Jabberwocky to get a hold of this yellowing paperback written by Roland L. Warren in 1987, and Nic was eager to learn as much as she could about this legendary woman who was the youngest daughter of Tristram Coffin, one of the island's original proprietors. Nic could hardly believe Mary Coffin was born in Haverhill, right next door to Newburyport. *Wow,* she whispered as she read the back cover under her breath, "As a teenager, Mary moves with her family and other pioneers from the Massachusetts Bay Colony to settle Nantucket. There, she marries Nathaniel Starbuck and experiences the early, rugged days of the settlement of that *far away island,* the encounters with the Indians, the revolt of the half-share men and the feud that split the settler group in two."

Nic looked out at the Merrimac River, the *same* river Mary Coffin grew up on before settling on Nantucket, getting married at age sixteen, and having ten children of her own — including *the very first white child to be born on the island.* Nic was a sucker for an honest love story. Growing up under her parents' umbrella of love had given her a solid belief that soulmates were real. Her crash-and-burn marriage to Brad notwithstanding. Goosebumps prickled her skin in the hot sun. She knew she'd be drawn in by this book and comparing women of her own era. While she welcomed being transported to the seventeenth and eighteenth centuries, it was going to be tough to reconcile the excessiveness of twenty-first century's Nantucket.

Ping, looking down at Cade's name on her phone shot her through with joy. While she was trying to be reservedly excited about their relationship, she couldn't deny her body's physical reaction to just getting a text from him. Even the ones that started with, *sorry...*

Hey Nic, sorry I can't make dinner tonight — supply chain issues persist — and Mark called a meeting here in town with the team to figure out how to keep the project on schedule. I'll make it up to you!

I'll take you up on that! And no worries — got a new (old) book on Mary Coffin Starbuck and early Nantucket history — will I be reading about your great-great-greats?

Maybe! Text u later. Xoxo
Xoxo

Emoji...no emoji? Ugh, technology. What were the rules? She didn't want to mess things up with this man. And while being completely honest with people was supposed to be the way to go, it was certainly not foolproof. Wasn't there such a thing as being *too* transparent, putting your every emotion out there on display? Who didn't like a little guessing, a little chasing?

She and her ex-husband had been together since college, they'd basically grown up together, knew everything about each other. Until they were *actually* grown up, and realized they were very different people from each other. That and he thought everyone deserved a little Brad in their lives. In their pants, specifically.

They'd met sophomore year at UCONN, at a frat party their first night back at school fall semester. Not being a sorority girl, Nic was dragged to SAE by her connected roommates who were rushing Kappa Kappa Gamma. They were already buzzed on Rubles vodka and Crystal Light when they arrived and promptly lined up at the keg. "I'll Follow You Down" by the Gin Blossoms was cranked and Nic couldn't tear her eyes away from the guy alternately taking his turn in a keg stand and playing pool. Brad. He had her at *stripes or solids*? And did she ever follow him down.

He'd always had a bad-boy streak that was irresistible to her. Naturally she was going to be the one to tame it. She was an English Literature major and he was Business. They complimented each other perfectly: her introspective curiosity and sunny beauty a beguiling match for his gregarious, self-assured (just this side of cocky), rugged charm. It worked. While she pursued a master's in education within the top ten percent of her class, he graduated *sorta*-cum-laude and reinvented himself again and again from one company to the next. He collected connections and colleagues while she changed diapers and mommy friends, juggling work and kids and a marriage. Hers wasn't an original story. The disconnect grew wider until they couldn't find their way back.

Nic was grateful that thoughts of Brad didn't bend her in two anymore. It had taken a while for her to reclaim her self-esteem after he blew the last chance she foolishly gave him and flunked out of marriage counseling. But he had an arsenal of sweet-talk, knew exactly what to say to her, and how to say it. And she fell for it, over and over, not willing to end their story. She tried not to revisit all the gut feelings she'd buried in the name of self-preservation. Exactly which self had she been trying to preserve?

Divorce had equaled failure in Nic's mind. And she couldn't bear to think of how her parents would feel about that, about her. They, with their big movie-love, had stayed married through thick and thin — why couldn't she manage to? So she did, for a while. Until she couldn't. Her mom had been gone by then but her dad supported her in her decision. She remembers the day she told her father that she'd asked Brad for a divorce, expecting disappointment and shame. But instead how he'd brought her into a fierce hug, resting his chin on her head for a long minute, how she'd almost folded right there at such a small and necessary kindness.

"What's that face for?" Evelyn appeared, standing over her mom's bench on the boardwalk in her black pants and shirt, hair in a loose bun, leather tote over her shoulder.

"Oh my God, you scared me Ev, yikes, I was deep in memories I guess. And not the most productive kind."

"Oh you mean Dad? Mom, look how much you've grown since then."

"Hey, who's the adult here? I don't know how you turned out so good, Evy, I was a wreck while you were at your most vulnerable, most angry. I mean do fourteen-year-olds even *need* a reason to be, how shall we say...?"

"*Bitchy*? Bitchy, I believe is the word your looking for, Mom, ha!"

"I was a mess," Nic said, "I'm embarrassed to think about it — all the crying and carrying on, how long it took me to do the right thing. Which doesn't always look like the right thing when you're in it. All I wanted was my mom, I felt rudderless without her."

Nic was reminded of the heart-to-heart conversations her own mother had trusted her with when Nic was just a teenager — when Sofia hadn't felt good enough, or *enough* of anything, for Gino, who had his whole career which grew and grew — along with his charisma. While Sofia's life revolved around her children who grew and grew, then outgrew her.

"There was no one to rock me and tell me it'll all be alright, you know, Ev? And your Auntie Mia is always somewhere else, somewhere far. Ugh, how did we land on this, looking out on this gorgeous day? Are you tired? You must be."

"I am. Tired of waiting on people, tired of wearing black, tired of screwing up and pissing off the cook. Ugh, are you sure I can't tag along with you to Nantucket?

"Awe, honey, it's not my place to invite you."

"I know, I know. I was kinda kidding — but kinda not."

They hit the gelato shop on the corner for waffle cones before heading home. Evelyn got her usual strawberry banana and Nic decided to try holy cannoli and not being sad thinking of her dad's love affair with gelato. They sat on a bench looking out at Market Square, people were so happy when the sun was shining. "So, what are you making for dinner tonight — Cade's joining, right?"

"That *was* the plan," Nic said, trying not to sound disappointed, trying not to *be* disappointed, "but now he has to stay late for a last-minute meeting. They're still having trouble getting materials. I swear to God if this screws up the Nantucket trip..."

"Mom, he *is* the Nantucket trip. It's a family wedding he is not going to miss," Evelyn said, turning her cone quickly to catch a drip with her tongue, "He's got a good team working for him, right? And no one is indispensable. Isn't that what you always tell me?"

"I know, and you make perfect sense. And why am I anxious and excited about this trip in equal parts? Rhetorical question. Meeting the parents and the whole rest of the family — and there is bound to be some kind of drama or another."

"That's the fun of it! Kick back and enjoy. Trust me, it will be all about *them*. Plus, Mom, you're one of the most chill people I know," Evy said, peeking into Nic's shopping bags. "Now show me what you bought."

They sat in the sunshine a little while longer before gathering up their things and digging for their keys. "Okay, this is me, Nic said approaching her Blue Flame RAV4 in a spot behind Sea Level. "Where are you parked?"

"Up behind Starbucks. And I brought my gym stuff so I wouldn't blow it off. I'll be home after Planet Fitness — are you still cooking dinner? I mean, no pressure at all, just planning. I could totally do a protein smoothie and be done with it."

"Good to know. But I'm sure your brother expects some side of beef or other large animal."

"Mom, stop. I swear to God or I'm going vegan."

"Right? Me too. It's just so easy throwing meat on the grill. But I hate myself for it."

"Lol, Mom. Okay, see you later, thanks for the gelato."

∞

Nic was glad, again, that Ben was out with friends, even if that meant he was eating a chicken finger sub or three. She'd made a big salad for her and Ev with all the fun stuff: walnuts, strawberries, goat cheese, arugula, and avocado, maybe she'd grill some chicken.

They were binge-watching Outer Banks. Again. "Oh, this reminds me!" Nic said to Evy, "I told you how John B looks almost exactly like my prom date right?"

"Yeah, Mom, don't rub it in."

"Going through Papa's photos I found some from the *grand march* of my senior prom — you're gonna die when you see the resemblance." Nic went to one of eleven boxes she'd labeled, stacked on the floor of the dining room, and brought back the exact photo from her memory."

"Oh my God Mom, look how blond your hair was! And omg he's so hot, how did you land him?"

"Thanks, kid. But right? I'm beat — he's all yours. Goodnight beautiful girl."

∞

Cool fresh sheets were everything. And as much as she loved snuggling with Snoopy, Nic was glad Evy had claimed him for a sleepover that night. Her muscles quietly buzzed from a long walk with the dog after Newburyport and her brain was just fatigued enough to allow her to drift off seamlessly without holding her captive. Somewhere between there and the thick molasses of sleep it occurred to her that she'd forgotten to check for a text from Cade.

Having been consumed by the sheer volume of her dad's photos, images started popping up in Nic's dreams from all the years, confusing the decades and her heart. Her dreams had always been as vivid as life but strung together clumsily without rhyme or reason. Recently, she'd welcomed especially the ones that brought her back to the house she grew up in with her parents, brother and sister. Her parents were always about forty years old in the dreams, young, robust, and with their whole lives ahead of them.

It could have been minutes or hours that she'd been asleep when she felt the bed shift beside her. Or maybe it was another dream. She caught the scent of fabric softener waft on the air as the sheet was drawn back, and the heady smell of Cade, shower-fresh, spooning her body. The feel of his muscled form against her back blended with her nocturnal musings and her mind never quite swam to consciousness. Her brain reached for concrete awareness but it slid away, leaving her in a filmy silken place.

She leaned her back into him, pressing herself deeper against the oarsman's body he maintained still as a forty-nine-year-old man. She kept her eyes closed wanting to linger in this space in-between. She felt a feather touch at her neck as he slid her long hair away. How could calloused, hard-working hands leave only a whisper of feeling? She stayed so still. When his mouth found her neck she felt it in every nerve ending.

Her breaths grew deeper, every shift of her body matching his. She pushed against him lightly, then harder, feeling the rush, the swell, the want. His body responded in kind. They were skin on skin as he slid her panties down her legs. She felt her own excitement on them as the wetness brushed her ankle.

Sometimes she worried too much about not coming, and she'd chase it away. She quieted her mind over the roar of her blood pumping as he slid inside her. Little bits of color started to float up, deep in her. A song and a laugh starting between her legs. Fully stirred and curved around her body he moved with her, until she clenched and pulsed around him.

Waves broke over her, and over and over her. Before they faded she turned to face him, leaving him briefly abandoned until she pulled him in, planting him deep inside her. The heat of his mouth on hers started a new song, a new ride. They rose and they rose, holding on and holding back, until the fountain firework, a million tiny sparks that lasted for long minutes.

∞

Nicolina woke up alone in her bed challenging her sleepy brain to give her the straight deal. She'd either had the most sensual dream of her life or a beautiful midnight visitor. She breathed in the pillow beside hers, Cade's spicy maleness lingered and she felt her body coming awake. With her eyes closed she laid back, letting her hand slide down between her legs to relieve the pulsing ache for him.

Chapter Five

AFTER A BREAKFAST SPLURGE of bacon, egg, and cheddar on a toasted plain bagel, Nic settled out on her deck in the soft morning with the box of letters from her dad's house. Since these were letters that her mother had kept, she wasn't surprised to find some from her own Gran in there too, one with a pencil sketch of a potato from her garden. She took a minute to appreciate that lost art. Today it was emails and texts, maybe a GIF on your birthday or a JibJab. There was something about a handwritten missive, preserved for all of time.

She looked back down at the small pile in her lap, thumbing through, when a jolt of recognition drew her eyes to her own printing. A letter from camp, she'd been fourteen and had long since abandoned her wildly illegible cursive. A whiff of pine and campfire rose up out of the envelope bringing with it her fear of swimming in the lake, mastering the gimp box stitch, bug juice, and Color War. It struck Nic how much could be packed into your brain and your heart, and how with even a whisper of a smell brought it back whole and unshakable. She folded it and tucked it away. It was this side of too much.

Taking a deep breath, Nic opened the top letter from her father to her mother. Judging from the date, it had to be from her parents' first year out of high school when her mom was away at college and her dad at a post-grad prep school year The return address was just a street in New York City, no school name. Her father's looped handwriting taxed her brain and made it slow going.

April 7, 1968

My dear Sofia,

My first class was canceled this morning so that gives me the opportunity to begin the day right and that is being with you. Bella, I think that spring fever of yours is contagious for I've been noticing some effects of it recently. For instance, this morning I had the most interesting dream concerning you and I. Hmmm!!! It was motto bene. Remind me to tell you next time I'm with you, I'm sure you'll enjoy hearing it.

Its going to be a wonderful day today, its funny but I just feel as though it will be, strange but true. It rained last night, and everything looks greener already.

Sweetheart, that weekend at Penn was fantabulous. I'll try to give you a few highlights but remind me to tell you when we're together, ok? We met all the football coaches and other scholarship candidates and then the drama club put on a little variety show for us. It really was very nice, both in thought and performance.

Darling, the bell just rang and I have to go. I'll write again very soon. XO How I wish you were right here!

Be good. God Bless You.
Love,
Gino xxooxx

Nic could hear her father's voice in it, though he was just a boy of nineteen. His handwriting startlingly familiar yet not fully grown. How she wished she had Sofia's letters to read in between her father's, the voice of her nineteen-year-old mother.

She went into the kitchen to pour herself a second cup of coffee and to get Snoopy a new bone, she didn't want any interruptions.

April 30, 1968

Dearest Sofia,

Hello Sweetheart, I couldn't help but think of our wonderful weekend together while driving back to school. Honestly, Hon, it really was fantastic! I know now I'd travel more than a mere five-hundred miles to be with you if only for a short duration. We have something many people wish they had, that something I know will last a lifetime according to God's will. I love you so much, Sweetheart, I only wish I knew what was in store for us both. But that wouldn't be very good, would it? It's best to accept life as it comes, for it's much better to be surprised. Don't you think?

Driving was slow and very foggy. We didn't arrive at school until 5:00 a.m. We went to our room without disturbing a soul except unfortunately Mr. Sloane, as he cast the beam of his flashlight across the darkness and I slowly pulled my blue blanket over my weary body. Knowing we had exams in a few hours didn't bother Vin and I a mere trifle for we knew we weren't getting up until real late. Being sure also of due punishment we both waltzed into the office. Well, we didn't get any demerits, but we have forfeited all our going-home privileges during our future, so-called, long weekends.

It was worth it, many times over. I know darn well I'd do it all over again.

Ah! Guess what? I heard our song coming over. I'll be darned if I can remember the title, but it was something about two young lovers who couldn't seem to say goodnight. Although it was 2:00 a.m. it sorta hit home. Don't forget your promise to get that record for me! I hope I don't have to wait six weeks before I see you again, but the way things stand I haven't much choice. But the next time we are together it will be for a much longer time.

Until then, we have such pleasant memories with which to keep us company, memories only you could create. So long for only a short while, my love, till I dream of you again. Stay as you are, I will never ask for anything more.

All my love,
Gino xxxooxxoxx

The letter fluttered in Nic's hand from the breeze and she tightened her grip. The devotion of her teenaged father rose up off the paper. But his words swam before her; *stay as you are, I will never ask for more*. How long, Nic wondered, after they were married had things stayed that idyllic and simple?

Their family adventures were too numerous to count, unforgettable trips and experiences under the sun and in the snow, on foot, on horseback, on bikes, skis, and skates. How much Gino and Sofia did for their children. Had there come a time when they no longer knew how to do so for only each other? Had Sofia given up dreams in order to raise the children so Gino could keep taking giant steps forward? What had been sacrificed after all?

One more letter, she told herself.

That Nantucket Summer

May 21, 1968

Hi Sweetheart,

I just don't know how to start, I really don't. After trying my best for an entire year and giving it all I had, it just doesn't seem fair. What I'm trying to say is that I flunked the Naval Exam. Yes, that's right, I said flunked! The test is comprised of several subtests in areas such as general science, math knowledge, arithmetic reasoning, word knowledge, paragraph comprehension, and electronics.

The competition was so rough the medians were all close to 600, far better than I'm capable of doing or did. Out of the whole student body here only 36 students passed. I don't know at this point if I'm really disappointed, I really don't. I guess I'm all mixed up, Hon. It seems everything I try to do never works out. It gets pretty discouraging after a while, wouldn't you say?

I called Mr. Boren, the scout for Penn here in O.C. a short while ago to ask him how things are looking for me at U Penn. He said he'd call the university tomorrow and would let me know next Wednesday how I stand. Let's hope this nitwit makes it!

I haven't heard from any of the other schools I've applied to as yet so I'm really sweatin' now. I haven't heard from my dad in over a week so maybe there's the possibility the colleges sent the notices home. If so, I hope it's good news.

I plan to get my transfer papers form the Naval Reserves next Tuesday for I plan to leave this dump sometime next week. I am supposed to go on two years active duty as of October if I don't get into college. If this horrible thing happens, I plan to join the regular U.S. Air Force for I couldn't bear being a swabby for two years.

If I'm not smart enough to get into college after all the effort I've put in studying this year I don't deserve hanging around anywhere, in fact I should be shot!

Sweetheart, if I don't make college, I don't know what I'm goin' to do with you, for I wouldn't want you to get involved with a flunky, for that's what I would be. I'm sure your father would agree with me on that point. You have many opportunities, I'm sure, to meet many intelligent college men. I advise you to take advantage of that fast, for I doubt I can even make a dog happy.

I think it would be best for you to forget about me for you want someone you can be proud of and I'm not the guy. I've tried, darlin', honest I've tried but its like runnin' against the tide; I just can't seem to win. I could never look you in the eye knowing I've failed. I could never walk beside you knowing I'm robbing you from a much better man than myself. You deserve a man far superior to me, for I am nothing, nothing at all.

A while ago I told you this exam would shape my life and it has. You may say its false pride on my part, and that may be so, but that's me and you know that better than anyone else. I love you very much, Sofia, and I want what's best for you and right now its not me. Sometimes I wonder why everything happens to me but I guess that's just self-pity for I'm fortunate to be alive.

I was going to call you when I was informed of the bad news, but then I thought it best if I didn't. I haven't told my dad yet but intend to call him tomorrow when things should be clearer in my foggy mind. Flunking the exam has been quite a shock as you can imagine; it'll take a little time to forget if I ever do. If only I could be sure

I'd be accepted to any college everything would be different. All I can do now is wait. Thats all I seem to be doing lately and I don't think I can do it much longer. For I want to start my life, my real life.

Well, this is it, sweetheart, this is the end of the line, this is where I jump off.

God Bless You.

Love, Always,
Gino xxxooxox

What? What even *was* this? Her father was the most disciplined and accomplished man she'd ever known. *And* a proud Navy man. How had she and her siblings never known about this failing? And there had to be a hundred other things they knew nothing of. It would be foolish to think they knew every little thing about their parents — *before* they were parents, never mind during. Nic felt oddly removed from this couple, asking herself stupid questions like; *did Sofia and Gino get back together, did they get married, have a family, live happily ever after*?

Getting to know someone, but in reverse, learning new things about her parents but with the film unspooling backwards had Nic's heart in a tailspin. Had she opened the proverbial Pandora's Box?

Nic's first instinct was to text her brother — but this seemed too big for a casual text, consequential, momentous in a way that she wanted to keep to herself. For now, anyway. She needed to switch gears, to cover ground, to move forward instead of back. Snoopy was certainly good for that. He would literally pull her onward, drag her out of her funk and a past that she wasn't going to be able to leave alone.

The air smelled sweet, fresh, with the ripeness of the earth waking up again. As her crazy animal hurried her along at a good clip, she thought back to his early days when six minutes into a walk, he'd pull a flat-Stanley on the side of the road, splayed like a bearskin rug, refusing to go on. Many were the times that they'd made it out twenty minutes only for Nic to end up carrying him home. Now, he maintained and unrelenting pace. Nic's thoughts were equally tenacious.

She worried about the burden Enzo was under as executor of their father's will, and deciphering their father's filing system, which while at one point was as meticulous and lawyerly as could be, had been reduced to a tangle of misnamed files and missing information. Bills and more bills needed squaring, accounts settled and closed, and service after service that would no longer be needed but couldn't be shut down just yet. Adding to Enzo's load was his wife's upcoming one-year-breast-cancer-free oncology appointment. Nic would keep the letters to herself for now.

Nic thought back to their first big push when Enzo was cracking the whip and she had sat on the floor by her father's bed in front of his night table. A relatively small piece of furniture but where she'd spent the rest of the day, traveling across his eighty years. While she couldn't believe her dad had imagined her going through his things this way, he had to know they would.

Breathless from Snoopy's pace, and the places her mind wandered, they slowed down as Nic replayed the night table's precious though random contents. Cloth handkerchiefs that their dad was never without, film cannisters filled with pennies, a laminated prayer card, a crayon and glitter birthday card from young Mia, an elementary watercolor of the beach Nic had painted for Father's Day, a baseball picture of Enzo, and a fragile and faded valentine from Sofia to Gino as a sixteen-year-old girl! Then a notepad from a fancy hotel Nic couldn't imagine him at, and a receipt for diamond earrings that was too recent to have been for her mom.

Memory Lane was long and winding.

An hour later Nic and Snoopy lay panting on the front lawn. Her exhaustion was thorough. Snoop's, she knew, was unequivocally temporary. She closed her eyes against the sun — she'd forgotten her sunglasses and was already paying for it with a swelling headache. Her eyes were so light that she felt blinded even on overcast days. Her dad had always told her she was a throwback to their Venetian ancestors with her light hair and green eyes, presenting old photos of the great greats in Northern Italy. But honestly, what details were to be gleaned from those archival, sepia-toned photographs?

A big bowl of water for Snoopy and a Pellegrino for her, she stood at the sink looking out on her perennial garden. Her daffodils grew more scant each year instead of multiplying — were rodents getting the bulbs? *I'm so sorry I can't grow jonquils like yours, Dad.* But her heirloom peonies from her Gran's garden were coming in thicker than any year before. They would bloom on Father's Day, like they did every year. Gran had told her that peonies could live 100 years. A longer life than most people.

She considered the timelessness of some things, living things like trees, and grass, that somehow managed to replant themselves, re-root, divide and grow for ever after. Human beings lasted five minutes in comparison, and their *replanting* was so fraught. Why was it ever thus? Seeing Snoopy blissfully passed out on the cool hardwood floor, she felt like she should make good use of the time. She sat in the fat chair by the French doors overlooking her garden with the letter box in her lap.

She sighed and opened the lid. She closed it again wondering if she was really in the mood for getting sucked back in. It wasn't something you did for just a few minutes. She weighed her fatigue against the list of things she still had to do and sighed again. Opening the lid, she ignored the olfactory pull built into the red felt and picked her way gently through to the bottom of the box. Not as many letters as she'd thought, but some unwritten postcards collected for souvenirs, a book of matches, a vintage John F. Kennedy campaign button, and a creased yellow prom program that she did not have the emotional armor to deal with. Snoopy startled her with a muffled *rooo* in his sleep and she bumped the box in her lap. Her nerves were raw and it was exhausting.

Scraping the letters into a neat pile within the box, Nic's fingernail caught on a corner of the felt interior pulling it away from the bottom. *What*? A false bottom? Her heartrate sped. Laying all the known contents on side table next to her chair, she carefully pulled away the felted bottom that revealed a letter addressed to Gino in her mother's immediately identifiable script and a chain with a silver pendant stamped with the letter "**S**" like a wax seal.

S for Sofia? It was very cool, and more Nic's style than her mother's preference for delicate gold. Why was it hidden? The postmark was faded and barely legible but it looked like it said *Nantasket Beach*. Nic turned the envelope over slowly in her hands, her thumb toying with the flap that stuck as though either never opened or glued by the years. She peeled the stuck flap open. Her mother's swirly handwriting undid her every time. The letter was on plain cream stationery and was undated.

My Dearest Gino,

I hope that this note finds you well, more importantly, that it finds you at all. Your father's address is the last one I have for you. I know it has been quite a while since we last spoke, it has taken everything in me to honor your request. How I have missed my best friend, my love! I have wondered so very often how you are, where you are in the world. I would tell you that my heart has healed, but that would be untrue.

That Nantucket Summer

I left the university to pursue my painting. I couldn't see spending my father's money on a degree I didn't intend to use. I never could see myself working for his company. And losing you, well I couldn't see much point in anything after that. I am what you'd call a starving artist, with a roommate and waitressing to pay my share of the rent. I don't know if this will make you angry with me or proud for going after what I wanted, for finding the strength to do that. I suppose that is neither here nor there. We can barely scrape by now that summer has passed. I kept praying that someone important would see a painting of mine in one of the pretty shops here in this magical seaside place and I'd finally have made it. But I'm afraid my time has run out for that.

Gino, I'm in a bit of trouble and I'm quite desperate for your help. You are the only one I can turn to. If I may still turn to you? We used to mean so very much to each other.

If you receive this letter, could you please call the telephone number I'm including?

No matter where or what you are, Gino, I will love you until the day I die.

XOXO,
Sofia
(992) 555-1735

Chapter Six

Nicolina's heart tripped over every one of her mother's beautiful, painful words. Snoopy's muffled pawing at the door broke through her pulse thudding in her ears. Nicolina hadn't known her parents had actually lost touch with each other at one point. She wondered what it had cost her proud mother to plead for Gino's help after he'd ended their relationship. And while they were destined to be together from the start, had their split come with sacrifice? At some point, that wasn't now, she would try to break down these new details that cycloned like dried leaves at a garden gate.

In a zombie state she rose to let Snoopy out, following him outside to sit on the steps leading down into the yard. The air seemed washed and expectant. Elbows on bent knees, she closed her eyes and massaged her temples, talking her heart back into its normal rhythm. She was picturing her mom as she would have looked back then, as a young woman of, what, twenty? Or had more years passed since she'd seen Gino. Yes, Gino and Sofia, she should think of them as some other young lovers instead of her parents.

Sofia, with her classic hourglass figure, was all female and would have had men falling at her feet. Her demure but proud way would have been obscured by the cascading waves of deep brown that fell past her shoulders and hid eyes of the same warmth and hue. Growing up, how Nicolina had wished she'd had her mother's exotic beauty. Nic's sister, Mia, got more of those genes while Enzo was the image of Gino. Nic and Enzo resembled each other in nameless ways — more in the way they looked at the world than what the mirror had to say. Nic knew she depended on her brother overly, he was her younger brother but an old soul, a protector, a leader. He was their moral compass growing up, possessing a clear sense of right and wrong even as a little boy. Nic felt unendingly safe with Enzo. She wanted to walk the beach by their dad's house with him and puzzle it all out. But there was no time for that, and her heart was aching for her brother who was not only grieving intensely for the loss of their dad, but also grappling with the ever-lurking fear of his wife's cancer coming back. She would not burden him further.

The too-quiet yard yanked her from her reverie. Snoopy. Gone again. Damn, he was a runner. They had way too much woodsy woods for him to find trouble in — did he really think he was going to catch a deer? If any dog could... The way he'd spring off the deck steps, all fours in the air like Dasher, Dancer, Prancer, and Vixen. And running toward her now, muddy from his undercarriage down. Her mother would laugh and say, *no rest for the wicked*!

Nicolina missed Cade. Between his working extra to keep the bridge project on schedule and her trips to Maine, he seemed more like just a really good dream. She was glad that Ben and Evy were keeping themselves occupied and fed, because she just didn't have it in her lately. But she was lonely. Her closest friend, Jen, was in Brewster on the Cape with her family opening up their summer cottage, and a quick text wasn't going to cut it this time.

Nic put the kettle on for tea and reached for a mug she'd chosen to keep from her dad's house. It had been her mom's, white porcelain with a pedestal. She pictured Sofia sitting in the breakfast nook of their home, sipping Earl Grey with her hands wrapped around the cup for warmth, tapping her wedding rings against it while they talked. They were looking out at the apple tree one late February day, snow still bunched at its bottom, under a low gray sky. Nic members her mom saying, "See? The buds on the branches are thickening already..." Nic looked in awe of that then, and every February after.

Her tea was hot and sweet and Sofia felt close. It was the perfect company to be in when Enzo called to say that the first open house was a rager with over fifty people showing up and they'd have their choice of bids. The biggest and the best coming from a couple who wanted it lock, stock, and barrel. The dream sale — every piece of furniture, the oriental rugs, paintings, every fork, spoon, knife, and wine glass. It was an enormous relief. But it hollowed her out beyond any expectation.

Nic thought of her parents' bedroom set that she'd wanted to take but with no place to put it, a wedding gift from Sofia's parents; dark cherry, that queen-size curved headboard with hand carved detailing on the posts that stood over them even after their move to a king. As if it held them together somehow through all the years. Nic had slept in it every time she'd visited her dad, had felt cradled and loved. She'd never see it again. Or put her clothes in Mom's matching bureau, in that top drawer where the keys to Sofia's very first car, a red VW Bug, were kept in an oval dish carved into the drawer.

She cried herself to sleep that night, VW keys on her night table. Something big was over, something that was everything. She reached for her phone in the dark and texted Enzo:

How did we get here? It took so long, but it's all mist and memory now. I'll lay my sadness down next to yours tonight...while remembering that it's born of all the things that brought us safety, laughter and love. In the words of Kahlil Gabran, "When you are sorrowful look again in your heart, and you shall see that in truth you are weeping for that which has been your delight."

How very lucky we are dear brother. XO

Chapter Seven

AFTER NEARLY SIX DAYS of straight rain Nic and Cade were on a fast ferry out of Hyannis bound for Nantucket Island under a limitless blue sky. Fellow passengers wore the same breezy smiles certain that now Mother Nature owed them a week of blue bliss. Nic had been reading enough early Nantucket history that when she looked up from her pages she half-expected to see demur women in long plain dresses with hair tied back under bonnets, and men in knickers with broad-brimmed hats. And no matter how she tried to force the vision to color, it stayed in sepia tones.

It was in comically stark contrast to the reality of the Louis Vuitton bags around her, artfully distressed jeans with gaping holes costing hundreds of dollars, Tory Burch flats with fresh pedicures, straight white teeth, and not so much *thee* and *thou* as me, myself and mine. Nic wasn't entirely exempt from her own observations, but this was definitely not an example of *the more things change, the more they stay the same.*

"You okay, Nic, seasick or something?" Cade said.

"Oh, sorry, no. Why, do I have resting-bitch-face?"

"Kinda — I can't place it. Do you see someone from high school who kicked you off the lunch table?" Cade said, looking around at what could only be entire bridal parties, or maybe the *real* housewives of New York maybe even a blonds-only club — stalkers of the cliché five-star weekend.

"Very funny. And no, I didn't have a big enough personality in high school to get kicked out of anything to be honest. I do now though, and I'm comfortable with that. I was just listening to those women and trying to understand the desire to be *pampered*. The word itself needs help. I can't think of a bigger waste of time and resources than a weekend of servants and spa-ing. I mean, really? Come to Nantucket to be holed up in your air-conditioned suite being serviced? No. Put on a bathing suit (that you can actually swim in), get your hair wet, your pedicure sandy, and leave your fake lashes in the box. Dive into the ocean, walk in the sand, lie in the grass and count the shooting stars."

Cade reached for her hand across their laps fixing his dark blue gaze on her. "And I love that about you, would not change a single thing, Nic, you're brilliant, beautiful, authentic, compassionate and forgiving. Remember that."

What exactly did he mean by *remember that*. Was he worried about what his parents would think of her, of *them*? She caught something in his eyes he was trying to hide as he looked out the long windows at the ocean. She wouldn't push it, suddenly nervous she might poke a hole in a good thing. She returned her attention to the book in her lap. Mary Coffin Starbuck's life was simpler, though by no means easier. She hoped to have time to continue Mary's nineteenth century journey in the midst of twenty-first century grandeur. So much juggling lately of then and now.

The letter to Gino from Sofia from the bottom of the wooden box peeked out from the book — Nic had forgotten she'd stowed it there. She never did have the opportunity to talk with Enzo about it before she left. Looking over her shoulder, Cade asked if he could take a closer look at the envelope. Caught off-guard and in no way ready to share anything about the letter, Nic tried to shove it back into the pages, but the postmark caught Cade's eye.

"What's this? It looks ancient but does that postmark say Nantucket?" Cade said, taking a closer look at the faded envelope.

"What? No, it's Nantasket, isn't it? I googled beach towns near home that started with an "N", since I couldn't really read the faded letters in between the N and the k-e-t, and Nantasket fits perfectly. I cannot picture my mother setting off for a faraway island, Cade, are you sure?"

Cade examined the letter more carefully to be certain, and while the middle of the town's name was illegible and the zip code smudged it looked like 02554 to him. The letter had come from Nantucket. Cade could also read the name, Sofia Fiore, in the return address which was otherwise blank. "Sofia Fiore?" he asked Nic.

"My mother, Fiore is her maiden name."

"Oh right," Cade said, "she became a Tucci when she married your dad."

"Tucci...you don't know how many times I've wished I kept that name," Nic said wistfully, looking into Cade's eyes.

"Wright's not so bad, and it's your kids' names."

"Yeah except that it turned out to be so *wrong*," Nic said.

"Ha! Funny, not funny. Sorry. Anyway — so this is kind of mysterious then, isn't it? Have you read the letter? What do you think this is all about?"

Nicolina felt her brain short-circuiting, sparks ricocheting off the things she thought she knew. Her mother had actually *been* to Nantucket... had she *lived* there? How had Sofia never mentioned that? Thinking back to what she'd read in the letter, telling Gino she needed him? After they were, ostensibly, broken up? What did she need him for? Rent? Roommate issues? Rescue from an island? Had her traditional, proper mother had this other perhaps more Bohemian side to her?

"Hey, that's an interesting medallion, I've never seen you wear that before. You've found all kinds of goodies haven't you," Cade said, noticing the distracted, quizzical look on Nicolina's face as her finger and thumb rubbed at the **S** pendant around her neck, "and cheer up, we're almost there!"

"Oh, good," she said, dropping her hand into her lap, "Yes, I really like this — I never saw my mother wear it. It was in the box with the letters my dad kept buried in the hope chest at the foot of the bed they'd shared. But that letter and this chain around I only found by accident."

"Yeah, you told me that box was squirreled away good."

"No, it was more than that, there was a trick bottom in the box."

"Ooh, this is getting juicy…"

"I don't know about juicy, these are my parents we're talking about, my conservative, very traditional, by-the-book parents. Who I've only ever known to be in love since the seventh grade! None of this is making any sense to me. I mean should I just let it go — under the category of *it's none of my business* OR do I try to figure it out, do some digging? I mean, when I came here during college, I couldn't say enough about how special it seemed, its timelessness and charm…and she never let on that she'd been here, *lived* here. Why not? I mean that's not weird at all…"

As Brant Point came into view, Nic couldn't believe they were already there. The high-speed ferry was notably faster than the steamship — one hour versus two hours and fifteen minutes. She would almost rather it took longer from the mainland, she liked feeling far out to sea. Or maybe she was just letting anxiety rise about meeting the whole family and all the wedding events. Cade squeezed her hand and they shared a quick smile. She knew he wasn't entirely without reservations himself about staying under the same roof with his parents and his sister's family. Rick, his brother-in-law, was as a gem he'd said, and he was the one meeting them on Straight Wharf.

Nicolina's heart leapt at the simple view of church steeples and what she could see of the weathered cedar-shingled cottages, silver in the sun. Then, at the spectrum's opposite, she took in the rows of yachts on their slips off the long pier. She could hardly believe the profusion of affluence, something that had to be seen to be believed. Past and present as ever trying to exist side by side.

She felt the ferry connect with the dock and the passengers around them all scurrying to exit with their stuff, voices loud and hurried with excitement, eager to disembark. It was Nantucket!

"Ah — there's Rick," Cade said, smiling and waving to his his sister's husband who was standing with other wildly waving people greeting the new arrivals. "He's the real deal, Nic, you'll enjoy his company, I promise." It occurred to Nic that while he'd been building up Rick, he'd said almost nothing about his sister, Lexi.

Looking out at the assembled crowd on the brick sidewalk in the sun on an impossibly clear day, Nic took in the charm. Not just the perfectly quaint and tiny shops, the artful window boxes and baskets dripping with blooms, but the sea of beautiful people. Maybe it was their wide smiles and huge joy that made them so — maybe that's what this place did to a person. She felt giddy suddenly at getting to be a part of the magic.

Rick's eyes held the smiling story his whole face was telling and she felt the pull of his enthusiastic wave. He clapped Cade on the back in that dual handshake-hug-thing guys did, smile never fading. He swept Nic up in a generous hug and she couldn't help but feel like she belonged. He carried her bags to his new Land Rover Defender parked in the Harbor Stop & Shop lot chatting the whole way. "Great day on the water for you guys, lucky, it's been nearly a week of *gray lady days* here. Some mornings fog was so thick, no flights coming or going."

"Let's hope that's over with," Nic added, "we've had a torrential week too." It was her nature to jump into the conversation while taking in everything around her. She was happy to be in the back seat as they rumbled over the ancient cobblestoned streets out to the family homestead on Pine Street. With all the history she'd been steeped in between Mary Starbuck and Nathaniel Philbrick's *Away Off Shore*, she was keeping her eye out for anything she might recognize. Nic couldn't pinpoint why she was so enamored with Nantucket's past — every place had a history — but Nantucket had her full attention. She could hardly believe that Cade's family was among the first to settle the island. His very existence could be traced back 350 years ago when a small group of hearty English settlers decided they could make a home here. One week would never be enough time.

With a particularly big bump over the cobbles, Nic nearly banged her head on the car door. "Sorry about that back there!" Rick shouted from the front seat, "So, Nic, any idea why all these cobblestoned streets here?"

Nic scanned the recesses of her memory for anything she'd read recently that might provide her with an answer that would impress Rick, but nothing sprang to mind. It's not that she wanted to impress Rick expressly, but she prided herself on knowing things, or at least being able to figure them out. "Ummm because they hadn't invented asphalt yet?" she said, laughing at herself.

"Ha!" Rick said, "Well, maybe in a roundabout way…they put cobblestones down to eliminate the great mud and puddle mess actually. And if you think it feels rough in a car, imagine how it felt for a horse and carriage!"

Rick's his enthusiasm and good nature put Nic at ease right away and she could tell he'd be a fun source of information. As if reading her mind, looking at her in the rearview mirror he asked if she wouldn't mind if he pointed out a few historical tidbits on the short drive. "See out to your right, those three identical brick homes? They have been standing sentry over upper Main Street for over 180 years, how cool is that?"

"Very," Nic rolled her window down all the way to make room for the huge view.

"Those are referred to as the Three Bricks collectively. They were built in 1839 by whale oil merchant Joseph Starbuck, one for each of his three sons." As Rick spoke, Nic noticed even Cade looking out and listening, though she was certain he had to know all about them. "They are identical, imposing, and built to endure, obviously — here they still stand. And if anything is a reminder of Nantucket's booming maritime economy, these are. And across the street too — see those gorgeous Greek Revivals? They're known as *the Greeks*. The one on the right, 96 Main Street, is the Hadwen House and you really have to visit, it's open to the public, and truly one of the most elaborate examples of Greek Revival architecture on-island, I mean just look at those columns."

Nicolina was getting swept up in Rick's passion, wanting to know everything, about every person who lived in these magnificent homes. She begged him to tell her more as they continued up Main as she filled him in on what she'd been reading about Mary Coffin Starbuck and the what little she knew so far about the island's earliest beginnings.

Rick smiled back at her in the rearview, "I love that you're so into this, Nic, most visitors are all about *let's go to CRU* or *who's playing at the Chicken Box*? I may only have *married* into descendants of descendants but I'll take it. So, where was I...oh yeah, the Hadwen House — built in 1846 by William Hadwen, silver retailer. The whaling economy was starting to suffer and these homes were the last true mansions constructed by a prosperous whale-oil merchant. Hadwen built the Newport-styled house for his wife Eunice, whose father built the Three Bricks across the street for her brothers!"

It was a lot to take in, Nic needed time to process. She was drawn to Rick's enthusiasm and was picking her brain for who he reminded her of. Probably Ryan Reynolds with a touch of Richie Cunningham. He already felt like someone she'd trust implicitly and who would make her feel brilliant even if she couldn't name the Speaker of the House. "Thanks, Rick, I really appreciate all this, so much to know!" She smoothed long strands of hair between her thumb and finger as her brain swam.

Nic had no idea what to expect of the Swain family home. It could be palatial, completely modernized, and bearing no resemblance to its origination, or it could be an old, musty, antique home with cavernous fireplaces, front and back parlors, plumbing that had to try too hard, with barely enough room for guests. It didn't matter even a little, she would love it either way.

Cade grinned back at her from the front. Rick pulled the Defender slowly into the short, white-shell driveway and Nic felt her heart gallop. The house was set close to the road as old homes often were, and it looked almost small from the front, its gray shingles making a stunning contrast to the white trim. There was a generous doorway with narrow vertical windows paired on either side as well as a transom window over the door. A brass latch and lightship basket knocker had been shined to a high gleam. Cedar steps led to a wide balustered porch, she wondered if the house had been erected here or had been moved somewhere along the line like many of the oldest houses. There was a date of 1756 over the transom. From the side she could see how much larger the home was than it appeared from the front as it went deeper back and turned small corners here and there suggesting additions over the years.

While she'd been staring at the details of the house, the men had been unloading Cade's and her gear. The front door opened to reveal a woman who radiated elegance with strong posture, a sleek platinum bob, gas-flame blue eyes, and whose age it would be impossible to guess. She was trim in white skinny jeans that came to the ankle, mules with some kind of bling, and the palest periwinkle knit sweater.

"Cade, *darling*, come give your mother a kiss," she said smiling with an unbelievably taut face and perfect peony colored lipstick, reaching out for Cade, clearly her pride and joy.

"Mom," Cade said, trying to extract himself gently from his mother's surprising grip, "I'd like you to meet Nic, she's the one I've been telling you about. Nic, this is my mom, Prudence Swain."

"*Nic*? Hmm what an curious name for a woman, dear."

"*Nicolina*," she and Cade said at the same time.

"Nicolina, much better. Are your parents Italian, dear?"

"Yes, they were, Mrs. Swain, my dad passed a month ago and my mom's been gone for nine years. But yes, they were actually both Italian American."

Nic would never get used to speaking of her parents in the past tense.

"Please accept my deepest apologies for your loss, dear, I didn't know," Cade's mom said, though feeling to Nic like the farthest thing from depth. And it wasn't lost on Nic that she did not offer for Nic to call her Prudence.

"Thank you, Mrs. Swain, and how generous of you to invite us to stay here with you and your family, seems as though you'll have a houseful." Nic tried not to sound like she was sucking up, but the harder she tried the worse it usually got.

"Well, dear, Cade *is* my family, my *dearest* child, the very wind beneath these old wings, aren't you darling," Prudence said smiling adoringly up at her only son, "There is always room for you."

Good Christ, Nic said in her head, following them both up the five steps into the house.

Chapter Eight

WHILE CADE VISITED WITH his mother Nic took in the details of the house, fantasizing about its history. No matter how much renovating you do to a place its wonderful old smell will give it away. In the wood that has swelled and shifted over the generations, the humidity that still lives in corners, the hint of orange oil polish, ages of apple pies and baking bread surely must linger in every cotton throw and curtain. The pine floor underfoot was aged to a deep amber and Nic wanted to take in every detail of the house that had been a home for over two hundred years.

"Hey gorgeous," Nic turned in the direction of the unlikely greeting and found herself standing face to face with a kid who she knew from Cade to be his nineteen-year-old nephew but with the cockiness of an entitled twenty-something. He wore khaki shorts, a pressed pale blue button-down shirt cuffed with precision, and loafers that looked more expensive than her entire wardrobe. He looked at her with brazen glacial eyes and with deep brown hair that was as slick as he was. The sister's son, Nic thought, oh this was way too much.

Putting his hand out to shake hers, "Tryp," he said, "at your service," taking her hand, though she hadn't offered it, and holding it a beat too long. Rick materialized in time to pop the awkward bubble and to take over introductions.

"I see you've met my charming son — do I need to apologize yet?" Rick asked, having missed Tryp's greeting. And to Tryp, "This is your uncle Cade's guest, Nicolina, who you will treat with the utmost respect, got it? Go get your sister."

Nic took the moment to regroup, and to lower her eyebrows back to where they belonged. One down, she thought, three more to go, the sister, the sister's daughter, and Mr. Swain. Where in the hell was Cade?

"Here," Rick said, leading her toward the staircase that wrapped around the center chimney, "...let me get one of your bags, I'm sure you could use a minute. I'll show you where you and Cade are sleeping." What a kind and thoughtful man, Nic thought, how did he spawn that audacious child? Ugh — judging again. *Be curious instead of judgmental*, she'd learned in more than one professional development seminar at school.

"You're the best, Rick, I appreciate it so much. Where is Cade anyway?"

"I'd be willing to bet old Prue has got his ear, ecstatic to have him all to herself, you know?" Rick said.

"I'm starting to understand that. No one is going to be good enough for him, am I right?"

"I know how you feel. Only certain people are allowed into that pantheon of affection," Rick said with a chuckle, "Give it time. She'll come around. She fully embraces her reign as queen of the castle, and we are all her subjects."

Fatigue zapped her body on the way up the narrow staircase, she bumped the walls with every other step, tipping with the weight of her bag. "Is Mr. Swain here at the house? I haven't seen him yet, or your wife for that matter."

Taking a left at the top of the stairs, Rick ushered Nic into the bedroom to drop her bags. "Lexi is out to lunch with her dad. Probably a good thing — spread the introductions out a bit, you know?" Rick said with a grin, then showing her around the upstairs.

Nic's heart lifted at the vintage spindle spool queen bed in her room with deep white bedding. She was sure if she lied down it would be dark by the time she woke up. Walls of the palest blue were in gorgeous contrast to the darkened softwood floor and the white sheers flitting in the breeze at the windows. The massive center chimney design created and abundant six fireplaces in the home, three on the first floor and three upstairs. She thought how what was easy to take as luxury began as the only source of heat in the home once upon a time. The lightship basket of dried hydrangea blossoms on the hearth was lovely, but what she'd like better would be to light a fire on a chilly night. Wouldn't she be just the one to burn down a 200-year-old home.

She was relieved to see a small bathroom in the room; a tiny sink and a toilet, and a larger bathroom across the hall with a white cast iron clawfoot tub and showerhead. "Hey *Nic Nack Paddy Whack*," Cade said, scaring her half to death, "I'm hoping Rick showed you around a bit?"

Nic melted into his big hug. "Yes, and his passion for the historic and most finite details is contagious. It's beautiful. And while it's so evocative of a time gone by, it also has an air of comfort and of being well-loved." Pressed against Cade's strength, Nic felt exceedingly safe, secure in the way her father had made her feel her whole life. His loss had left her feeling exposed, raw. Was this new vulnerability pushing her closer to Cade too soon? The power of her feelings scared her. She'd become bad at trusting the future.

Rocking as they stood together, his smile felt like the full sun on her skin. As his hands slid down her body, pulling her close, she pushed harder against him. He scooped her up and walked across the hall to their room, closing the door with his foot.

Nic woke up alone in the heirloom bed with a sheen of sweat on her forehead. And while she felt utterly sated, it had grown stuffy in the room with the door closed and the humidity pressing in through the windows. Sunlight measured itself in rectangles across the pine floor telling her a couple of hours had passed. She breathed in the smell of fresh-cut grass sweetening the air and tried to recall the dinner plan, if she'd known it at all, and wondered if she had time for a swim in that big tub. Just as she was gathering a towel and robe a text came in from Cade:

> *You were out cold, I hope you don't mind my sneaking out, figured you could use the sleep. No rush at all but my parents would like to do drinks and a little spread here at the house before our reservation at Straight Wharf. Text me when you get this. XO*

Nic smiled, returning his text, still smelling him on her skin, she almost thought twice about washing it off.

> *Yeah, quit disappearing on me, will ya? Taking a quick bath — what does one wear to Straight Wharf?*

> *I'll be up in a few — don't sweat it.*

Did that mean he didn't trust her to choose a suitable outfit? Ugh — she needed to stop. A shower would be faster. Once she figured out the knobs on the watering can showerhead, she relaxed into the pulsating heat while flipping through her wardrobe in her mind. You could never go wrong with a sundress, she thought, but she should have hung them up before her afternoon delight. A quiet knock on the door snapped her out of it and she rinsed the conditioner from her hair.

"Hey Nic, it's just me, you have a towel?" Cade said.

"I do, be out in a sec." That guy was something else she thought, smiling to herself as she turned off the faucets and wrung the water from her hair. Robe secured and hair wrapped in the towel, she opened the door to whoosh of cooler air. Relieved no one was around, she hustled into their room across the hall where Cade had started to unpack.

"I forgot to tell you about the outside shower — it's the best thing — and no mildew with the moist air and lousy ventilation."

"Trying to tell me something? Yeah, no, I didn't get the memo on the outside shower or the mildew farm I may or may not have started in there." Nic was good natured about it but she couldn't help but feel slightly scolded. "Next time, okay? But I am *so* taking a long bath at some point in that gorgeous tub..."

"Of course! I'm sorry Nic, I didn't mean anything by it, forget I said anything, and you take as many showers inside as you like." He kissed her button nose and returned to his unpacking.

There were satin hangers in the small closet, an unexpected touch, Nic could swear they were lavender scented. There were also traditional wooden hangers which pierced Nic with a quick sorrow thinking of her dad's closet, empty now but for the stretch of naked hangers. As Cade hung a Navy blazer, she noticed he was also hanging pink pants.

"I see that look," he said to Nic, "they're not pink. They're called *Nantucket Reds* and they are as traditional as it gets here — they can be worn anywhere but a funeral and can only be bought here at Murray's Toggery Shop."

"Okaayyy, but what's so special about them?" Nic asked, touching her fingers to the faded, softened fabric.

"Let's see...I've always just accepted them as a staple in a man's wardrobe here on-island, you know, my dad and all the men wear them to dinner, the golf club, especially weddings these days. I'll admit I didn't wear them as a kid — didn't put a pair of long pants on the whole summer — but these are great actually. They start out as a deeper red, and stiff like canvas, but fade to this soft, perfect dusty rose color over time."

"Well, listen to you...I love it. I love how this island is all about embracing that weathered look, like the silver-shingled cottages — the salty wet weather will indeed have its way, right? So, are you wearing those tonight?" Nic asked, hanging the last of her things up.

"Actually no, I think I'll save them for the wedding. Tonight, I'll be wearing these with a white shirt," Cade said holding up a pair of Nantucket Red shorts.

"It's too easy being a dude," Nic said laughing, "please tell me they don't make bikinis out of that stuff too?"

"Ha! Come to think of it, I don't see as many ladies wearing the Reds, but I won't stop you!"

"I'm all set, thanks," Nic said grinning, and tucking her underthings in the bureau and trying to close the stuck drawer in the fat air, "but I bet you look very handsome in them, if a bit preppy — are you unpacking a whole new you?"

"Hey, no labels," Cade said teasingly, "my parents had me in private school before I could say *no thanks*. Summers here you kinda fall back into the look I guess."

"It's a very classy look, I'm not knocking it at all. How's this then?" she said, holding up her new sleeveless Tommy Bahama dress; blush-pink linen with a ruffled v-neckline, hitting above the knee with a flirty fringed hem. "Will I pass inspection?"

"First of all, there's no inspection, Nic, second of all, you are going to slay in that dress, it's perfect, and perfectly you," Cade said crushing her in a hug.

"Oh my God, Cade, I don't think *slaying* is quite what I'm going for! And cut it out, you'll wrinkle it," she said, turning away from his smooches and the magnetic forcefield that was him, "shouldn't we be getting dressed now anyway, it's 5:30."

"Ooh, you're right, hey, I'll give you some privacy, it won't take me long to get dressed," he said, walking toward the door.

"What, are you kidding me? It's not like you haven't seen me in my undies before, you do *not* have to leave the room," Nic said, kicking out of the shorts she'd put on after her shower and sliding her t-shirt off over her head."

"Um, YEAH I do, be back in a few," he said, "before I change my mind and make us very late for drinks and apps."

∞

Descending the bare stairs creaking underfoot behind Cade, Nic bit back her adolescent angst about not being good enough. They would smell her fear anyway. She was an eloquent conversationalist and with a glass or two of Prosecco she'd be just the right amount of breezy. Deep breaths, she told herself, and then she saw Tryp, standing at the island with one hand in his pocket, the other wrapped around a bottle of *not soda*, and a shit-eating grin on his face. *Who did this kid think he was?*

"Finally, *darling*, we were about to start without you," Prudence Swain said with a smile that didn't quite reach her eyes. Everyone, get a glass, will you? John has just topped the flutes off and we must make a toast."

The early evening sun slid in, as if on cue, gilding the fizzing stemware and bouncing off however many carats of diamonds ringing Lexi's finger. "To my wonderful son, Cade, welcome back to our beloved island, it is never home here without you."

Without missing a beat but waiting a few for his mother to welcome Nicolina as well — which she did not — while glasses were still poised in the air Cade added, "and welcome, Nicolina, to Nantucket — my favorite girl in my favorite place."

"Cheers!" Rick said, setting off a concert of tapping crystal. "Nic, who haven't you met yet? I know Tryp has graced you with his presence," Rick said with no small amount of sarcasm, as Tryp raised his glass to her with his precocious grin, "but I don't believe you've met Lexi, my wife, Cade's sister of course."

Nic switched the glass to her left hand and offered her right to shake Lexi's, but none was forthcoming. Was shaking hands still not a thing? *It was 2023 and she still wasn't sure which protocols that involved touching people were gone for good.*

Lexi raised her glass in the air just a touch and said, "Any friend of Cade's..." then gulped what was left of her rosé. "Mother, we must have another bottle of this, yes?"

She wasn't entirely sure what to make of Cade's sister, but Nic was all about opening another bottle. *Keep it comin,* she thought. The next thing she knew John Swain, Cade's father, was taking her hand in both of his large warm ones, cerulean blue eyes shining on her, telling her how very lovely it was to meet someone who means so much to Cade, that he was quite looking forward to getting to know her and being a part of her Nantucket experience. His kindness soothed her spikey edges and she felt instantly at ease. The heavy screen of the front door slapped shut and they all turned to watch Tryp's sister walk toward the kitchen and join the party.

"Ah, my gorgeous girl where have you been," Prudence said, taking her granddaughter's face in her hands, "we were just celebrating the arrival of your uncle Cade. And his friend, Nicolina." Nic took in the stunning young woman, tall like her father and with his kind eyes, sun-kissed and with a confident yet authentic aura about her.

"Hi everyone, pleased to meet you Nicolina, sorry I'm late!" Nic was struck by her easy grace and open smile and Nic felt redeemed when Poppy reached to shake her hand.

"Please, call me Nic, and I'm so happy to meet you too, Poppy, and to be sharing this beautiful home with you all." Nic's shoulders settled and her smile brightened. She was letting herself be happy and in the moment, which, of course, was the only way to be. Poppy's dress was similar to her own, casual linen, but in a shade of green apple. And rather than feeling like she shouldn't be dressed like someone half her age, she decided instead to feel that she looked just right. P-O-P another bottle of Whispering Angel was opened, a fine pink mist rising up and disappearing in the air and the happy hum of conversation.

"Poppy, your dress is the exact color of Nic's eyes," Cade said.

"Oh my gosh, you are so right — and Nic, you really do have incredible eyes!"

"Well thank you, very much."

"That lovely color sets off your gorgeous chestnut hair, my darling Poppy," Prudence interrupted, shifting the spotlight to anyone but Nicolina, "now let's get going before we're late for our reservation, they don't seat just anyone with a harbor view you know."

Nic was thrilled when Tryp and Lexi wanted to ride with John and Prudence, that meant it would be Rick, Cade, Poppy and her in Rick's Range. "I love your bag," Poppy said sitting next to Nic on the short drive, and I'm glad you got the memo on wearing wedges — cobblestones have no mercy, ha!"

"I got lucky, I guess! So, do you live here in the summer or are you just visiting for the wedding?" Nic asked, the bumpy ride adding to the effervescence of the evening.

"I wish I were here for the whole summer, those days, *years*, were the best. Impossible to appreciate until they're only a memory. Nope, I have a big-girl job now at a marketing firm in Boston, which I love, but summers are tough. Bye-bye surfing days and beach bonfire nights..."

"Which is a huge part of the reason I'm a teacher," Nic said, "I need my summers! So, I hear you, but good for you, a real grown-up career. Do you mind if I ask how old you are?"

"Not at all — I'm twenty-four so I've been at this almost two years. The money is nice but rent in Boston, UGH." Nic was pleasantly surprised at Poppy's unexpected appreciation for earning a living having come from so much. Old money had an aura of mystery to it, and she never did really understand why it didn't enjoy the same reputation as *new* money — she guessed that was a debate for the people with *money*.

Rick offered to let the ladies out while he and Cade circled for parking, but Nic declined, and was glad when Poppy did also. What a spectacular thing the sky was doing as the sun sunk into the sea. She didn't know where to look — the raspberry-lavender sky, the harbor reflecting it back, or the white fences turning shades of sherbet.

"Hard to believe isn't it," Poppy said, under the spell, "It never gets old, the golden hour. It's something you take with you when you go, this color, this feeling — even though you will be certain that you imagined it all."

Chapter Nine

THEIR PARTY OF EIGHT was seated in time for the sky's last hurrah over the water. The candlelight took over from there, dancing in the stemware and pooling in the plates. Restaurant guests stopped by their table on their way in or out across the evening —the Swains knew a lot of people. A sweaty hand on her thigh got her attention and made her jump in her chair.

"Dear? Are you quite alright down there?" Prudence asked from the head of the table, "you'd think she had a snake in her chair."

Exactly, Nic thought, If only Prudence could see for herself that she'd hit the nail squarely on its head — something Nic would *love* to do to this Tryp seated beside her. Holy effing shit, *where did he get the cojones?* She removed his hand without batting an eye and looked across the table at Cade to ask what he'd recommend from the menu. Which started an animated discussion of everyone's favorites and who was getting what. Nic decided to start with the pear and celery salad with pecorino — whatever that was — walnuts, and lemon, then for her entrée, wanting something local, she chose the day boat scallops with sweet potatoes, haricot verts, watercress, squash mole, gooseberries, pumpkin seeds, and sesame-pine nut salsa Macha.

Tryp had switched gears and his attention to the hot server, thank God, freeing Nic up to chat more with Poppy. The waitstaff floated in and out of the shadows to replenish their water and wine, she was feeling sublimely buzzed while conversations hummed around her. "So, Poppy, tell me more about what kind of marketing you do, like who are your big clients?"

"Well, the Museum of Fine Arts in Boston is my personal favorite. It's been a challenge lately though with a decrease in visitors on top of a shortage of sponsors."

"Oh — why has there been a decrease in visitors do you think? The MFA has always been a favorite spot for locals, and tourists too I'd imagine," Nic said.

"Absolutely, but there has been a series of adverse economic events that really impact people's ability and desire to spend money on entertainment, you know? It's been a tough few years for everyone. And add to that the sponsors — private corporations that used to have their headquarters in Boston — were bought by larger companies based in other states, making fundraising way more difficult," Poppy said with the confidence and poise of someone much older.

"That's a shame…trips to the MFA were such special outings for my mom and me. I'd kept a sketch pad since I was about nine, adding watercolors to my repertoire in middle school. She thought I had this incredible talent — but sometimes it felt like she was more excited about it than I was. So I started to feel this sort of pressure to be really good — better than I thought I'd ever be — so I gave it up for a while. Anyway, Sofia, my mom, had an appreciation for most paint genres, but I'd say her favorite was Impressionism," Nic said, with a faraway look, remembering her mom then, the quiet transformation in her face, her posture, when she stood in front of certain pieces. They seemed to transport her so thoroughly. How unreachable she seemed in those moments, but then how she'd loop her arm through Nic's on to the next exhibit with joy in her step.

"That's wonderful, Nic, what a beautiful memory. And you're an artist? That's amazing. But did you notice how you said you *used* to go?

I guess that's what I mean. It's a *big* place, it needs staff, security, and it has to be affordable at the same time. And it's no easy feat generating spectacular events, with rich visual content that contributes to culture on the large scale in order to appeal to a larger number of visitors."

"That's quite an undertaking - I can appreciate the challenge," Nic said, "but kind of exciting, right?" Salads and appetizers were served and Nic hoped she wasn't monopolizing Poppy or talking with her mouth full. "Are you an artist yourself?"

"I wish. I'm more of an art history buff — not much good in the studio though," Poppy said in between her Nantucket oysters."

"I was exactly the opposite in college. Loved the studio classes: drawing, painting, and film photography. I signed up for one art history class and was asleep before the tenth slide. I knew I could never memorize all that, and I just didn't see the point." Nic said, suddenly realizing that the *pecorino* in the salad was like a Romano cheese.

"It's not for everybody," Poppy said, wiping the corner of her mouth with her starched napkin and washing that last oyster down with a sip of her wine.

"What's not for everybody?" Tryp leaned over Nic to ask Poppy.

"YOU, Tryp, boundaries, kid! You don't just lean into someone's personal space like that," Poppy said. Then to Nic, "Please excuse my brother, he's a neanderthal."

"Now children, *please*. What *is* the fuss about?" Prudence asked, her face looking like she'd eaten a bad clam.

"Nothing Mimi. How were your oysters?" Poppy said, changing the subject.

"Quite good, darling, thank you, and yours also I trust? Mm, this Sauvignon Blanc is the perfect pairing, is it not?" Prudence cleared her throat and placed her hands in her lap. The seven of them turned to face her. How well trained she had them, Nic thought.

"As you all know, the rehearsal dinner is tomorrow night. And as my brother George is the father of the groom and hosting the event, he has at the *last minute* decided he is able to accommodate the eight of us after all. Now I know what you're thinking, how very boorish of him not to have included his sister's family from the beginning. But that's George for you. He means well, of course, my darlings, so we will all be good-natured about it and have a marvelous time. Do I make myself clear?"

Nicolina felt like she was nine years old being told not to make a pyramid out of the creamers. They were all adults for God's sake, did *Grandmother* think there'd be a revolt? Nic needed and elastic on her wrist to snap for being snappish. *Did she need another dress*? Could she keep up with the drinking? Yes and hell yes.

Over decaf-cappuccinos Nic and Poppy got to finish their conversation about the challenges associated with marketing strategies for the Museum of Fine Arts.

"So, what can happen," Poppy concluded, "is that the bringing of all sorts of artistic works to new audiences, you know, more trending events, is that the classic collections can end up taking a back seat — resulting in a conflict for some visitors feeling and unwanted shift from the museum's original direction."

"Wow. You cannot please everyone, that's for sure. So many people with so many opinions. With some making a career out of their opinion being the *only* one."

"Right? We're getting more and more stuck. So much divisiveness with *cancel culture* off the rails."

"I agree, it's sad. How did you get so smart for twenty-four, Poppy?" Nic said, thinking how her own kids felt much the same way. What kind of world did they have to look forward to? So young and already so jaded. Who could blame them?

The rest of the meal passed uneventfully and, sadly, Tryp was unable to procure the digits of the hot waitress. Everyone passed on dessert and John and Prue decided to call it a night along with Lexi who complained of a headache. That meant Rick, Cade, Tryp, Poppy, and Nic were left to pub crawl or stand in line at the Juice Bar for the island's most famous ice-cream. Nic sighed with relief when Tryp separated from them to meet up with friends. She did not want to have to, one; be looking over her shoulder for his unwanted shenanigans and, two; have to witness him and his fake ID crash and burn. He was the same age as Ben.

The air turned moist and Nic thought how cool the misty fog looked swirling under the saffron glow of the streetlamps. Rick and Cade wanted frappes at Nantucket Pharmacy while Nic and Poppy wanted to check out the paintings in the window of the gallery across the cobblestoned street. Nic looked back to appreciate the view of the guys sidling up to the chrome-edged stools of the vintage soda fountain in the pharmacy, like they'd probably done since they barely came up to the counter. Completely adorable, she didn't want to look away.

"Wow, this is amazing," Poppy said of the Forrest Rodst painting front and center of the window of Quidley & Company, *Lunar Surf* it's called. Just look how that moon is reflected again and again down the waves rolling in, how white the foam is in that light, the depth of the greens and blues in the waves..."

"It's so intensely realistic but with something else too — a splash of a dream or wish," Nic added. They both stood and stared, each alone in the private place the painting summoned. "What this man does with acrylic paints — such a different vibe from watercolors."

Poppy turned to Nic, "Do you ever work with acrylics?"

"In high school I dabbled, but I wasn't achieving that wow-factor that I get from watercolors — I didn't feel any movement in my work — the images just sort of sat still on the canvas, uninspiring. I mean if *I* didn't feel transported then I wasn't going to be moving anyone else, you know? I just love the brush work of the wash style, the unexpected blending, the surprise of what I end up with."

"That's amazing, Nic, I envy you. To be able to do that, it's pure magic," Poppy said.

"Did somebody say pure magic?" Rick startled them from their trance."

"Yikes, Dad, way to sneak up on someone and, wow, so that's where Tryp gets his cheesy one-liners!" Poppy said reaching for his frappe cup to steal a sip.

"Save any for me, handsome?" Nic asked, waggling Cade's cup to see, "Mmm, mocha, my favorite." The creamy blend of coffee and chocolate reminded her of her dad. He'd been crazy-strict about how it was made: with coffee ice-cream and chocolate syrup, *not* the other way around.

"Like it?" Cade asked.

"It's heaven." Nic said, adjusting her expression, "mocha frappes were my dad's go-to. Even laid up in the hospital hooked up to a machine scribbling out his heart's secrets, he'd put in an order when I was on my way to visit." It always took a minute to believe he was really gone. Grief was like that...sometimes it just got you behind the knees.

The four of them stood looking at the canvases in the window. Poppy was drawn to a smaller one set back too far out of the spotlight to see clearly, but Nic honed right in on it. It was a sepia-toned piece with an old-fashioned postcard look to it. Nic moved as close to the window as possible, focusing as hard as she could in the dark. An obscure shadow of recognition walked up her spine.

"Why is that so familiar to me," Nic said softly, mostly to herself, up against the glass, cupping her hands around her eyes to block out glare from the streetlight. "I'm getting this weird feeling...but the harder I reach for it the further away it gets...like I've seen this before, or something like it."

The others gathered closer to take a look and Poppy said, "Well, I mean, maybe that's what we're kind of supposed to feel? You were just talking about paintings, good paintings, having the ability to move you, conjure a feeling, right? I mean the sepia-toned look of this, the old-fashioned bathing suits, nostalgia at its best, it's absolutely bringing us back to the 1920's."

"Yes. And no, it's more than that… Let's remember to come back here to wander around inside, okay? I know things will ramp with wedding stuff but I really want a closer look at that one. How long are you here for again?" Nic asked Poppy.

"Ugh, I have to head back late Sunday," Poppy said, "but we can make it happen. Also, remind me to get you the names of some other galleries here, Nic, you'd probably enjoy that since you have, what, a whole week here with Cade?"

"I do and I would love that, thank you!"

"What do you say, ladies, night cap or head home?" Cade said, wrapping his arm around Nicolina, "You know I'm down for either."

"After that frappe, are you kidding me?" Nic said, filling her cheeks out like a puffer fish.

"Right?" Poppy agreed, "bottomless pits you guys, home please, I'm beat. If that's okay with you Nic."

"Absolutely. Long day, I just want to get cozy. It's so weird for me to have only myself to think about — I'm not used to not being needed for something. I mean my kids are wonderfully independent, for the most part, but I miss my crazy puppy!" Poppy wanted to hear all about Snoopy on the walk back to the car, saying she couldn't wait to get a pup someday. But finding a rental she could afford that allowed animals was impossible.

"Don't do it! *Yet*, I mean," Nic said, "what you don't expect is really how much they demand of you, it's way more than you think — money, yes, but mostly *time*. Well, depending on the breed of course, but you'd want an active dog, right? One to walk and hike with you? But right now in your life, when you're going to work every day, he'd be alone all day — not a great situation. And it will tie you down to a degree, you know, like when you want to travel."

"I hear you, and I know you're right, Nic, we've just always had dogs growing up and I miss that. But I know there's a big gap between the reality and the fantasy. Ooh it still gets chilly at night doesn't it," Poppy said, rubbing her arms.

"I was just thinking the same thing," Nic said as they climbed into the Defender.

"It's June-uary on Nantucket," Cade said, laughing at his own joke.

"Yikes — the fact that it has a name!" Nic said from the back seat, "So, do the fireplaces work in the bedrooms at the house or...? That would feel so good." Her question hung in the air for a minute. Then Cade and Rick answered at the same time.

"Yes," Rick said.

"No," Cade said.

"Well thanks for clearing that up," Nic said.

"It's complicated," Cade said, "technically the fireplaces all function, but I guess the only thing that matters is that my grandmother forbids use of the upstairs fireplaces — claiming she hasn't had the chimney swept — she says this every year — but the real reason is she doesn't trust anyone not to accidentally burn the house down by being careless and falling asleep with a fire blazing when an ember could jump out — you know what I'm saying."

"When you put it like that, it makes perfect sense. Oh well. I don't suppose candles are allowed then either in the bedrooms?" Nic said as they were pulling in the driveway.

"You catch on quick, and don't you worry my little Nicolina, I will keep you plenty warm." Cade said with a wink.

The house was quiet when they returned, the four of them said goodnight and went to their rooms. Nic toyed with the idea of reading a little before sleep — she was captivated by the juxtaposition of Mary Coffin Starbuck's mid seventeenth century life challenges settling the island with the extravagance and leisure of today's Nantucket.

Tension mounted in Tristram's face. The earlier expression of frustration and defeat gave way to anger.

"You won't believe this...it gives the Gardner brothers the right to purchase land directly from the Indians."

"But that is illegal," interposed Mary. *"Wasn't there and agreement for all time that none of the proprietors would be allowed to purchase directly from the Indians for their own private use?"*

"Of course there was!" Tristram snorted. He tossed the papers down on the table. *"These orders are an infamy. I can't understand what got into the Governor's head. How did those Gardners do it? They betrayed the rest of us. We've got to fight this...How can those Gardners claim that the original proprietors who bought and settled this island have no more rights than any off-islander who decides to come here and live...we'll fight this one. And believe me, we'll win."*

These developments would have been much easier to endure if the Gardners had been obvious rascals, hungry for power without scruple. But this was not the case. They were clearly honorable men and attractive leaders...the Gardners were good people. No denying that. How is it then that good people can disagree so heartily, if they are really good and really searching for the right way?

"We were together in our struggle against nature — to gain a foothold on this rugged island; and we have done well in that struggle," she said to herself softly. *"But now we have a new and more threatening struggle — against each other."*

Mary walked along sadly. She sensed that a new leaf was being turned in the story of the people of this small island. Things would never again be the same on Nantucket.

Cade was softly snoring beside her; she was relieved the lamplight hadn't kept him awake. She wanted to keep reading, to know it all, but it was past midnight and she was still in the mid 1600's. Setting the book on her night table and clicking the lamp off, she settled deeper under the cloud of down, appreciating its simple luxury. She tended to think of people who lived hundreds of years ago as different from her. But people were all the same. Same basic needs, feelings, desires, and fears. *She* wasn't afraid she'd be too cold to sleep, or have enough food on the table, or have the medicine she needed. But people were people — with the everlasting struggle to live peaceably together and for the greater good.

Chapter Ten

FRIDAY DAWNED CLEAR AND warm, a perfect day to rumble out to Great Point. For breakfast Cade spoiled Nic with a mushroom and spinach omelet and toasted Portuguese bread with blueberry preserves. "Oh my God, this *bread*!"

"Right? Baked fresh here on-island. And don't even try to compute how many loaves you'll consume while you're here," Cade said.

"Great, I'll be wearing muumuus the rest of the summer," Nic said patting her belly. Lexi, who had been drinking her coffee at the marble island and scrolling on her phone throughout breakfast paused, looked over at Nic in a way that suggested she was imagining Nic getting fat. It seemed to give her pleasure.

"What does everyone want for our picnic lunch on the beach?" Rick asked, getting ham, turkey, Swiss and cheddar out of the fridge and lining up more bread.

"After that breakfast, I do *not* think I'll be eating until dinner. But then again I always say that in the moment and end up scarfing down a whole sandwich at lunch — Turkey please!" Nic said.

"I'll throw some yogurts in there too," Rick said, "and hey, Cade, can you grab the chips in the pantry and I think we have a bag of pistachios too."

"You guys have it down to a science," Nic said, watching the men pack the cooler and Lexi continue scrolling. Nic could see the outline of a bikini beneath Lexi's crochet sundress, she looked pretty, if a bit furrowed in the brow with hair pulled tightly back. Poppy was in the outside shower after her run and Tryp had yet to surface. Prudence would be having lunch with friends and John was golfing, that left the six of them to squish into Rick's Defender. Nic wanted to call shotgun if for no other reason than to not have to be in the lap of Tryp. But then she remembered that Lexi was joining them.

Lexi finally got up to supervise the packing of the beverage Yeti. She had to be sure her Miraval Rosé got in there with the Cisco beers and High Noons. Nic was starting to see what Lexi's priorities were and thought, well, okay! When in Rome...

Nic took the narrow steps two at a time upstairs to brush her teeth and make sure her beach tote had sunblock, a towel, a book, sunglasses, and a hat. Then hurried bac out to the truck — she did not want to be the last one ready.

"Shotgun!" Tryp called.

"Rub a lamp dear son," Lexi said sliding into the luxurious front seat of her husband's Defender.

"Ha, you fell for it. I wanted the way-back anyway — closer to the Yeti," Tryp said with a good-natured chuckle.

"Such a child," Poppy said, sighing and closing her door, "entertainment I guess — at least he's good for something."

Nic waited for a retort from the backseat, but none came. She almost felt bad for the kid, but not quite. He was just a little bit too smug.

Cade put his arm up on the back of the seat around Nic's shoulder and gave her a quick squeeze. "Are you excited? Great Point is really something," he said, "there's this narrow section where we'll be cruising on the smoothest sand with the blue ocean on both sides of us, it's incredible."

"Is there a map back here somewhere? Yeah, yeah, I know I'm the tourist but I need a visual, like where exactly on the island we're going," Nic said, peeking in the seat pockets.

"Oh, you won't find anything in there, Dad is a little crazy about *stuff* in his truck," Polly said.

"Oh boy, one of those, huh?" Nic joked, then hoping her sarcasm didn't sound critical.

"Oh, you would not believe" Lexi said, looking back at Nic with something of a conspiratorial smile, opening the glove compartment and fingering methodically through the items until she landed on bicycle map of the island. "But he is also exhaustively thorough and will doubtless have whatever you need, even if you didn't know you needed it." She handed the map back to Nic.

"Thanks Lexi, this is perfect," Nic said feeling hope bloom about a possible friendship with Lexi. She opened the map of the ironically whale-shaped island, "Ah, so we'll be driving out on the tail of the whale, I see now, interesting. How has that area not been washed away? It looks pretty vulnerable."

"They limit access at times due to erosion, but it's been pretty good the last few years," Rick said from the front, meeting Nic's eyes in the rearview mirror. His smile always reached his eyes.

"Hey Dad," Tryp shouted from the back over the summer wind coming through the open windows, "why didn't we bring the rods?"

"*We?*" Poppy said, "what exactly did you contribute to this outing?"

"Shut up Poppy," Tryp said more to himself than his sister.

"Hey, next time, buddy, okay? There are a lot of us packed in here today. And can you imagine your grandmother's face if we brought home a giant Bluefish to be gutted?"

"With the rehearsal dinner tonight? I can't even..." Poppy said.

Everyone got a laugh picturing that, and as they turned onto Polpis Road there was a companionable quiet as "The One That Got Away" by Jake Owen had them each in their own worlds. Lexi cranked the volume to an insane level when "Wishful Drinking" came on next. Was she already pregaming, Nic thought, what exactly was in her Yeti turquoise tumbler anyway?

They pulled into the gatehouse at the end of Wauwinet Road to take the tires down to about 13 PSI with Rick giving her a detailed description why. Sounded like it was going to be a wild ride — Nic felt as excited as a little kid in line for Space Mountain and was glad she didn't get carsick.

"*Woohoo*," she couldn't keep it in, it was such wholesome fun, like catching air in the last seat of the school bus. "Wow, what is that place?"

"That is called the Wauwinet, named for one of the original Native American chiefs, or sachems I believe they were called," Cade told her, "Coastal elegance at its finest, since about 1875, I think. One of the oldest and most historic hotels on Nantucket."

"And definitely one of the priciest, if you can't tell," Poppy said, reminding Nicolina of her daughter, down-to-earth and seeing beyond the conspicuous consumption of the absurdly wealthy. For Nic, while she could appreciate the idea of something so extra, it actually made her uncomfortable to imagine living in that kind of aggressive luxury, she would never be able to relax with it, or enjoy it in the way she could in a deep fat chair with a cozy handmade blanket, a wooden table with a story in a kitchen with lots of windows and someone to play Bananagrams with. She was becoming more enamored with sweep of sand with every passing mile under their doughy tires.

"What do you think so far, Nic?" Rick asked, meeting her eyes again in the rearview. Nic could tell he was the kind of person who got excited to show people new things, appreciated the pleasure he'd see in their eyes, and that it magnified his own. Cade was like that too, in fact, he and Rick were more like siblings than he and Lexi. Lexi was a lucky woman.

"I'm speechless, breathless, all of it," Nic said over the sea breeze, taking Cade's hand in hers, "like I'm on the other side of the world. How lucky are all you guys for having grown up summering here."

"The Swains, yes," Rick said, "but my first visit here wasn't until I was about twenty-one — I came with my college roommate for a couple weeks, his family has a summer place. Or had, if memory serves, they sold it."

"Who would ever sell a house here? I mean it's something that will only ever increase its value, right?"

"Oh, you have no idea," Poppy chimed in, "pick the tiniest shack you can find on this island and I guarantee you it would sell for no less than one million dollars, and I am *not* exaggerating, am I Dad?"

"I wish you were, honey, I wish you were."

"Helloo?" Lexi said, "What do you care? We have a place here. Well, Mom and Dad do, that will be ours one day."

Ouch, Nic thought. People with not one, but two living parents just didn't realize the luck in that. Especially healthy, able, and generous ones.

"And one day, MINE," Piped up Tryp from the back.

"Alright, alright," Cade said, "Let's just enjoy this beautiful day." No sooner did Cade say that than they were cruising in the soft sand tracks with true-blue ocean on both sides of them, with white-sand dunes rising and falling out of view.

"Okay, this is officially my new favorite thing, view, place, mood, *everything* in the whole wide world, right here right now," Nic said, leaning into Cade to get closer to the window with her sunny hair waving in the wind like the silvery green dune grass. "So how did you two meet, was it here on the island?" Nic asked Lexi and Rick.

"Cutest. Story. Ever." Poppy said.

"It was here alright," Lexi said, "on a hot summer night at the Muse, *where the music never stops.*"

"We still got it, don't we, Hon? The music?" Rick said looking over at his wife.

"Stop," Lexi said, "I'll tell it. And you are as tone-deaf as ever." Turning to face Nic, she continued, "The Muse is this local bar with live music, pool tables, pizza, and yes, karaoke night. And once upon a sweaty summer night, this big lug was dared by a bunch of his drunk friends to get up there and sing Ricky Martin's "Livin La Vida Loca." It was so pathetic, it hurt. I had to rescue him."

"Come on, Mom, you're leaving out the part where you thought he was so hot — like Ryan Reynolds-hot," Poppy said.

"Awe, I love that," Nic said, "and you've been together since then?"

"*Oh, no*," Lexi said, like Phoebe from *Friends*. "He was working for a moving company out of Boston then — I mean, sorry but Gentle Giant was *so* not lining up with my expectations, ha! To be fair though, he did have a Bachelor's degree in computer science but he burned out on the IT jobs. And then his car obsession morphed into airplanes. Am I getting it right, Ricky Martin?" Lexi said.

Rick's incandescent charm lit his face, "Livin la vida loca ever since."

"That *is* the cutest story ever," Nic said.

"A*dor*able, now can we pick a spot already?" Tryp said from the way back.

"How do you pick a single spot with miles of this natural beauty?" Nic said.

"Anywhere we want," Rick said, "We can pull right over up ahead, no one in sight, or we could get closer to the light house? What's your pleasure, you choose, Nic."

"If we make camp up over there, are we close enough to the lighthouse for me to walk?"

"Sure, I'll just get a little closer," Rick said, cruising another one hundred yards. "How's this?"

Nic got out of the truck and stood, looking out at the cobalt sea set against the powdery sand under the denim sky, as far as the eye could see in both directions. "Just — oh my actual God — where do you even go from here? How does any other beach, in the universe measure up? I mean I've been to the south of France, I've been to three islands in Greece, Sicily, Saint Thomas — and I'm telling you — this is *it*."

Cade stood next to her, seeing it through her eyes, for the first time. She loved that about him, being fully present, his largesse. She did that too when she was somewhere familiar to her but new to the person with whom she was. Seeing something again for the first time, letting those first impressions trip your heart.

Rick smiled as he unpacked the beach chairs, setting them up in a friendly arc facing the ocean while Tryp wasted no time running straight into the water. Poppy was uncharacteristically checking her phone, self-conscious about it, announcing, "After this last email check, I'm putting my phone away, I promise."

"Why?" Lexi said, "who's judging?" Was she looking for permission herself, Nic wondered? "The service is surprisingly awesome out here," she said turning to Nic, whose only thought was — why would you want to be anywhere else?

Rick followed his son into the waves to frolic while keeping an eye out for the errant seal. They loved Great Point too. And where there were seals... You had to pay attention. Cade and Nic lathered each other's backs in Coppertone before plopping down — Cade in a chair, Nic on a big towel.

"We have plenty of chairs," Lexi offered, displaying the lovely arc they'd set up with her arm extended like a Price is Right model.

"Oh, thanks, maybe in a bit. I just love spreading out like this, feeling the hot sand under me." Nic felt a zing of pleasure at being included.

own at her from her over her Ray-Ban Jackie Ohh's
:val, then said under her breath, "whatever, it's your

Cade caught Nic up to speed on the bridge project in Boston, Nic only half-listening since his relaxed demeanor told her all she needed to know. The sun was working its magic — warming the air to a perfect seventy-five degrees — and bathing her in a slow tickling heat that made her sleepy. She was deliciously anchored on her wide towel on Nantucket's Great Point but also adrift in memories. She remembered something she read that went something like; *there are no days more full than the ones we go back to.*

She thought also that there is something especially nostalgic about summer days at the beach. Things rushed back from old hiding places as new as that yellow and white daisy bikini she had at age six, filling her waxy dixie cup from lunch with sand, carefully turning it over to pat and release, over and over until she had a castle. Playing Four Square on the hard sand with her dad, spiraling a mean football to Enzo, but dropping every frisbee Mia flung her way, while her mom looked on from behind her trademark black oval sunglasses buried in her latest book. They bodysurfed the waves because they didn't have boogey boards and waited for the tide to go out to float the wooden boats their dad had made them in the warm tidal pools left behind. And nothing in the world tasted better than peanut butter and jelly on Wonder Bread with Pecan Sandies for dessert.

"Is it lunchtime yet?" Tryp shouted as he jogged toward them, shaking his wet hair like a dog, startling Poppy and Nic who'd been half-asleep."

"What is WRONG with you, doofus? You just got everyone wet — does it ever occur to you to *think* before you do something?" Poppy scolded.

"You're at the beach, wuss, get a grip, now where are them sandwiches at, I'm starving," Tryp said, carelessly kicking up sand on his way to the cooler in the back of the Defender. Nic thought how Tryp would be a different boy, man, if he had a brother.

"Hey bud," Rick said coming up to the truck pointing down the beach, "check it out. Looks like he's got something pretty big on his line." They both looked twenty-five yards down the beach to see a guy surfcasting with his rod bowed by the weight of something big. Tryp and his dad walked toward him for a closer look, Cade joining them, then Nic jogging to catch up. They watched the man reel in hard then lean forward, reeling in harder. Nic could feel the tension and the thrill — and she was suddenly torn between wanting the guy to haul a huge wriggling Striper out of the water and having it break away, free.

She was probably the only happy one that it broke free. "Awe DUDE, I totally thought you HAD that thing, sucks man," Tryp said.

"Yeah me too. Son of *bitch*."

"Have you been out to the point? I hear the rip's been pretty good — blues and bass running," Cade offered, "Catch the right tide on the right day and you're pretty much guaranteed top surf casting action." The man thanked him then headed off toward the point.

"Hey Dad, when can we go out on Bubba's boat for some deep-sea action, we haven't even done that yet this summer," Tryp asked Rick.

'We'll see, bud, I know things have been a little crazy this summer, but it just started! Let's get past this wedding stuff, okay? And didn't you say Max would be giving you more hours down at the pier? That was the deal you know — if you were going to live here for the summer — full-time hours. And if you can't get them as a dockhand, you'll have to supplement with a second job, a deal's a deal."

Tryp didn't have much in the way of a response for his father and wanted to get back to his lunch. While the men all reached in the cooler for a sandwich and a beer, Nic was surprised she actually felt her stomach growling. That was another thing about the beach, the ocean, and summer — your appetite for everything was insatiable.

She grabbed a container of cantaloupe chunks and sat in a chair. She offered some to Lexi sitting beside her and was pleased when she accepted.

"So sweet, right?" Lexi said, "is this all of the melon from the fridge?"

Nic couldn't tell if Lexi was passive/aggressively accusing her of eating all the cantaloupe but she decided to play it as if not. "Nope. Plenty left. And honeydew and watermelon. It's weird with melon, though, one day it's perfectly sweet, next day it stingy like vinegar. I still don't know how to buy a decent melon, no idea what to look for. Do you smell it? Press that spot where the blossom was — but how do you tell the difference between *that* and the stem end, is thumping involved?"

"You thump a *watermelon,* you kook. A cantaloupe should be tan in color with light green lines across it," Lexi said, "A ripe melon has a sweet smell that's fruity and a little musky, and, yes that spot should yield to the touch but not be too soft or too hard."

"Well, listen to you," Nic said, mildly surprised.

"Two summers working at Bartlett's Farm, don't look so shocked. We had summer jobs here like anyone else. Anyway, don't eat too much of that — shit bloats you. What does *not* make me bloated, bitches, is rosé." Lexi stood up from her chair and headed to the Yeti, asking Nic over her shoulder, "you in?"

Nic really wanted to get some reading in before she started drinking. But she was kind of enjoying the camaraderie. "Hell yes," she said, because, well, it was *summahtime...and the livin was eassyyyy.*

Naturally they wouldn't be drinking out of solo cups, but Nic didn't expect such fine stemware, plastic of course, but still. And she had to admit, it was more fun getting to see the pink bubbles in action. "Hey Poppy, how about you? Ready for some fizz in your day?"

"It's barely noon you lushes. Thanks, but maybe later, the sun feels delicious."

"More for us," Lexi said tapping Nic's *glass* as they sat back in their chairs, mesmerized by the sea, how the wind rippled the surf with streaks of foam.

Nic picked up her Mary Coffin Starbuck book and out dropped the letter from Sofia to Gino. Lexi did another of her over-the-sunglasses looks.

"What in Holy Christ are you reading? That thing looks like it was typed on a Smith Corona at the kitchen table like a hundred years ago," Lexi said bending down to retrieve the yellowed envelope before the wind took off with it. "Oooh what do we have here? Wait, is this, a Nantucket postmark? From nineteen-sixty....? Can't read the year but what is this?"

"So you think Nantucket too? It's so faded and I was sure it came from Nantasket — more my mom's style — but then Cade caught the zip code. Sofia was my mom and this letter is to my dad, Gino. Although they weren't my parents yet. Barely in their twenties! Going through my dad's things my brother and I found an extreme amount of stuff — a mashup of Antiques Roadshow and Hoarders if I'm being honest. Seriously, photos that when stacked in boxes towered over me, not including the boxes of slide carousels, letters, keepsakes, and cards celebrating every milestone known to man, woman, and child.

"Back up, back up," Lexi interrupted, "Get back to the letter from Nantucket. And note to self — burn all journals and letters before I'm trapped in the memory ward literally losing my fucking mind for real — and the whole family's digging through all my private shit. But back to you. What's with the letter —why is it stuck in that tome you're reading? Sorry about your father and everything, I can't imagine it, but go."

Nic's heart was beating in her throat so she took a healthy slug of her pink drink. "I tucked it in the book so my dog wouldn't get it — but I'm glad I did, maybe you guys can help me puzzle it out."

"Mom, seriously?" Poppy interjected, "Is this really any of your business?"

"No, it's okay," Nic said, "I haven't really had time to think about it — why my mom would have spent time here without ever sharing that. I mean she knew I'd been dying to get back here after that college daytrip, to see the roses climbing whole cottages and rooftops for real instead of on a postcard, to capture it all with my paints. *Why the secret*? That's what I don't understand."

Nic tried to reign in her thought parade. And just be present, there on the edge of the world. Every single person had secrets. It's not like her parents, *or* her children for that matter, knew anything about the time she did too many shrooms in Morocco and misssed the train from Casablanca to Marrakech. Or that night in college when her roommate Holly crashed her car and Nic switched seats with her and told the cops *she'd* been driving to save Holly from big trouble with her father.

She took a loud breath like she was coming up from under water. "So, *this* was in an old box with some other letters, but I found it by accident because it was under a fake bottom."

Poppy sat up to listen more intently, even Lexi had leaned in. "Interesting...," Poppy said, "I guess we don't think of our parents as having secrets from us."

"But that's just it — they weren't always our parents. They were kids once just like anyone," Nic said.

"True," Poppy said, "I'd love to know what *you're* hiding, Mom, ha! Wait, scratch that, I probs do not want to know."

"And you never will because I won't keep incriminating evidence!" Lexi said, emptying the last of the bottle into Nic's cup. "I mean, if this was meant to be all hush-hush why hide it and not burn it?"

"Unless," Poppy said, *"unless* you were meant to find it, exactly now, when both of your parents are gone."

As the guys came up from the water, Nic stared out at the candid and endless horizon, considering that possibility, that she was meant to be there, that all roads led to Nantucket. A ripple of something curled down her spine.

"Not to be nosy — well, of course to be *nosy* — but what's in the letter?" Lexi said.

Nic handed Lexi the envelope. "Have at it. It's not much."

Lexi put the letter in her chair while she got up to root around in the Yeti for a second bottle of Miraval, popping the cork in dramatic fashion on her way back to her chair.

"Mom, are you kidding me?" Poppy scolded, first for leaving the cork where it had blasted and *then* for the second bottle.

"What do you think this is, *amateur hour*? Come on Pop," Lexi said scooping up the cork and topping off her glass and Nic's to just this side of overflowing.

Cade surveyed the scene with a chuckle. "Yeah, we're definitely intruding on noon-is-the-new-happy-hour. Let's toss the football," he said to Rick and Tryp.

"Make it a frisbee and I'm in," Tryp said.

As they walked down the beach Rick shouted over his shoulder and the sound of the surf, "Pace yourselves ladies, we have a long night ahead…"

"Talk about amateurs," Poppy said, "Okay, I'm in, Mom, hit me." Poppy had to help herself to the sparkling wine since her mom was engrossed in Sofia's letter.

"Well, I love a juicy story and a good mystery but we have precious little to work with here," Lexi said, setting the page in her lap. "Okay, so I'm confused — this letter sounds like Sofia and Gino were not a couple, but more like best friends, right? So, help me understand… And what do you think Sofia meant by *I need you*? Did she need someone offed and Gino had like some mafia connections from the old country?

Or more like *I can't make my life work on this little island and I have nowhere to go?"*

Nic choked on her bubbly. "*Mafia*? Oh girl, you are going down the wrong road. Gino was like this pillar of the community, you're way off!" Nic took another sip. Too big, it circled back up her nose. She didn't really know where to start. This part of her parents' history was a mystery to her. She'd started to ask herself if she'd known them at all — or just the versions they'd allowed her to see.

"They were high school sweethearts," Nic said, "Or, if we're being technical, middle school. Separated only by geography after graduation when my mother went to college in Providence and my dad was doing a post-grad year in New York — that's the story I grew up with anyway."

"Seriously? Jesus H," Lexi said, "middle school? That's a long time — of course there had to be a split in there somewhere. And not to quote Ross Geller or anything but they were clearly *on a break* when this letter was written, am I right?" Lexi said, as the letter in her hand fluttered in the breeze.

"Seems so," Nic said, "there was another letter in the main part of the box where Gino confesses to Sofia that he failed some entrance exam for the Navy. He sounded really wrecked by it — writing that he was *worthless*, not even good enough company for a dog, or something crazy like that, and that she deserved so much better, and that he wouldn't embarrass himself by even considering approaching her father for her hand knowing he was such a failure. So, yeah, it sounded like he was ending things. But for how long? And he was definitely in the Navy! That's where he met his best friend that he had for the rest of his life. And my mom used to put us in his old regulation sailor caps at the beach — those thick white canvas ones, they were legit. And his name was stenciled on each one."

"Well what the fuck then," Lexi said.

"That's sad, how hard he was on himself," Poppy said, "what a waste. I know more than a few guys who could use a shot of humility to break up the arrogance. Well, thank God Gino and Sofia were reunited somehow then and went on to have your perfect family, right?"

Nic took another sweet swallow looking out at the thin seam separating the blues of the sky and the sea. "Nothing is perfect but we had it pretty good. I had a great childhood with parents who loved us and put our needs before their own, who spent time with us, taking us on all kinds of adventures. The most important thing to them was how we treated each other — Enzo, Mia, and me — that we loved each other and would always support each other. They didn't tolerate fighting, or worse, indifference."

"That sounds wonderful," Poppy said, almost wistfully.

"Oh, don't get all weepy like I didn't care about you and your brother just because instead of taking you to Niagara Falls and Disney World we brought you to Paris and London," Lexi said.

"And shopping at Harrod's and *high tea* at the Palm Court in the Ritz was just every seven-year old's kid's dream? You don't get it Mom."

"Save me the poor little rich girl song and dance, Poppy."

"Forget it. I've had an abundant childhood, you are right."

"So, what do we know?" Lexi asked, turning her attention back to Sofia and Gino's love affair. "One: your parents were high school sweethearts. Sorry, middle school, whatever. Two: Sofia went to college while Gino did a post-grad year. Three: at some point during that first year out of high school Gino failed some Naval entrance exam and was ready to throw himself off the Potomac — and we have *no* idea what Sofia was going through because Gino didn't save all her letters stacked and tied in a sweet satin ribbon for his future progeny to exhume. Four: at some point they married and had three perfect children. Am I getting this right so far?"

"You are," Nic said, feeling pleasantly buzzed and as though they were talking about characters in a novel. Which was working for her. Beautiful Sofia and handsome Gino — young lovers who lost their way and spent God knows how many months or years apart before finally getting married and having a lovely family for their happily ever after.

"What we *don't* know," Lexi began again, enumerating on her fingers, "Did they really break up or just take some time apart? Sounds like they definitely lost touch. Did Sofia quit school to move Nantucket? When was Gino in the Navy? And you said he was an attorney so that means not only undergrad but law school too — when did all that happen? HOW does your mom being here on Nantucket once-upon-a-time fit into the story, WHY did Sofia write to Gino all of a sudden asking for help, WHAT kind of help, and is that when they got back together? Our list of unknowns is decidedly longer."

Nic, Lexi, and Poppy each sat back in their chairs, lids heavy with the wine and the sun. Nic felt like a bubble bursting on the surface of a dream. With two bottles down, the sharpest moments for mystery-solving had long since passed. They dozed separately but together under the golden sun with lazy low waves rolling in and rushing out.

A frisbee landed just short of Poppy's foot spraying a generous amount of sand on the ladies wrenching them from their collective beach coma.

"*What* is the matter with you, Tryp, you total dingus — and you seriously wonder why you don't have a girlfriend? You're a *child*, that's why!" Poppy scolded.

"Okay, okay Pop, take it down a notch, I'm sure it was an accident," Rick said.

"Really, Dad?" Poppy said, shaking her head trying to dust the sand off her sunblock-slick skin.

The breeze had picked up and carried off the spat — Nic catching only snippets of voices as her brain came swimming up out of sleep. "Wow, hey guys, what time is it — how long have we been out here?"

"No, the question is how many bottles did you guys go through, jeeze" Tryp said.

"Zip it, Tryp," Rick said, "and help me start loading the truck."

"Already?" Lexi said, stretching, forcing herself awake. "But this feels sooo good, we can't leave yet..."

"And will you be the one to tell our dear mother that we'll be late?" Cade said to his sister, "it's rehearsal dinner night for Cousin Lincoln don't forget."

"Could we, though? Forget?" Lexi said.

Rick came up behind his wife to kiss her on the head before unceremoniously tipping her out of her chair so he could start loading the truck. Nic looked over at an advancing Cade with a smile playing at the edges of his mouth. "Don't even think about it Swain," she said But before she knew it Cade had scooped her up and was jogging with her in his arms straight into the water.

"Oh, my fucking God, don't *you* even think about it," Lexi said to Rick. Who wasn't even thinking about it. But he was enjoying, vicariously, the sight of Cade tossing Nic into the sea.

It was impossible to be mad at Cade, Nic thought, coming up for air and sweeping her long wet hair off her face, she was so damn attracted to him it scared her — his energy, a smile that dazzled, and the way his eyes lit up like a kid getting away with something. Sexiness could be hard to quantify but Cade was a bona fide member of the one percent. She did a dolphin dive then surfaced to face him. "Whew, it gets deep fast," she said with her arms around his neck as he scooped her close, his heart flush against hers kicking hard. He pressed salty kisses on her neck making her giggle and squirm.

"Stop! You know how ticklish I am. Plus, let's not start something..."

"Fine, fine," he said releasing her, "race ya back!"

Nic was a strong swimmer and kicked it into high gear back to shore. She knew Cade was powerful and good at just about everything, but he was a lead weight in the water. She never looked back until she could stand in the sand and high-step it the rest of the way to shore.

Reaching up to squeeze the water from her hair, she turned in time to catch Cade rising up out of the waves like Aquaman.

"Alright you two, do you think you could keep your hands off each other for five minutes," Rick said, "you need to dry off and we gotta fly."

"Yeah come on Uncle Cade, this is a family show, jeeze, show some restraint bruh," Tryp said, leaning against the truck with *not soda* in his koozie.

Poppy gave her towel a final shake before packing it in her Lily Pulitzer beach tote and loading it into the back with Tryp. "Oh my God did you just fart?" She said to her brother, waving the air in front of her nose, "You seriously had to save that for inside the car — are you *kidding me?*"

"Oooh yeah, that's got some hang-time, sorry!" Tryp said.

Nic quaked with silent laughter in the middle seat. As they turned to go fog was stealing in, painting a lavender line at the horizon and slowly swallowing the sun.

Chapter Eleven

POST-BEACH SHOWERING HAD to happen in short order if they were to be dressed and coiffed in time for the dinner. And Nic only gave in to *showering with a friend* since the windows above the cedar plank stall belonged to an empty room. Cade had been so right about the open air sweetened by Rosa rugosa, cedar and sun. Heavy hot rivers streamed off her body as she backed into the rainfall shower head rinsing the salt and sea away, tickling down her spine. When she opened her eyes, Cade was staring into them, his deep ocean pools darkened by desire. She felt the hairs on her arms lift, the air was charged.

She watched emotions chase across his face as he squeezed lavender body soap into his palms then onto her shoulders. His calloused hands and perfect pressure made her weak. She turned to face him fully and soaped his chest, reaching down to feel him. A muffled groan escaped him as her grip tightened. He parted her with a slow ease.

He lifted her effortlessly as they moved to the small bench, she was only distantly aware of the risk of being caught. Nic stared into his eyes and lowered herself onto him. "Shh…." She whispered into his ear as she took him in, rocking at an achingly slow pace with her breasts rising up to his mouth. Time collapsed, and she was flooded with a pleasure she wasn't used to feeling.

∞

No one was the wiser as everyone gathered in the kitchen at six o'clock for a glass of wine and a small cheese board before heading to Ventuno. Nicolina was stunning in a black halter-neck jumpsuit and black platform Bernardo Raleighs that buckled at the ankle. Her hair was sun-kissed and an elegant combination of sexy and sophisticated in a sleek low knot with a deep side part.

Prudence looked like she didn't know quite what to say, but her husband did. "Why, Nicolina dear, aren't you an absolute vision, bellissima."

"Wow," Poppy said to Nic, "can I be you?"

Nearly at a loss for words Nic said, "I'd say being you is pretty great, Poppy, but thank you. And, John, I'm very flattered, thank you."

"Well, dear, you know what they say about flattery..." Prudence said.

Nic sipped her wine and weighed the fairness of Mrs. Swain's remark.

"Oh Prue," John said, "I mean it in the sincerest fashion. You're a breathtaking young lady, Nicolina, and my son has superb taste." Nic would have done anything for the attention of the room to be directed elsewhere.

"Thanks Dad, I couldn't agree more," Cade said with his arm possessively around Nic's small waist while his mother leaned against the counter, in cream linen slacks, legs crossed at the ankles with her pale rose pashmina slung artfully across her shoulders, as if she liked her pose too much to undo it.

"Bottoms up darlings, we will not be late," Prue said finally, gathering up her Hermès purse and handing the keys to John.

"Hey Mimi, how about I drive so you and Pops can relax," Tryp offered, hope raising his eyebrows nearly up to his hairline.

"Over my cold, dead body my dear boy, now chop-chop, let's go."

"Better luck in your next life, kid," Lexi said, "maybe Dad will let you drive his Defender." Once again Nic found herself feeling bad for Tryp — it had to suck being the youngest, the last to do everything. How were you supposed to ever grow up when you would be the baby forever after? Mia never let her forget it. She was starting to understand him better and his subconscious craving for attention.

"No, you can't drive Dad's car because then who would sit in the way back? Just go with Mimi and Pops, Tryp, stop making things difficult."

Tryp flashed a hand gesture for his sister's eyes only on his way out to his grandparents' car.

Nic was pleased she'd gone with the slicked updo as the fog was thickening and her hair would have otherwise been more bozo than bellissima. She felt good. Beautiful even. And she decided not to let what anyone else was wearing change her mind about that. Cade was handsome in cream linen trousers, pale pink shirt and navy sport jacket.

They found parking on the first lap and didn't have to walk far to the restaurant. Ventuno looked polished in an elegant Greek Revival building downtown in the Nantucket Historic District on Federal Street. Nic realized she was ravenous and excited for the renowned handmade pasta with Nantucket Bay scallops. Their group was led upstairs where she could see the party had started — she was eager to have a glass of wine in her hand so she wouldn't fidget.

Prudence and John were already there, talking and laughing with guests, Nic wondered if one of them was Prue's brother, father of the groom. She'd already forgotten the name of the bride and groom, if she'd ever known them. She would meet maybe thirty people tonight, most of whose names she would not remember. She figured she'd only be known as Cade's date anyway so she wouldn't sweat it. The only young people present appeared to be the bridal party, which, as far as she could tell, added up to an abounding nine maids and nine groomsmen. Nic wouldn't have even five close enough friends to fill the bill. She'd kept three close friends across the years and that was enough for her. Women had become so competitive in her experience, the time wasted comparing made them pinched and old.

"A lot of old-timers here," Poppy said standing next to Nic.

"Yes, that's because this is a tradition really meant for the parents," Nic told Poppy, "You know, and their people. So, does your cousin have siblings or are these kids in the bridal party all friends?"

"They must be — Lincoln is an only child. I'd bet most are from the bride's side. It's a lot, isn't it?"

"It is to me, but I haven't been to a wedding in forever. And you probably haven't been to many yet, have you? Your friends are still too young."

"Correct. I am *not* ready for all that. There's this girl at work who's like twenty-nine and you should hear her, she's hysterical — and let me get the Boston accent right; '*First* it's the engagement *pahty* — need a bougie dress for that, *then* the freaken bachelorette, right? Always like a *total* destination thing — I mean, *really*? It just should *not* be that *hahd*! It would be so much *smahtah* to just go to a *bah*, you know? Drink a few beeahs, maybe some shawts? And then dinnah, right? SO much *cheapah*! Then there's the WEDDING. Don't even get me *stahted* on the bridesmaids dresses... And then in a year or two it's the *baby showah*, and then the friggin *gendah reveal*! BOOM I'm out TEN K! I sweah to gawd.'"

Nic was laughing so hard she almost spilled her drink and peed herself. It would have been worth it. She hadn't noticed Cade wander off but she guessed he had to make the rounds to family he hadn't seen in a while. Lexi came back from the bar to stand beside Poppy and Nic, a drink in each hand. "Thanks, Mom," Poppy said reaching for one.

"UH-UH, get your own. I had to pretend to know who your Great Aunt Mary even was for like ten minutes waiting for these," Lexi said, taking a healthy slug out of one glass, while scanning the room.

"Really, Mother, double-fisted?" Poppy said.

"How else are we getting through this shitshow? I don't know why we need to be here," Lexi said, on her way to emptying the first of her two drinks, "I wish we'd stayed uninvited. Isn't having to go to the wedding enough?"

"*Having* to go to the wedding? What's your deal, Mom? It's at Galley Beach for God's sake — the most beautiful spot on the island, *on the water*, and it's closing just for this wedding!"

"Wow," Nic said, "that sounds amazing, I can't wait to see it. Tell me more, Poppy." Nic said, her face soft with wine, wholly enjoying the mini tuna tartare cones and the prosciutto-wrapped persimmons with goat cheese. Absorbed in the moment and trying to work out how Prue's nephew was marrying John's niece, she listened to Poppy describe the Galley at Cliffside Beach...the candle-lit tables on powder-white sand that stretched to the sea, rolling out as far as you could see in both directions. And then how the sun, red as an orchid, planed down toward the horizon line, casting its firelight across the sky.

Nic was startled by the buzz of her phone in her purse. She hated to be that person on her phone at an event but seeing two missed calls and a text from Evelyn, she couldn't ignore it and excused herself to the ladies' room.

Mom — sorry to bother you, Ben and I are fine but Snoopy's on a freedom run or something. He never does this with me — I always let him off-leash and he never runs off! He's such a knucklehead I know but he always comes back! Ugh. Dad says he has deer that traipse through his back yard and that Snoop's probably tracking like a bigshot. IDK — It's been two hours and the neighbors haven't seen him! I'm so sorry to bother you Mom but I don't know what to do! And I hate to say this but Dad says there have also been coyotes hanging around. Tell me what to do. Sorry! GAH! PLEASE call me when you get this!

Nic felt the blood leave her limbs and nausea roil. She lowered herself to the toilet which thankfully had a lid. Her sweet puppy, she could not lose that sweet boy — her empty-nest baby who rescued her in so many ways. She tried taking deep breaths but swallowed them when a couple of women came into the ladies' room talking.

"I don't know who she is," one of them said at the sink, "but if she's with that Cade Swain, she is one lucky lady. Doesn't he just get more handsome every time we see him, Carol?"

"Oh Joyce, you *cougar* — he's Tom's nephew for cripe's sake, and he's half our age!"

Nic would have laughed if she weren't so close to throwing up. She couldn't call Ev back from the toilet. She'd have to get her shit together and step outside. The sink was running, she hoped the ladies were wrapping it up.

"All I can say, Carol, is God only knows how that uptight Prudence gave birth to that lovely man. She probably lost her virginity in World War II for Mercy's sake — and not to one of our guys!"

"Oh shh, you never know who can hear you Joyce, let's get back to the party, have another drink, and see if we can't find a more appropriate man here for you to get your panties in a twist over."

Their cackling followed them out into the hall and Nic had to make her move. Willing her legs to carry her down the steps outside, she turned the corner waiting to press Ev's contact. The air had a chill now that the sky was darkening and it plucked Nic out of her happy buzz. What was she waiting for? *No news was good news* did NOT apply to this situation at all.

Nic's cell number was on Snoopy's tag, if someone had found him, they'd call. No news meant that Snoopy was still missing, possibly lost in a neighborhood he wasn't used to, or laying with a broken leg in the middle of the woods, or being shredded by a coyote or a Fisher. *Please let him be okay, please let him be okay*, she chanted over and over in her head then hit *call*.

What was her phone doing, what was happening, another call coming in at the same time? This always messed her up, the red symbols, green, the choices: End and accept, Send to voicemail, Hold and accept, GAH, what the fuck was she supposed to hit godammit?!

Breathe.

"Mom? Mom, are you there? Hello?" Okay, it was Evelyn, breathe, listen, and don't be hysterical, she told herself.

"I'm here, honey, I'm here," Nic kept saying to stymie bad news. Denial was her go-to. She let Evy talk, let her say things. Other things. Then jumped at Cade materializing by her side mouthing *are you okay?* She didn't have an answer for him but took comfort in the heat emanating from his body.

"Mom, *Mom*, we don't have Snoopy yet, but while we were out looking a neighbor of Dad's said they saw him sprinting through their back yard."

Nic let go of the breath that was stuck in her heart and grabbed Cade's hand, staring through him as she concentrated on Evy's voice. "Well, that's good, right? He's not hurt if he's running and he's still nearby then, right?" Nic could hear hysteria rising in her voice, asking Evelyn if she'd tried shouting, 'TREATS'. Then catching Cade's confused expression she moved the phone away from her mouth to clarify and whisper-shouted, "Snoopy ran away!"

Nic ended the call with her daughter making her promise to call or text with ANY updates then filled Cade in on Snoopy's latest mad dash through the swampy woods in the back of Brad's property.

Cade had his hand on her lower back as he told her to try not to worry. Which was always the dumbest thing to say and to have to hear. Her puppy was racing around an unfamiliar neighborhood that coyotes frequented and it would be dark soon. Yes, he had ID on his collar with her cell number and, yes, it was more cul-de-sacs than deep woods. But still. Worst-case scenarios always barged in.

There was nothing she could do. Except not let Cade down. She let him hustle her up the stairs and back to the party to catch the speeches. And another round. "I'm surprised Ev let him off his leash knowing the property is not fenced in," Cade said.

"Um, *I'm* not. She sees me do it all the time, it's *my fault*."

"No, it is absolutely not your fault, Nic, you know he only comes when *you* call him. Ev should know that too, right? You really have to stop taking the fall for everything that goes wrong." It looked to Nic like Cade was biting his tongue. She was pretty sure he wanted to add *and Brad is an irresponsible asshole*. But he didn't. Boundaries were still in the navigational period. And while Brad may have been a lot of things, Nic knew he was a good dad. "Sorry, none of my business, just looking out for you," Cade said, "And you know what, I'm sure that crazy dog will find his way back sooner than later, out of hunger or boredom anyway."

They entered the dining room just as George was dinging a champagne glass with is fork, ready for his father-of-groom speech:

"Good evening, everyone, I'm George Gardner, father of our groom, Lincoln, and I'd like to thank you all for being here tonight. Actually, you should be thanking *me*, because, well, here you are at Ventuno's on Nantucket! I'm kidding, I'm kidding. No, I'm not. Ha! Seriously, though. The Gardner family has enjoyed a long history as successful whalers and fishermen — and we're happy to see Linc carry on the tradition in obtaining the finest catch in Christina."

Nic was looking around at the other married couples, wondering if they might be reliving their own rehearsal dinner nights and weddings. She felt like an extra at this event, unnecessary, a plus one, which, of course, she was. But it was a voyeuristic opportunity to study at least some of Cade's family. It seemed that Cade was more Swain than Gardner, more like his father; disarmingly honest, unfailingly kind, open, generous. And, she'd yet to wrap her head around the fact that there she was, a part of a group made up of two of the founding families of Nantucket. She was pretty sure she was the only one weighing the coolness of that. *And* the only one questioning her own lack of archival lineage. Guests appeared to be soundly planted in their abundant present.

Nic wasn't sure exactly where Lexi was planted, besides at the table with her two glasses in front of her. They'd started something out at Great Point that day, Lexi had come to life contemplating the mystery of Sofia and Gino — had seemed attentive, animated even — Nic wanted more of that. They'd created this esprit-de corps and it felt good. Having lost both parents made her feel adrift. Like all of a sudden she doubted her ability to steer, to navigate. It's not a feeling she'd predicted, no one probably does, but it was real.

"What's eating you?" Lexi asked. Nic really wished she didn't wear her thoughts on her face so much. And then she burst out laughing like an insane person.

"*What's eating you* — you know what that reminds me of?" Nic said, "No, don't guess, I'll tell you," Was she slurring? "One year, my ex-husband's idiot brother, Luke, actually wore a t-shirt that said *Eat me, I'm organic* to Thanksgiving dinner!"

"Stop it, I fucking love that — Luke is my hero."

"Ha! So, Lexi, where's a good spot for a drink when things wrap up here?" What was she doing? Did she really need to keep drinking? Yes. Yes, she did. She liked how her heavy thoughts had a pillow now. She couldn't let her mute phone torment her — she had to eclipse the *worst-case* shit barraging her brain. She filled Lexi in on Snoopy.

"That little asshole. Sorry. I had a dog who liked to run like that — we called him Houdini the way he'd get himself free. What a dick. No, we loved him, he was awesome, but my mother would stay up all night sleeping in the living room until she heard him at the damn door.

She wanted to punish him and hug him all at the same time. He always, always came back."

"Prudence did that? I'm trying to picture it..."

"Oh she loves dogs, believe it or not. After her last one passed though she said she couldn't go through it again."

"I can see that, " Nic said, "and thanks for not saying *don't worry*."

"That's what my fucking brother said, isn't it — Jesus. Okay — well, let's see, there's Gaslight, there's Club Car — we've done Straight Wharf..."

"You forgot Cru," Poppy said, joining them.

"Nope. Didn't forget it. Cru needs to get over itself. Yeah, no, I am all set with Cru, thanks," Lexi said.

As distant and uninterested as she presented at times, Lexi was badass. "You pick," Nic said, "I'm down for whatever." Honestly Nic just wanted to get out of that small dining room — as quaint as it was, the walls were closing in. She was thrilled when Lexi stood up and reached for her bag. "Let's check out Gaslight, they usually have live music. Beats hanging around here with the parade of Chads and Beckys."

Nic was all in, Poppy too, but what about Rick and Cade?

"Hey beautiful ladies," Rick said approaching them, "were you sneaking out?"

"Not sneaking, just leaving," Lexi said in her unvarnished way, "let's go girls."

"Wait, wait, wait," Cade interrupted, "where you all headed? And where's your brother, Pop?"

"*Not it*," she said, "and looks like he's found some friends over there anyway. Plus, he's underage and packing a fake ID, so yeah, not it!"

Everyone laughed and Rick squeezed Lexi's shoulder, kissed the top of Poppy's head, and told the group he'd square Tryp away and meet them at Gaslight. "Sure, you will," his wife said. Explaining to Nic as they headed outside that what that meant was *maybe* they'd see Rick in an hour or more. He was a charming conversationalist and as a pilot he knew a lot of people in a lot of places.

"Which is totally fine because we don't need him," Lexi said, "or you, little brother, if you'd rather be somewhere else."

Cade attempted to get his arms around all three as they walked, "Where else in the world would I want to be?"

"So, tell me about Gaslight," Nic said, checking her phone *again*, double-checking that the ringer was all the way up."

"It's actually a pretty fun spot," Poppy said, "it's only been Gaslight since 2019 — used to be Starlight. They've always had live music though, you know, indie bands — local and national — with more of a Japanese Asian fusion vibe now. Killer drinks and of course Saki if you're into that. I personally think Saki is disgusting but that's just me, I mean fermented rice? No thanks. But it's a cool spot. Hopefully no line."

As they turned down Union Street Nic could tell by the clumps of people hanging around the entrance that it was a hot spot. "Looks like the place to be."

"Oh fuck this line," Lexi said, "I'm going in — Fitz is probably behind bar, hang on."

"Ugh, I hate when she does this diva routine," Poppy said, "like she's Mariah Carey — humiliating."

Then next thing they knew a big bald dude with a short dark beard in a t-shirt and jeans with a bar towel over his shoulder was waving them in, ahead of the kids in line. "And that must be Fitz," Nic said, "right? Cutting in front of people makes me so uncomfortable," she whispered to Cade. But looking around, no one seemed to notice or care.

Cade walked behind her with both hands on her hips moving her through the entrance with a low-key fist bump for Fitz, "Thanks, man."

"Your sister can be very persuasive," Fitz said, "what are you drinkin?"

Nic heard Poppy order whatever Cisco Brewery beer was on tap, Lexi got a Thug's Passion, whatever that was, Cade was getting his *usual* which was apparently bourbon neat — Maker's Mark — and having to decide fast Nic went with the Cu-Cumba (tequila, cukes, lime and mint).

"Tequila? Are you nuts?" Lexi commented, "you're in charge of your woman," she said to Cade.

Nic looked back and forth at each of them, "something I should know about?"

"Oh nothing," Lexi said, "it's just that some of us can't tolerate the devil's juice — it's a Swain thing."

"What, are Swains collectively allergic to tequila or something?" Nic said, with her finger and thumb rubbing her **S** pendant, a habit she'd noticed recently.

"Ha, NO, it's more of a Swain aversion I guess you'd say," Cade said, "Or maybe just a Lexi-problem. You're safe. But you know that song, Nic, you're a country music fan — doesn't tequila make your clothes fall off?"

"Very funny, Cade, and you should know better than anyone — I do not need tequila for my clothes to..." Oh shit, was she saying that out loud? How much had she had to drink already, *Jesus*. Cade kissed her to shut her up, giggling into her mouth and tasting like caramel, oak and cloves.

"Here you are, pretty lady," Fitz said, putting her drink in front of her on the bar, "Wow, cool pendant, looks like a wax seal."

"Wax seal?" Poppy asked, "It's silver, right? I don't get it."

"Yeah," Fitz said to Poppy, "I guess you wouldn't — we don't exactly seal letters with a wax stamp anymore."

"What's a letter? Ha!" Poppy said, "But now that you say that — I can totally picture it. I've never seen a piece of jewelry stamped that way, though," she said taking a closer look at Nic's pendant, "It has a very old-world feel, and sort of secretive too —like if the wax seal was broken on a letter, that meant it had been opened and read, right?"

"Exactly," Fitz said, mixing and shaking a long line of drinks, "It looks familiar to me for some reason, like I've seen it somewhere before."

"Whatever, dude," Lexi said, "I'm ready for another."

"Mom, Jesus," Poppy said.

"Well, which is it, Mom or Jesus?"

"I *cannot* with her right now..." Poppy sighed, turning her attention to Nic, "hey let's go check out the band, Crooked Coast is onstage."

Nic was glad for the distraction and the volume to pull her out of her torment over her missing dog. She checked her phone constantly, convincing herself he was found and safe but word hadn't reached her yet. Maybe the service was bad — that *had* to be it. Of course! She held that fiction in front of her like a shield. Then wondered if the booze was bringing out an untrustworthy euphoria.

Chapter Twelve

COTTON MOUTH AND EYES dried shut was not how Nic wanted to wake up the Saturday of the wedding, but she'd earned it. Disoriented, she sat up and looked around the room as flashes of memory sifted in. She didn't *do* black-out-drunk, never had, but last night was at least a qualifier. It could have been the tequila — or more probably just the alarming quantity of alcohol consumed. Why did *one more* always seem like the best idea? Some kind of evil mind game. Quitting while one was ahead was the simplest advice, but somehow the most impossible to follow. Water, coffee, and getting vertical were all in order. She looked over at Cade, sleeping like a puppy without a care, and she envied him that level of bliss.

Puppy...SNOOPY! In a cold sweat she fumbled for her phone that Cade had apparently plugged into its charger. Hands trembling, head pounding, she unlocked her phone and stared at all the little red notifications. Missed calls, voicemails, texts.

> *Mom — where are you? I've been trying to reach you all night! We have Snoopy! He's fine — nothing that a bath won't fix. Please CALL ME!*

Nic laid heavily back on her pillow, accepting the full weight of her throbbing skull as penance along with the waft of sweaty hair and regret.

The white lace curtains lifted, waved, and settled back again, revealing peeks of the sideways spill of the rising sun. Slowly she pressed herself up off the bed so she wouldn't disturb the gracious man beside her who was more than she deserved. She needed to move her body and give her brain things to do. A walk would feel too lonely without Snoopy and her body would reject a run. She grabbed a white t-shirt and jean shorts, found her flip-flops and tip-toed out the door into the bathroom. She was surprised to find she looked better than she felt. Those days had to be numbered, the collagen collapse was already in progress. She brushed her teeth and hair and smeared moisturizer on her face before heading downstairs.

"Morning!" Poppy said, chugging water at the sink after her run. "So, I was thinking — you wanna grab some coffee at the Hub and then check out Quidley's?

"Yes, definitely!" Nic said trying all the cabinet doors looking for a water glass."

Poppy opened the cabinet to the left of the sink and handed her a glass. "Awesome — I'll just grab a quick shower outside, give me ten minutes."

"You can take more than ten minutes, girl, don't you need something to eat? How far do you run?" Sometimes youth seemed very far in the rearview.

"About four miles," Poppy said, "I'll just do a protein shake, I'm fine. You should sit outside down on the patio, it's gorgeous out this morning."

"Well okay then, I will," Nic said, perusing the glossy coffee table books in the living room to take one outside with her. She couldn't land on just one so she picked up Robert Gambee's *Nantucket Island* and a newer one called *From Nantucket, With Love* by Sadie Wilson.

Why was that name so familiar to her? A parent of a student maybe? It would come to her eventually. Or it wouldn't.

The island's earliest history had become familiar to Nic as well as its whaling prowess which lasted almost 100 years. What she didn't know was that no other town in America today had as many homes (over 800) built in the period 1740-1840, almost all of which are located in their original settings. And that during a 100-year span, Orange Street was the home to over 125 whaling captains.

She'd read about the Great Fire in 1846, which eliminated an entire third of the town and vast stores of whale oil. That reminded Nic to pick up a copy of *Daughters of Nantucket* — the story of three women in the aftermath of the fire battling to put their lives and the town back together.

Then there was the California Gold Rush and the Civil War which bled the town of many of its able-bodied sailors. If that weren't enough, shifting sands then made the island unnavigable, and adding insult to injury, the discovery of petroleum put an end to the need for whale oil — the island's only major economy.

Nic wanted to skip ahead to all the polished photos of today's island homes and lush gardens, beyond the empty shell it had become in 1870. But she wanted to understand the journey too. Unfathomable that in the late nineteenth century, houses on Nantucket had no market value, the decline had been swift and thorough. *Inconceivable* when confronted with the real estate market on-island today, Nic thought. And it was that depression that caused many of the buildings to remain in their original condition, leaving a living museum for today.

It didn't take people long to realize the value of their beautiful open space, sandy soil, and Gulf-Stream warmth. By the turn of the century tourism bloomed along with the island's variety of vegetation. The Population increased, the season of tourism extended, and lifestyles on Nantucket changed. Nic allowed herself to turn the pages ahead to peek at the gray-shingled cottages that belied the timeless treasures inside. And the terraced gardens tucked behind gates, cultivated to exquisite perfection.

She could imagine where once sea-side yards swayed with simple dancing eelgrass in the ocean breeze now existed curated gardens of clematis, gladiolas, Queen Anne's lace, hydrangea, and Rosa rugosa. The variety of gardens and houses on Nantucket was enormous, and odd to think that what began as fishing shacks and whale huts in the seventeenth and eighteenth centuries were now vacation homes. The juxtaposition was staggering.

"Are you ready?" Poppy's voice yanked Nic from her reverie.

∞

It was a short enough walk into town from the Swains on Pine Street and Poppy and Nic tilted their faces to the sun as they navigated the uneven brick sidewalks and cobblestones into town. The day was delicious, salty and sweet, the light looked drinkable. Long points of sun splintered out from behind cotton ball clouds and Nic knew there was no other place in the world she'd rather be.

"If I owned a home here, I could never leave," Nic said, like a child wishing for a pony, promising to feed him and muck his stall every day.

"So, it's got you, huh?" Poppy said, "under its spell so soon?"

"How could it not?"

"You'd be surprised, folks who step off the ferry and don't stop complaining about the price of a burger, a beer, the fog, the parking, *whatever*."

"Well, then they should just get right back on the ferry."

"Agreed. Okay," Poppy said, this is the Hub, and it is *the hub*. Has a little bit of everything, a sweet book selection, adorable souvenirs, plus the best lattes. Let's get our coffees and find a bench outside and people-watch okay?"

"Sounds perfect. So, what's your mom up to this morning? I haven't seen her?"

"Barre. She's hard core about it. That, and Peloton."

"Oh boy, one of those..."

Poppy laughed, "right? It is kinda culty isn't it? I don't get it. I need to be outside, actually moving my body forward, covering actual ground, you know?"

"I do, but I'm not exactly an exercise addict," Nic said, "but anything outdoors, hiking, swimming, smelling the earthy air, hearing the birds, and feeling the sun in any season is a gift."

"Then, tell me, please, how are you so, like, tiny? And I mean that in the best way, like lean, and well, perfect curves too."

"Good genes, I guess. And I like to be busy — just without the rigor of a gym or exercise classes, you know? And look at you, Poppy, you're beautiful and *disciplined* — that will always serve you well."

"Thanks, I hope so. How are you doing with your latte, I'm dying to get a closer look at that painting we saw Thursday night, you ready?"

Once inside Quidley's they worked their way to the back left of the shop, but nothing there looked even remotely like that sepia-toned painting they'd seen two days before. "Do you think they rotate the art that quickly?" Nic asked Poppy.

"Only one way to find out," Poppy said before turning to an employee, "Excuse me? Hi, two questions: one, can you tell what happened to a painting we saw in the window here on Thursday night, and two, what was the name of the artist?"

"Good morning," she said to them, "you know what? Let's find Bruce, this is actually my first day back since my vacation and things change quickly around here. Let me see if he's out back."

"Hello there," Bruce said, "Lori says you ladies have a question about a piece you saw here, is that right?"

Poppy began to explain the painting again to Bruce, and before she could finish it was like watching a lightbulb ding over his head. "I think I know exactly the canvas you're referring to, the Stella Fera. Yes, a gentleman was in here just yesterday and bought it."

"Stella Fera, okay, do you have any other pieces by her?" Nic asked.

"Afraid not. She didn't produce very many pieces, comparatively speaking. That one was just under fifty years old I believe. My boss recently acquired that particular canvas in an estate sale. Since homes on Nantucket change hands dramatically fast, estate sales happen frequently.

"Of course," Poppy said, "What do you know about her? I've never heard of her. And would you know of anyone else on-island who might have any of her work?"

"Not off-hand, I'm afraid, but you know what? You could try Estate Treasures over on South Beach. He has quite a collection over there; furniture, paintings, scrimshaw, jewelry, all kinds of things. It's like a museum in there, quite interesting."

Nic and Poppy made their way from Quidley's to Estate Treasures over on South Beach Street. Bruce had told them that typically what doesn't get purchased by interested homeowners and local dealers, Philip at Estate Treasures would sell on consignment.

"Good morning ladies, I'm Dorothy if you need help with anything or have any questions." She was seated being an enormous cherry desk reading. She peered at them over the glasses she wore on a beaded chain. She was a large woman with iron-gray hair and a generous bosom — it looked like it might take some effort to rise from behind the vintage desk and Nic was relieved she didn't feel pressured to rush to her feet. Nic was eager to poke around on her own.

Poppy and Nic started out together but slowly moved at their own pace in different directions. Nic liked to imagine what the eyes in the paintings had seen across the centuries, and for whom the scrimshaw jewelry was carved. Framed artwork was spread throughout the space in the different little rooms of what had once been a home. They were hanging here and there while some stood leaning, the eye was drawn every which way, by design, so customers wouldn't miss a thing.

Poppy heard Nic's quick gasp and looked over to where she stood. She was staring up at a sepia toned painting at the rear of the shop that might once have been the parlor. Poppy hustled over to look then with wide eyes turned to Nic, "It has to be the same artist, right?"

"A real beauty, isn't it?" Dorothy said from behind them, having materialized like vapor, startling them both. "Reminiscent of summers from my parents' day — just look at those bathing costumes."

"Right?" Poppy said, "When exactly did women start wearing bikinis anyway? Never mind topless... Which I still *cannot* believe is a thing here now."

"Don't get me started, young lady..."

Nic studied the painting entitled *Beach Day* — women in skirted tank suits, straw sun hats, some cloche style, and men lounging in the sand under a slanted striped umbrella. It was a moment in time long gone. Nostalgia for a time she knew nothing about fluttered in her heart. The faces were blurred if visible at all and could have been and image from a vintage postcard.

"What do you know about this artist?" Nic asked Dorothy, her voice little more than an exhale, as she stood, rooted with certainty that she'd seen something so like it before.

Nic reached into her memories spinning on a reel, filmy and as elusive as the curled edge of a dream. Then she was eleven years old, sitting in the dark of her mother's side of the closet, out of breath from hide-and-seek. She was afraid her heavy breathing would get her found by Enzo or Mia, so she sat still as a stone with her arms wrapped around her bare knees that were tucked up under her chin. Long minutes passed in the dark space that summer day, nothing. Their parents' closet was off-limits.

Her eyes got used to the pitch black of the closet, and with her heart beating in her ears she looked around, breathing in her mother's perfume that lingered on her blouses and dresses. There were so many shoes; in boxes and hanging shoe shelves. Nic had never seen her mom in most of them. Sitting crouched for so long made her itch. When she reached around to scratch her back, her elbow hit something hard that was leaning against the back of the closet.

She thought of Narnia, wondering how far back the closet went. Contorting her body to see what she'd bumped, she pushed aside the long garments hanging in thin plastic. And there was a framed painting, brownish mostly, of an old-fashioned woman at the beach, sitting close to a man like they were telling secrets, under a striped umbrella. Nic had thought how dumb it looked without colors.

"GOT YA!" Enzo's nine year-old voice yelled into her black den, exposing her as he rolled the heavy door open, blinding her with the light of the summer day pouring in through the window of her parents' room.

"Miss? MISS?" Dorothy said, pulling Nic back to the present. "If Phillip were here, he'd be able to give you more definitive answers, but he is not in today. All I can tell you is that at some point, this painting was hanging in a home on-island, the house was sold, an estate sale followed which is where Philip would have obtained it. Can't tell you when exactly or anything about..." Dorothy pushed her glasses higher up on her nose to get a closer look at the signature, "Stella Fera. Never heard of her. This piece has a very 1920's or 30's feel, see there with the cloche hats and so forth, but that doesn't necessarily mean it was painted then. Mr. Barnard will be in tomorrow if you'd like to come back and pick his brain."

"Is this the only one you have?" Poppy asked, coming to stand beside Nic. "We were just at Quidley's asking about one we'd seen in their window Thursday night and it's already gone."

"Curious. I wish I could provide more clarity for you. But as I said, come back tomorrow ladies."

Nic noticed Poppy sneaking a photo of the painting with her phone. Dorothy was already on her way back to her chair behind the desk. Poppy looked up and turned to Nic with a mischievous grin, "I'll just shoot this to my friend, Sharon at the MFA — if anyone will know something about this artist, Sharon's our girl."

Nic continued to stare at the painting, her curious memory toying with her. "Poppy, you're not going to believe this but I just had this weird memory flash…of seeing something so much like this painting in the back of my mother's closet."

"Umm, so, did you spend much time hanging out in your mom's closet?"

"Ha, no, it was actually a hard no-no for us kids — but caution to the wind when it came down to hide-and-seek, right?"

"I'll take your word for it," Poppy said wistfully, "being a kid these days is so not like it used to be. But that's crazy, you think your mom had a Stella Fera?"

"I don't know! I mean, there could be other artists who worked with this sepia-tone kind of wash style, right? I can't stop looking at it."

It was the kind of painting to be viewed from a bit of a distance — with the facial features blurred or nonexistent, it was more about the whole feeling than the details. Moving closer to try out this theory she caught the price tag, it was $4,500. Her parents would not have owned expensive art. "Hey, Poppy, do you see how much this is selling for? Who decides the price of artwork anyway?"

"Well, if it's a well-known artist, I'm sure there are standards, certain values calculated, that only increase with time. Whatever the market will bear I suppose, who's willing to pay the most for a piece, I'm not really sure. I mean art auctions would be a whole different ballgame with people outbidding each other. And if a thing is part of some limited collection? Well, there you go, people pay more for rare. What I DO know is that we better head back for lunch and to just be present before it's actually time to get ready for the wedding festivities. You know how Glammy gets."

"Wait, what did you call her? *Glammy*? As in glam-Grammy?"

Poppy let out an unexpected guffaw, "Exactly. That is what she *wanted* to be called — but it didn't stick because I couldn't say that! I called her Mimi and that's what stuck."

"I have no words..." Nic laughed.

Chapter Thirteen

NIC'S BREATH WAS SWEPT away with her first step onto the powdery sand of Galley Beach. She'd never seen a more spectacular backdrop for a wedding. Rows of white chairs with wide ribbon bows lifting in the wind arched to face the blue-green sea. A white birch trellis stood as an altar wrapped in fluttering tulle secured at the corners with creamy white hydrangeas wrapped with grapevines and greens.

Cade was quintessential in his Nantucket Reds, white shirt, ice-blue tie, and navy sport coat. Nic complimented him perfectly in her champagne pink dress; raw silk, sleeveless, and with a full A-line skirt that fell in wide pleats to the knee accentuating her small waist. She wore her hair in a loose chignon with sunny tendrils framing her face.

"Going all Audrey Hepburn on us, eh?" Lexi said walking onto the beach with Rick.

Nic looked down at herself for just a microsecond before Lexi tapped her on the arm with her purse, "In the best way, Nic, you look beautiful. Although you're not allowed to look that good without being a slave to the almighty Peloton."

Nic let out a small laugh wanting to come up with a genuine compliment that wouldn't sound back-at-ya. "You look so pretty in blue, Lexi, it suits you, and I love your hair down with those beachy waves."

"Okay no more gushing, I'm gonna puke, where are we sitting? And I don't suppose they're passing out beverages *before* the ceremony, are they?"

Rick held out his arm for Lexi to take and they headed to sit. Cade and Nic followed. Nic wondered if there was a bride's side and groom's side — or was that old school. How long had it been since she'd been to a wedding? The June sun was just right that late in the afternoon with a few high clouds passing over it every now and then. Prudence and John were a few rows in front of them sitting beside Poppy and Tryp.

Nic was excited to see the nine bridesmaids walk down the aisle. The groomsmen were already lined up in front of the altar in navy tuxes, white shirts with pale sage neckties. The harpist began Claude Debussy's "Claire de Lune." And all eyes turned to watch as one by one, the bridesmaids began their procession down the white sand aisle. Each young woman wore a unique dress of her own choosing, one that made her feel the most beautiful, perfect for her own individual size, color, and shape — each as stunning as the last. They carried blush peonies wrapped in white satin ribbon, wisps of styled hair rising and falling at the whim of the air off the water as they drifted to their spots at the altar.

Guests rose to their feet when the bride appeared, watching in shared awe as she took the last steps of her single life on her father's arm. She was radiant in a white gown with a sweetheart neckline, delicate straps, lace bodice and a luxurious chiffon skirt that flirted with the breeze as it lifted and draped to the ground. As she floated by them, Nic noticed the demure scooped back of the dress and the striking silhouette it made.

It was emotional every time, Nic thought, bearing witness to people promising their whole lives to each other. Her throat ached remembering. It doubtless had every person there reflecting on their own wedding day, or one they held hopes for in the future. Guests wiped the corners of their eyes behind their Ray Bans, Fendis, and Tom Fords then faced forward to listen. The ceremony was a traditional one and seemed all too short for what it was meant to accomplish. Nic wished she could have heard more clearly the vows the bride and groom had written for each other, that intimate devotion, but those promises had been carried out to sea on the wind.

Husband and wife were pronounced and delivered to the world beginning with their walk together up the aisle. Sentimental family and friends offered discreet celebratory waves, thinking they could capture the magnitude of the moment with their phones.

Nic guessed there had to be almost 200 guests and she enjoyed the parade of youth and beauty. And the wealth that had a high hand in that. Outside of Cade's immediate family and the few people she'd met at Ventuno the night before, she knew no one. It wasn't awful being an invisible observer. There was something in the Swain men collectively that struck her as familiar, an indescribable characteristic they shared that she couldn't put her finger on. It was staggering to think of the generations that could be traced back to the two original Swains who first settled the island of Nantucket. And she shone on the arm of a link in that historic chain.

It snuck up on her again that both of her parents were gone. She leaned into Cade's solid presence as they weaved their way through all the pretty people. Grief didn't leave you — time sanded down the edges, planed over the worst of its knots, but it was ever there.

"You look like I need a drink," Lexi said, coming over to Nic, "you having a moment?"

"You could say that. Big family love happening here, it hits you, the time you take for granted, thinking it'll last forever."

"Come, let's eat, drink, and be merry."

Lexi was definitely growing on her. Which was good because Cade was a social butterfly flitting here and there. "You don't have to babysit me if you'd rather hang with family you know, I'm a big girl," Nic said to Lexi.

"Don't worry about me. If I want to talk to any of these biotches, I will."

Nic almost snorted out her sauvignon blanc and choked on her crab puff. "You know Lexi, I wasn't sure we'd get along, but I was wrong."

"Good. Then don't fuck things up with my brother."

"Is that your way of saying you like me too?"

"Too far. Cut the shit. And bottoms up, I'm ready for another."

The sun felt delicious, the day was gorgeous and the venue was bar none. Nic watched the wedding party photo shoot happening down by the water's edge thinking how much of a challenge it was to keep a real smile on through so many photo groupings. It was too much. Everything about weddings had become too much. Scandalous cost aside, it seemed the size of the party was no longer commensurate with the length of the marriage. If it ever was. The perfect dress that cost more than the downpayment on a car — or the car itself — worn for eight hours, flowers that would last only slightly longer, linens to match the flowers, the favors, the music, vegan, gluten-free, Keto, Kosher, the toasts and timing. No wonder the world was on Prozac.

"What the absolute fuck?" Lexi said, with her glass halfway to her mouth.

Nic shielded her eyes from the sun and followed her gaze over to where Cade was standing talking to a beautiful woman. "Who is that?" she asked Lexi.

"That is Cade's fucking ex-wife — what in the fuck is she doing here? I swear to God this is Mother's doing. She LOVES that bitch, never got over their divorce, but seriously this is going too far."

Nic took a minute to absorb what she was looking at. Did Cade know she would be there? Is she trying to get Cade back? What was going on? Her festive mood popped like so many champagne bubbles in the air.

"She can't stand not being a Swain anymore. Of course, she'll keep the name until her dying day, that skank." Lexi started marching over toward Prudence but with Nic reaching out to stop her.

Nic grabbed Lexi's arm in time to redirect her, "this is so not the time or place, Lexi, you can't do this now."

"I know! But I'm so pissed. And I'm certain that Cade did *not* know about this. This is all Prudence manipulating those puppet strings. Reagan is JUST like her, probably why she's so in love with the bitch. I mean get over it, Mother, it's been almost three years since they split."

Nic was determined not to jump to conclusions. Cade was a man among men, one of the the finest she'd known. And just because his ex happened to be friggin gorgeous, and *present*, and perhaps adored by his whole family — what could there possibly be to worry about? Did his mother wish Cade was still married to her? Did Reagan? Nic's connection with Cade had developed so seamlessly that she hardly thought about his ex-wife. But what if he still had a pocket of love for her somewhere? That he didn't know he had...until seeing her again! Alcohol was probably not going to be her friend in this.

Before she knew it, Lexi was steering her toward the table of place cards to determine who was sitting where. Each name was painted in gold script inside a white scallop shell, Nic barely had time to appreciate them in her search. She jumped to feel hands on her waist and turned to find Cade's face inches from hers. "Hey there *Saint Nic*, can I get you a glass of something or maybe a fig and scallop skewer?" His eyes were practically cartwheeling with mischief.

Oh, he was just way too cheery. "Ok with the cute NIC-names buddy, what are you all jazzed about anyway?"

"Whaddya mean by that? It's a wedding — the happiest and most festive of occasions!"

"Nothing to do with your ex-wife being here? I mean, come on Cade — why is she here and did you know about that?" Oh God, she did *not* like the sound of her own voice right now. Jealousy was not her gig — she already had green eyes. "Never mind — sorry, rewind. I'd love a glass of bubbles and a fig and scallop thingie, thank you."

Cade went to hunt down a server giving Lexi the opportunity to show Nic that the table number on their scallop shells matched Reagan's. "This is positively diabolical!" Lexi said. "How well does my mother even know the bride to pull these strings for fuck's sake — this is just pure evil."

"Lexi, come on, this has to be simply seating families together with people who are connected to them in some way, right? I mean how much can seating arrangements hope to accommodate? Nic wasn't sure who she was trying to convince more, but it didn't really matter. There they all were, and why ruin such a beautiful evening in the most gorgeous setting there ever was.

The sun dipped ever so slightly changing the light by tiny degrees leaving them with a couple of hours of lavender-blue skies before the fire of sunset. Nic was tempted to get out her phone and take photos of everything to text Evy — the enormous turreted tent with all sides open to the sea and sky, elegant tables around a gleaming dance floor, ivory linens and crystal stemware glinting in the lemony sunlight. Blush peonies and white roses gracing each table surrounded by ivory pilar candles in glass hurricane chimneys. And at every place setting there was an antique-bronze compass under an overturned wineglass as a wedding favor, each with the inscription;

> *Go confidently in the direction of your dreams. Live the life you've imagined.*
> *~ Thoreau*

This was a long way from the white box of matches from her wedding, with their initials in pink above the date. That she would remember with a glad heart, no matter the ending.

She'd have to get Lexi to take a photo of Cade twirling her on the dance floor in her dress — it was made for dancing. She was choosing joy over jealousy.

"There you are," Cade said, balancing her glass of champagne, his beer and two canapes.

"You've got your hands full, thanks! So, do you guys come here much, for dinner I mean? I can't imagine a more beautiful spot."

"At least once a season. It is a spectacular setting isn't it, hard to believe there's nothing else quite like it on the island. How much do you think one of those rooms overlooking the ocean go for?"

"I don't even want to know — it would spoil it for me. Just let me dream..." She felt the sensual purr of the wine as she smiled at him with a heart that had no borders.

"Well, you are looking very dreamy, Nicolina, if I may say. I must be the luckiest man here."

"I'd say so," Lexi said coming up to where they stood.

"Second only to me, that is," Rick said with an arm around Lexi's shoulders.

"Cut the shit, Rick," Lexi said, "you're just trying to get lucky later. You know that means you'll have to actually stay awake, right?"

"How about this — you put your phone away and I promise not to get sleepy, deal?"

"Yes, dear. Aren't they done with the pictures yet — they need to get this show on the road."

"*Are we there yet?* You sound like you're six. Quit complaining sis, at least ceremony and reception are in the same place, right?" Cade said.

"I love when that happens," Nic said.

Before they knew it they were all being ushered to their tables for the couple's grand entrance. Twinkly lights lined the ceiling of the tent swathed in tulle while three chandeliers dangled lower as if suspended by magic. Impeccable countless details, more than could be known, Nic thought, appreciating every little thing. She felt like a princess herself and could only imagine how the bride was feeling. Cade's hand reached for hers on her lap, under the table. Lexi and Rick were to Nic's left which left four empty seats. Guests were taking their time finding their tables, which was fine with Nic, her heart was beating a bass drum in her stomach.

She saw Reagan making her way over, walking and talking to a man Nic hadn't met alongside another couple. *Please do not sit beside Cade*, she recited in her brain. Reagan took the seat next to Rick, which was almost as bad — Rick didn't have it in his genetic makeup to be anything other than attentive and considerate. Reagan was unfortunately *rocking* a Lily Pulitzer number, a fitted V-neck dress in pale pink and blue with a wrap skirt with tie, long voluminous sleeves and a ruffle hem. She dazzled. Her aubrun mane fell to just above her shoulders in a straight gleaming curtain that swung when she turned her head. Nic had to force herself to look away.

Once everyone was seated, the MC stepped to the microphone and the crowd hushed. "Ladies and gentlemen, may I please have your attention as I introduce, for the first time, Mr. and Mrs. Lincoln Swain!" Loud whistles and applause lasted throughout the introductions of all eighteen members of the bridal party — Nic's hands were stinging by the end.

"Enough already, right?" Lexi leaned in to say to Nic while Reagan cast a pretentious glance their way. "And ignore that stupid bitch." The first dance was next, the song was "A Thousand Years" by Christina Perry — Nic loved that song and couldn't help but think back to watching *Twilight* with her daughter, when Edward and Bella finally got married. She and Lexi shared a knowing look — okay, so she they were getting emotional over fictional vampires, but *still*, that song!

While Nic appreciated the sentiment surrounding father/bride and mother/son dances, she wasn't invested terribly and not even remotely close to that moment with her own children for it to resonate. The same was true of the speeches which were thankfully interspersed with food. And drinking. Was Reagan there with a plus one? Who even was the guy sitting next to her, all they knew was that his name was Vince, and that he'd used too much hair product, but that you forgave it when you noticed his front teeth crossed over each other just a little. The couple next to them was engaged, Lindsay and Marc, and thank God were talking the ears off Reagan and Vince. The voice in Nic's head spoke too soon.

"So, *Nicolina*, is it? Is that Italian? Cade tells me this is your first visit to Nantucket," Reagan said, "what do you think?"

Jesus, when did Cade tell her that? And did she have to answer the questions in order? "Yes, to the first two questions, but I was actually here for a day back in college." That sounded lame even to her.

Reagan's head tilted ever so slightly skyward as she laughed, "A day? That hardly counts I'm afraid. How do you like the island so far?"

Nic did not feel like herself around Reagan. Nic figured that was probably by design. Nic envied her control, elegance, and her I-had-him-first aura. Then she hated herself for that.

"Give it a rest, Reagan, why are you even here anyway, don't you have your own family?" Lexi said, surprising everyone, maybe even herself, though she refused to show it. Damn, that Lexi was someone to have on your side.

"Okay," Rick said standing, "who needs something from the bar, Vince, Cade?"

"I'll take a gin martini please, Rick, *extra dirty*," Reagan said, dripping with promiscuity. Vince wanted a Manhattan and Cade stood to accompany Rick. Lexi all but pulled Nic out of her chair to hit the ladies room.

"Is life really just a non-stop replay of fucking high school?" Lexi said, "Rhetorical of course, I'd like to slap that fake smile right off that amazon's Botoxed face, Jesus H. Christ."

"Why is she so haughty? What did Cade ever see in her? Well, okay, she is pretty, I'll concede that. And tall."

"In a RuPaul kinda way, sure. She's gotten more obnoxious with age, I can tell you that, bitter maybe, though what the fuck? She blew it. She was the one who wanted out, deciding that her fast track to partner was more important than having a family. I don't think she ever thought he'd actually let her go. She's loaded."

Reapplying her rosy nude lip gloss in the powder room mirror, Nic felt free to keep talking since they were alone. "Why would that matter to Cade? He does great financially. Plus, he wouldn't care about money anyway, would he?"

"Nope. And it's not like our parents are exactly poor, if you know what I mean."

Walking down onto the sand before heading back to their table Nic was about to ask Lexi if she ever liked Reagan. But changed her mind. It was none of her business and none of it mattered. And no good could come of going back in time, or wishing she'd met Cade a long time ago instead of having married and divorced Brad. She'd never have had Evy and Ben, who were everything. She took a big gulp of salty air and noticed the sun dipping lower to meet the sea, changing the sky's blue palette to purple. "We'd better get back to the table, we don't want a search party sent out."

"Are you fucking kidding me?!" Lexi said, upon re-entering the tent and seeing the twirl of Reagan's dress and her swingy hair out on the dance floor with her brother. "Just what the absolute fucking bloody hell does she think she's doing?"

Nic would be lying to herself if she pretended that view didn't crack through her like lightning. It seemed above and beyond the call of duty for Cade. What duty? He owed her nothing — it's not like they had children together. But it wasn't a slow dance so who cared, she told herself. Their bodies weren't pressed together moving in tight circles to Ed Sheeran's "Perfect". But it was Abba's "Dancing Queen", Nic's favorite. Yeah, so, no, this wasn't nothing. She felt PTSD coming in hot. Flashbacks to Brad saying he'd be working late — while she cooked his favorites, lit candles, poured wine, and he never showed. And all the travel she didn't entirely understand but was too consumed with raising their children and maintaining some semblance of a career to dig too deep.

How many signs had she missed? She swore she'd never put herself in that position again. Not that she thought she was in that place with Cade — *never* — he didn't have it in him. It was Reagan's intentions she didn't trust. And what if there was unfinished business between them that even Cade didn't recognize?

Nic willed the song to end, for Reagan to release Cade. Even as her pulse sat at the bottom of her throat she couldn't tear her gaze from them, how well they looked together, tall, glamourous, how people stopped to watch. Tears were hot and close as thoughts swam in her head looking for a place to land. Why was she fishing for information in his posture, his eyes, that might break her heart? An unerring flaw of the human condition.

When the dance ended, Reagan turned off the dance floor with a smile that ate up her face. Cade walked toward Nic. She wanted nothing less than to burden him with her insecurities but her face was hardly a mask of glee. His smile faltered. But she noticed his eyes in that light were the color of foreign oceans full of warmth and good intentions.

"Awe, Nic, come here," he said, folding her into his arms. "That was your favorite song, I'm sorry. Reagan grabbed my arm and dragged me out there, she didn't leave me much of a choice. Which, yes, I'm sure was her intention. But *please* know it meant nothing." Cade stepped back to look into Nic's eyes, holding her loosely but for all he was worth.

Nic swiped a tear from the corner of her eye, willing her makeup to stay. "You were married for twelve years, Cade. I understand that, and it hasn't even been a fraction of that since your divorce. It didn't look like *nothing* to her. She was a part of this family for a long time, and she, well, she fits in here — maybe I'm the outlier?" Hearing herself, *God*, how she resented her uncertainty and lack of emotional hubris.

Cade pulled her in again, his body flush with hers and spoke into her ear, "Nicolina, if you could take a swim in my heart, my mind, you'd see how much of me you fill, and you'd know that there is no room for anyone else." Pulling back just enough to be eye to eye, he said, "Reagan and I are over the divorce and over the marriage. We're just people who used to know each other. As strange as that sounds."

Nic raised her hands to touch his smooth face. She knew exactly how that was possible. But she hadn't counted on needing to hear it. Her chest filled with thick spirals of pleasure. She closed her eyes and met his lips with hers.

∞

The bride and groom beckoned everyone out onto the cool sand to watch as the wavering red ball sank in ripples into the sea, igniting a dramatic sky of the boldest crimson slashed with violet. Galley Beach diners did this every night, Cade told her, walked out from wherever they were seated to stand in the sand to watch as day traded places with night. Nic slipped off her sandals and felt the night spill onto her bare feet. Everyone clapped as the sky deepened, pooling into the ocean. Glasses were raised again, to the couple, to the moment.

The mood was loose and as free flowing as the wine. Table assignments were abandoned, conversations amped, the dancing in overdrive, and the selfie cringe-o-meter reduced to an embarrassingly low level. "That dress must have been made for you," Cade said to Nic, adoration shining in his eyes, "the way it flares like that when I spin you." The music slowed and he pulled her in tight. "You're the most beautiful girl here."

"We won't tell the bride," Poppy said, leaning into them as she danced by with some cute guy to Etta James's "At Last".

Nic wasn't thinking of a single other thing besides being in the powerful arms of such an enchanting man, feeling his heart beat against hers. Rick and Lexi were swaying in time to the song a few couples over — Nic wanted to wrap the night up on this perfect note. Couldn't they?

Chapter Fourteen

NIC WOULD BE GLAD when all things wedding were behind them, and she could just enjoy the island and its many gifts instead of stressing about another outfit. Part of her wanted to beg out of the post-wedding brunch the next morning but Cade brought her around. It would be a smallish gathering, relatively speaking, at his uncle's home out on Eel Point Road. And Nic had to admit, she was excited to see the northeastern part of the island that was nothing at all like the close houses and trellised patio gardens in the historic downtown, and very different from the big surf of the south shore.

Windswept moors rolled on forever and homes got bigger and further apart heading northwest of town. Eel Point Road was long, narrow and amusement-park bumpy once it turned to all sand. Nic couldn't decide which way to look as cedar shingled, mansion-sized *cottages* rose up out of the dunes. Acres of eel grass swayed and hedges of hydrangea bloomed in blues and pinks. Glossy white trim and seashell driveways caught the sun and kept it while the blue-blue sea stretched infinitely before them.

As Rick steered his Defender up the long shell drive off the sandy road, Nic noted that she was the only one paying any particular attention to the grandeur unfolding outside their windows. How, she wondered did you get so used to it that you didn't see it anymore? She imagined herself in one of the oversized rockers, on the sprawling front porch that spanned the length of the house, with a glass of wine and a book. There was a quarterboard over the door, dove-gray, with the name "Sandcastle" carved in gold.

"Is this more your style?" Lexi asked, noting Nic's expression. "Way too much house for me, and not a damn thing around here but the ocean. Give me a place in town any day."

"Oh no, I'd take this. Nowhere near this size but look at this wide-open sky and — oh my God, the ocean as your backyard!"

"Um, like I said — nothing here but nature and wind and shit."

"Oh Lexi, nothing can be too far from anywhere on an island fourteen miles long by four miles wide, get real, woman! The peace of this setting, are you kidding me?"

"Whatever. Time for some mimosas sans orange juice."

The brunch was set up on the back lawn with the Atlantic reaching as far as the eye could see. Running sheets of light skipped on the ocean's surface and lazy ripples rolled. One long table was set up perpendicular to the shore below with creamy linens and stems of ranunculus of the same rich cream in crystal vases. They were a flower almost too perfect to be real with their rose-like blossoms and layers and layers of tissue-thin petals. Beyond the emerald stretch of lawn, steep steps led down to the beach where kayaks and paddleboards lay waiting.

There were bloody marys and oysters, mimosas and pastries, and a grazing table of salted meats, cheeses, hummus, nuts, breads, and fresh citrus. And for the truly ravenous, an omelet station, waffles, sausage, and bacon. Nic was on the fence between coffee or a little hair of the dog.

Tryp looked particularly worse for the wear and most likely hadn't showered that morning. But glancing around at the other guests Nic found herself envying the tight supple skin of youth. It was such a slow disappearance, that, impossible to put a finger on just when it started to shift. What she did know was that in the mirror of your late forties after a day of gluttony, your face didn't keep that secret. That it took a few hours for the puffiness to recede, for your eyes to look familiar again. But then they didn't see as clearly as they used to — so there was that little blessing in the mirror. At least women had makeup — men had little more than sweeping their hair back with some product and a smile.

Poppy was radiant in a cute sundress and her dark hair loose. Her trademark Swain-blue eyes sparkled in the morning light as she sipped her lemonade. Nic didn't feel ready for food yet, but she hoped to get there soon with such a spread. "This property is beyond amazing — do you guys get together much out here?" Nic asked Poppy, trying to figure out the relationships — all the uncles and cousins.

"Not so much. When all us cousins were younger Uncle Tom and Aunt Celia lived in a much smaller place near Madequecham, which was perfect because everyone surfed. No waves here on the north shore."

"Oh, that sounds fun, so do you still surf? Does your dad? And Cade for that matter — I don't remember him mentioning it."

"Legends in their own minds, *ha*, but actually they were pretty good. They can still rip out there — you should def get them to go to Nobadeer or Cisco Beach while you're here."

"Oh, absolutely! Thanks for the tip. I'm bummed you can't stay — you really have to get back to work?"

"Unfortunately, yes, I do. But I shouldn't really say *unfortunately* — I love my job and, lucky me, I can come to Nantucket any weekend I want."

"I cannot even imagine having a place here...," Nic said dreamily, "I don't think I could ever leave." She collected photos with her phone, knowing justice would not be done, but impatient to capture what she could to bring to life later with her paintbrush.

"Could never leave what?" Lexi appeared, mimosa with the leanest splash of OJ in hand, her Ray-Ban Jackie Ohhs in place, "Nantucket? Oh yes you could. You'd be bored off your ass in time, trust me."

"I don't think so Lexi — it's so inspiring here. I mean I can see why artists and photographers and writers flock here. *Anything* to capture this beauty, this light, this feeling."

"Awe, a dorky romantic," Lexie said, "that ain't gonna pay the bills, sister."

Nic sighed, "I guess I'm getting all swept up, you're right."

"Don't listen to my mom, she's too practical. That predictable, left-brained, analytical type."

"Why, thank you." Lexi said as she headed over to the grazing table.

"I'm definitely more right hemisphere, that's for sure — numbers are not my thing."

"Well, Nic, that's why you appreciate the beauty and the history of this place so much. And why you experience it so intensely that you need to create versions of it with your own art. That's an enviable thing. Hey, I need to use the powder room, want to come in and check out the house?"

"Um, YES," Nic said, following Poppy through the back deck into the kitchen. Miles of gleaming white quartz counters and antique white cabinets greeted her, set against dark walnut flooring that made a spectacular contrast. Three glass pendants hung over the massive island that looked handblown and had an aqua swirl pattern on slightly iridescent clear glass globes. It was just the right splash of color. Tom's wife, Celia, was an interior designer, which was evident from every single angle.

Poppy disappeared to use the powder room and Nic had no idea in which direction that was. She found herself staring at the photographs in the hall off the kitchen and ending up at what looked like the master suite. Feeling wildly self-conscious, she turned quickly to retrace her steps but something caught her eye on a wall of the master bedroom. It had to be a Stella Fera painting! There couldn't be another artist whose work so resembled a vintage postcard in sepia tones. It was another seaside scene; young men and women in 1920's bathing suits — like beachy art deco flappers — with men in sleeveless tanks and striped trunks. Nic could feel their camaraderie as they posed by a vintage dory. That same shadowy familiarity walked up her spine again seeing this Stella Fera piece.

She was startled to see she'd wandered all the way into the bedroom and was standing right in front of the painting when a male voice made her jump.

"Pardon me, is there something I can help you with?" Tom Swain said, plainly and without judgement, kindness darkening his eyes.

"Oh, Mr. Swain, please forgive me — I was looking for Poppy when I was just drawn in by this painting — it's a Stella Fera isn't it?" It occurred to Nic that she was unapologetically standing there in the man's bedroom for God's sake.

"Tom, please, call me Tom. Mr. Swain was my father. And grandfather for that matter," he chuckled good-naturedly, "and that's quite an eye you have, although of course she is an original isn't she, Ms. Fera with her unique retro style? She was apparently inspired by old photos she went through when her parents died, and then became somewhat obsessed with estate sales and post-cards and photographs from the 1920's and 30's." He turned to look at the painting, as if beholding it through new eyes, "This piece, and what few others exist, are from the late sixties if I'm remembering correctly, but then nothing thereafter."

Nic was quiet for a long minute, surprised and intrigued by what Tom knew of the artist. But she filed it for later, wanting to lose herself in the painting. "I can't help but feel like I am part of that group there in the sand, holding that parasol, what were they talking about do you think? Having supper at the yacht club later?"

Tom laughed and Nic saw Cade in his smile. That was when Poppy stepped in to say she'd been looking for Nic everywhere. "What....? Uncle Tom, *when* did you get this painting? Oh my God — this is so crazy! Nic did you tell him how we've been on a Stella Fera hunt since seeing that piece in the window of Quidley's?"

"No, she didn't mention that," Tom said, "but to be honest we were both imagining ourselves in this moment here on the canvas, wondering what those ladies and gentlemen might have been talking about. I don't believe I've appreciated it with more than a passing glance. Were they posing for a photographer or maybe a painter? *Our Gang* it's entitled, how wonderfully reminiscent."

"Did you acquire it recently? I don't remember ever seeing it before," Poppy said.

"And would you have noticed, dear child? We've had it for quite some time actually. But when we moved into this house from Madequecham, much of our art was in storage. This beauty was lost in the shuffle for a bit. It's like getting to enjoy it for the first time."

Nic noticed Tom's eyes cloud and his expression shift from one of pleasure to something more melancholy. She turned back to the painting, along with Poppy, wondering what about such a lovely capture could induce sadness.

"There is, of course, a story behind my acquisition of the painting," Tom offered. "Now, Poppy you've never met your great uncle Theo, my brother, also your grandfather's brother, because almost fifty years ago he left the island and has never returned. I'm embarrassed to say it's as though he never existed."

"What?" Poppy said, confused, "Granddad has another brother besides you and Uncle Charlie? That's really weird, Uncle Tom, why don't we know about him?"

"Because the whole thing made our mother deeply sad. Even though she brought it on herself. We weren't allowed to speak of him once he'd left the island. He was younger than me, I was busy with my own life. I suppose the family grew around the hole he left until we didn't notice it so much anymore. Selfish and terrible it sounds to hear myself say it. Anyway, this and I believe a couple other paintings by Stella Fera belonged to Theo. He left them behind."

"Well, *here* you are, for goodness' sakes, Tom," Celia said clucking her tongue as she entered the bedroom, "what on *earth* is going on in here? I've been looking everywhere for you — don't you want to say something to our guests? The host can't be hiding in the bedroom."

"Quite frankly Celia, I'm all speeched out — why don't you go ahead and do the honors, I'll be right out."

Celia clucked again scrutinizing the odd group, You could actually see her medication stop working. She turned on her heel leaving a waft of something expensive in her wake.

"I've spoken out of turn, said too much already, please excuse me," Tom said, leaving the women more curious than ever about this painting, this artist, and the mysterious and absent Uncle Theo.

Chapter Fifteen

NIC WAS EXHAUSTED BY the time the brunch wrapped up and wanted nothing more than to lie on the beach and soak in the island's summer sun. The guys were not tired at all and down for a surf session at Nobadeer if the swell was any good. That would be great with Nic; sun, sitting, and a show! They had only to change into swim suits and pack beverages and snacks — there it was again — that insatiability of summer.

Poppy declined, wanting instead to crash a bit before her flight back to Boston, and Lexi needed a spin class before everything she'd eaten and drunk in the last seventy-two hours went straight to her ass. Weren't big asses *in* now? That's what Evy told Nic when she felt her curves getting curvier. Whatever, Lexi wasn't having it, her body was not going to be allowed to morph gracefully with menopause knocking on her door.

Rick, Cade, Nic and Tryp rumbled over the hilly sand in Rick's Defender onto Nobadeer Beach. Nic whooped with laughter like a kid on a roller coaster — feeling like they would *definitely* pop a tire. Cresting the last rise Nic couldn't believe what she was looking at. The spot was a *scene* — Jeeps and SUVs of every kind and color backed up to the tide, with enough sandy real estate before the water for the rainbow arc of beach chairs, towels, umbrellas, cornhole, Kan Jam, and Spikeball.

They got lucky for a late Sunday afternoon and squeaked in between an orange four-door Jeep — doorless and topless — and a Ford F-250 SuperCab. The waves looked huge to Nic, yawning massively out there before tumbling down hard into whipped froth. *They'll do*, they guys agreed as they freed the boards from the truck and waxed them.

Nic knew a fair amount about surfing having a close cousin who'd become a hardcore enthusiast. He'd started in New Hampshire, like all New Englanders, but eventually moved to the west coast to compete — even sponsored by Rip Curl the last she knew. Nic had loved photographing him but had never been bitten by the bug. Looking out at the crowded waves she could see it was more popular than ever.

Surfboards under their arms and leashes lashed to ankles the three of them walked to the water's edge then jumped into the waves atop their boards to begin the paddle out past the break. Nic felt a surge of excitement and a trickle of fear — surfing was sexy but things could go wrong. She stood at the edge of the ruffling tide loving the water that was not freezing. Tryp caught the first wave — Nic was sure he was about to steamroll some boogieboarding kids in front of him — but he expertly ripped to the left, executing flawless cutbacks like a pro. Of course he did, he was probably up on a surfboard as soon as he was walking. It shouldn't have surprised her at all, but it was hard to reconcile the smart-mouthed kid she'd come to know with this insight and splashy skill.

Then Rick was up, but tossed in the drink before he got any kind of ride. She was dying to see Cade catch a wave. Finally it looked like he'd timed his paddling perfectly, picked a wave and popped up. While he did not look anywhere near as fluid as Tryp, neither did he look too rusty as he pumped down the line until the shallows. *Who was this island boy?*

"WooHOOO," Nic yelled through cupped hands that carried her voice — Cade's smile told her he'd heard. She watched them for a few more minutes, more wipeouts than rides, but exciting still. Sexy. As. Hell. A couple of girls next to them were tandem surfing on a big old paddleboard which looked like crazy fun. Then It looked like Cade was trying to wave her in to give it a go. Yeah, NO. She drew her hand across her throat in the universal symbol for *no fucking way*. She spread her big towel out on the hot sand and lied down, wriggling her body into the sand to make it a perfect fit.

In that dream-space before sleep, she heard the roar of the surf and clips of conversation the wind carried to her then whisked away. Laughter tripped on the breeze and a dog's bark echoed while the sun soaked her limbs and pinned her deliciously. Snoopy flashed in her mind and she almost bolted up to look for him until she remembered he wasn't there, that she didn't have to worry or watch him. He was safe. Her children were safe, she was safe.

Cold droplets of water rained down on her pulling her to consciousness. Cade and the guys thinking it cute to shake their wet hair like dogs — fresh from the surf and in search of liquid refreshment. "Classic male behavior," commented the lady camped next to them from the orange Jeep, "like that's hilarious or something. That'll be these two clowns in a few years," she said, laughing and gesturing to the twenty-somethings funneling beers at the foot of her Jeep — one standing, holding the red funnel high, the other on his knees sucking down an obscene amount of beer from a thick hose. "Just holy shitballs, right? And they've named it! *Ginger*, or more affectionately, *Gingey*," the woman said, more in admiration than apology.

Nic didn't know whether to be shocked or to laugh out loud at the frat party throwback that she wouldn't have expected on Nantucket. She decided it was hilarious and she instantly loved that mom.

"Sorry, don't mind our neanderthal sons. Hi, I'm Val and this is Sadie," orange-Jeep-mom said.

"Not at all," Nic said, "I mean are you kidding me — I think it's hysterical, so wholesome! There are enough of us out there sipping chilled Whispering Angel from stemmed plasticware masquerading as crystal. Some good old-fashioned beer funneling balances things out." Nic felt an instant comradery and could see the appeal and energy of families all piled together. She looked more closely at the woman named Sadie, "wait a minute...I think I know you..."

"You look familiar too," Sadie said, "wait — did you teach at Bishop Academy in Byfield? I think you had my son Henry, maybe?"

"Yes! *Yes*, I teach Sophomore English, a course called, Finding One's Voice as well as your basic English Lit. I think I remember Henry, last name Wilson! And *you* have a gorgeous new photo-essay book out! Now I recognize you from your author photo. Oh my God, I was just looking at it the other day, *From Nantucket, With Love,* right?"

"I'm so glad you like it, thank you! That's a project I've wanted to do for a long time, I finally said, it doesn't matter how many other amazing photo books are out there about Nantucket, there's room for everyone, right?"

"You are so right. And you live in Newbury, Sadie, right? I'm surprised we haven't bumped into each other in Newburyport. I live in Amesbury but we spend a lot of time in Newburyport."

"Well," Val said, not to be overlooked, "that's because Miss fancy-pants here travels all over the place now for her books."

"Well, cheers to that," Nic said, "congratulations on the new book. I will definitely be picking up my own copy — It's at Mitchell's I assume?"

"Absolutely! And autographed." Val said, "You need a drink to cheers us, doll, grab one from the Yeti over there. There are some High Noons and some Nantucket Crans. Or Tito's if you're goin down that road."

"Tito's? Ha — that's pretty hardcore for the beach," Nic laughed.

"Oh, she's not kidding," Sadie said.

"What's a Nantucket Cran?" Nic asked, opening the Yeti and choosing a Cran.

"Aah — a newbie? Those little beauties are legit cocktails in a can, sister. Made with real vodka from the Triple Eight Distillery here on the island flavored with natural cranberry and blueberry flavors. Not like White Claws, ugh, so *basic*. Don't tell me you haven't been to Cisco Brewery..." Val said.

"Mm, this is amazing. Did you say brewery? Yo, Cade!" Nick yelled to where the guys stood at their cooler, "there's a brewery on this island? How do I not know about that?"

"Oh shit," Val said to Nic, "that's your man? He's fucking hot. Jesus, Sadie, look at him. Look at the three of them! Oh Christ, they're coming over, how do my tits look?"

"Oh my God Val, stop! Please excuse my cougar — oops I mean, friend, Nic — she's married and harmless."

"Speak for yourself, biatch, do you see any husbands here?"

"This is a husband-free weekend," Sadie said, "and that was your idea, now calm your titties."

Cade, Rick, and Tryp sauntered over, beers in hand to meet everybody. Noticing the guys sucking beers at the back of the Jeep, Tryp laughed out loud, "No Way dudes, a funnel! That is epic."

"Don't get any ideas, kid," Rick said, "that's all I need is to bring you home smashed. That's what your mother would do to me."

"So, Cade, this is Sadie Wilson, your mother actually has her latest photo-essay book of Nantucket on her coffee table — she lives in Newbury and I had one of her kids in school once upon a time!"

"Small world, and wow, your book is gorgeous, congratulations," Cade said.

"Okay, quit changing the subject surfer boy — why haven't you taken your woman here to the brewery for Christ's sake?" Val said.

Cade put his hands up, "whoa, whoa, in my defense, it's been non-stop wedding events since we got here — no time!"

"He's not lying," Rick added.

"Rick? That's your name, right? Is that an empty in your hand? For fuck's sake keep up. I'm fully stocked," Val said pointing to her cooler while Sadie sat shaking her head.

"It's true," Nic conceded, "welcome-to-the-island dinner, rehearsal dinner, wedding, morning-after-wedding brunch — relentless schedule. But it's over! And here we are. I mean I'm not complaining, it's been one stunning magazine-worthy event after another, but I'm down for some unscheduled time without planning an *outfit*."

"Amen," Val said, "I say we all hit the brewery from here in a couple hours latest. Outfits not required!"

Tryp started to object — apparently the Cisco Brewery bouncers were Gestapo and underage drinking was NOT a thing — until he got a look at the tandem surfer girls walking up with that big paddleboard under their arms. Nic could see him sizing up his chances with Sadie's and Val's daughters — and realizing that the one they called Teddy was way out of his league, but that maybe there was hope for the younger one.

Rick and Cade could come up with no reason why they shouldn't hit the brewery after the beach. They dragged their chairs over to Val and Sadie's camp and widened their circle.

∞

Whatever Nic had been expecting for an island brewery, Cisco blew it away. An open-beer-garden-style with cobblestone pavers spanning out to include a winery, distillery, and brewery all right there. Dogs wearing as much merch as humans, live music, and a long list of fun drinks — a total vibe. The guys stuck with beers and Sadie and Val got their favorite, the Pineapple Express.

"I'm getting you one, don't argue," Val said, Gucci wristlet swinging, Mahogany hair in a high bun, on her way to the bar.

"You'll love it, don't worry. And sorry, I know Val is a lot..." Sadie started to say.

"Oh my God, don't apologize, I love it, she's *hysterical*. How long have you known each other?"

Sadie filled her in on how she and Val met right there at the brewery years ago. How Sadie and her family had been renting out in the moors of Tom Nevers for fifteen years, and how they learned that very day that Val's husband's company bought the house right next door! They'd never have known, with all the scrub oak separating the houses they could have gone forever without seeing each other.

"And you're besties now? Wow. Truth really is stranger than fiction..."

"Here you go bitches, bottoms up!" Val said, back from the bar and raising her cocktail to lips that matched her vermillion nails. "So, what's the story with Hot and Hotter over there," Val asked pointing to Rick and Cade who, had of course, bumped into friends.

"Ha! They could be brothers, right?" Nic said, "They're brothers-in-law anyway; Cade Swain and Rick Adams."

"Swain as in original-Nantucket-family status?" Sadie asked in awe.

"Don't mind Sadie — she's a nutjob about that stuff. Nantucket history anyway. Do not get her going. Next thing you know she'll be dragging you out to the Oldest House, Hadwen House, all of it."

"I would love that actually!" Nic said, "I started *Mary Coffin Starbuck and the Early History of Nantucket* before I got here but haven't had much time to get back into it but YES, I want to see that oldest house! With that upside down horseshoe on the chimney?"

"YES!" Sadie said, "That was one of the first books I bought too my very first time here. This is awesome — Val here doesn't quite share my enthusiasm. And I love your pendant by the way, Nic. It reminds me of a wax seal on a letter to the royal court — or Lord Bridgerton anyway, ha! What does the "**S**" stand for?"

Nic's eyes dimmed as her hand reached for the pendant at her throat. Instant guilt at partying and feeling joy on such close heels of losing her father.

"Oh I didn't mean to upset you, Nic, I'm so sorry — just being nosy — forget I asked."

"No, no, it's okay. It's just that I lost my dad a month ago and I found this necklace of my mom's, going through their lifetime of stuff. They're both gone now and I guess I almost forget sometimes and then feel guilty for being happy. It's a tangled business, isn't it..."

"It is, believe me, I know," Sadie said, "My husband passed away about five years ago, and while I am happily remarried now, it can still knock the wind out of me knowing that that person is just gone, and that part of my life is over."

"And I lost my dad when he was only fifty-four years old, he was the closest person in the word to me," Val said, "I could be the president of *that* fucking club. It sucks. Who's ready for another round?"

The band was doing a cover of "No Woman, No Cry" — there was just something soul-soothing about reggae. With its bass-heavy heartbeat rhythm and lyrics about love and redemption you couldn't help but sway and smile along. It was a natural high. The place was magic. And while it had no claim on the island's fabled past, it had a clear hold on the present.

The cocktails, sun, and fatigue had Nic leaning on Cade walking back to Rick's truck. One more stop, Cade had said, he wanted her to see Bartlett's Farm, right around the corner from the brewery, Nantucket's largest family-owned farm. Nantucket did feel like home, like family in so many ways — she was already in love with it.

The market was adorable. Not in a tiny cute way as much as with perfect little sections of everything. It smelled like her grandmother's garden, green vegetable tops pushing up out of the earth and freshly watered tomatoes in the sun. They bought steaks to grill, basil, big farm-ripe tomatoes, burrata cheese, and green beans. But it was a month too early for their famous corn. "We'll just have to come back," Cade leaned in to say, steeling a satiny kiss.

Nic felt dizzy with the pleasure of the moment, the day, the prospect of all the tomorrows with Cade. "I'm gonna need a nap before we make dinner," Nic said to Cade.

"I was thinking the same thing, but only if I may join you…"

Rick texted Lexi for some intel on her parents' dinner plans — would they need more of everything or were the senior Swains dining out? He didn't sound disappointed to share the news that it would just be the five of them — Prue and John were eating at a friend's house. How the hell did those old-timers keep the pace, Nic thought. Tryp added some ice cream to their pile at the register and then they were off to Pine Street. Clouds move in on the drive back and Nic noticed how the light chose unexpected details of the landscape to trick out in gold…before a shadow would sweep it away.

∞

Nic went directly up the creaky stairs with her beach tote. She knew it was wrong to slip between the silky clean sheets all suncreened and salty but her body was making the choice for her. She was asleep before she could pull up the covers.

Cade, having indulged in an outdoor shower first, turned the door knob of their room as slowly as possible. It wouldn't have mattered. He slipped naked under the covers beside her, breathing in the scent of her, the sun, salt, and Coppertone.

The feel of Cade's front molded to her backside stirred her from loose dreams. She noticed the room still held an amber glow — then remembered that it was the summer solstice, the longest night of the year. She wanted to stretch but decided she wanted the feeling of Cade's body formed to hers even more. How her head fit neatly under his chin against his throat, with his heart beating slow and strong against her back, how the curve of her bottom tucked into the hollow his hips made, while his knees nestled into the backs of hers.

∞

The steaks and caprese had long since been prepared and eaten, with leftovers wrapped for Nic and Cade. The kitchen was quiet with hardly a trace of activity but for two place settings and a decanted bottle of pinot noir standing sentinel on the island. Nic could picture Rick arranging them, anticipating their delight. She was instantly ravenous and decided the starlight shower would have to wait. Dinner tasted better than anything Nic could think of in recent memory. The magic of the place seemed boundless.

"So, *Nicolina-Thumbelina*, what should we do tomorrow?" Cade asked.

"Thumbelina? Better watch out or I might fall in love with a tiny flower-fairy prince."

"Never," Cade said grinning, taking a slow sip of wine," So, how do you feel about kayaking?"

"I feel good about kayaking. I, in fact, love kayaking. But to be clear — not flying down rapids, rolling, snapped in with a spray skirt — none of that crap. Just simple recreational paddling for fun and a view. That I can do."

"Well, you're in luck — no rapids on Nantucket. And we won't be paddling through the surf of the south shore — I was thinking we could do a picnic on Coatue, maybe take off from Washington Street where the Sea Kayak rental place is, I think there are a few parking spots over there."

Nic tried not to let even a hint of fear show in her eyes. She was used to small lakes and paddling sections of the Charles River with her brother, but that was all super low-key. Being out on the ocean was a different ballgame. "Um, sure! It's not rough water, right? It's basically the harbor, the Sound, right?"

"Right, very chill, not open-ocean stuff. Would I do that to you, *Nickelback*?"

"Okay, that might be enough with the cute little nicknames," she said staring him down through her wine glass as she sipped. "Let's do it. Is this an early morning thing or...?"

"I think we can play it by ear — weather being the only real consideration."

After their dishes were cleared Cade grabbed the bottle and their wine glasses and moved into the living room to catch what was left of the Red Sox game. It was nice having the place to themselves, Nic thought, reaching for Sadie's glossy book next to Gambee's. Gorgeous photographs and stirring essays. Nic would love to know Sadie better, they were practically neighbors back home. And her wild friend, Val, who was actually a lot like Lexi now that she thought about it. Maybe like a Lexi on steroids.

Chapter Sixteen

THE NEXT DAY DAWNED with a soft coral glow. Not clear sunshine but trying. Nic pulled up the weather on her phone and it looked like it would burn off by noon. She was excited for their little adventure, she really enjoyed kayaking and wanted to see as much of the island as possible in the time that remained. She was so pleased with Cade for not being in constant touch with his engineering team back on the mainland, for trusting that the project was in good hands and could progress without him, for being fully present with her, for honoring her in that way. She picked up her Mary Coffin Starbuck book to get a little reading in while he still slept. It was wild going back and forth from the seventeenth century to the twenty-first. What would it be like hundreds of years from now? And how long did they say before Nantucket Island sank into the sea?

The kitchen was in full swing by the time Cade and Nic came down dressed in swimsuits, shorts and t-shirts in search of coffee. Prue and John were enjoying their breakfast out on the blue-stone patio. "Is that my darling boy's voice I hear?" Prue said, "Come out and give your old mother a kiss, I feel like I've hardly seen you." Dutifully, Cade stepped out onto the patio off the kitchen and leaned over to kiss his mother's cheek. She pulled him to sit next to her on the rattan loveseat, "Tell me, what have you been up to?"

"We've seen each other every day, Mom, with one wedding event after another, how has there been time for you to miss me?" Cade said, leaning back into his seat. Nic saw them from the kitchen window as she made a simple egg and bacon scramble for the two of them — his parents would have eaten hours ago.

As she moved about the kitchen, she noticed John out there reading the newspaper, old school, Nantucket's *Inquirer and Mirror* — the island's newspaper for over 100 years — with the *Wall Street Journal* on deck at his feet. How fortunate Cade was, she thought, again, to have both parents living into old age, healthy and under their own steam.

Lexi walked in dropping her keys on the marble island, startling Nic. She was clad in spandex, hair tied back in a low pony tail, and still sweating from whatever torture she'd put her body through. "How can you still be sweating even after driving back from whatever you were doing?"

"The sweat pours harder once you stop. Spinning is no joke — Peloton people are insane," Lexi said, refilling her water bottle at the sink.

"Well, that makes you insane too. Do you want some eggs? Bacon?"

"Umm, no. You can keep your nitrites and your saturated fats to yourself and I'll see you at your funeral. So, thanks but no thanks."

"Alrighty then. Coffee, vodka, rum?" A quick thrill rippled through Nic at their easy banter.

"Ha, ha. Coffee. Please, black."

"Darling, is that you?" Prue called out. Lexi rolled her eyes, took the steaming mug of coffee from Nic and stepped out to the patio to see her mother. "Well, it certainly looks as though you had quite a workout dear, don't you think you're overdoing it just a bit?"

John bent a corner of his paper forward to peer at his daughter, then to tell his wife to leave her alone. That Lexi was almost fifty years old for Pete's sake, she knew how to take care of herself by now. He was a man of few words but Nic could see that he knew when his wife was stirring the pot for no other reason than to get under her daughter's skin. Cade waved his hand in front of his nose when his sister took a seat in a chair beside him, "Maybe you should grab a shower first before interacting with humans, whew!" Hearing the exchange from the kitchen as she spread beach plum jam on the toast, Nic almost spit out her coffee. She'd never heard Cade behave like an annoying little brother. It was endearing.

"Good morning," Nic said to the group, arranging the breakfast on the low table. "Can I refill anyone's coffee or orange juice?"

No one responded at first making Nic feel like she was intruding. Which is probably exactly how Prudence wanted her to feel. "How thoughtful of you Nicolina," John said, "you just go ahead and eat your eggs before they get cold."

"Wow, thanks Nic," Cade said moving his chair closer to the table, "this is awesome. We'll be all energized for our paddle. Oh, and I was thinking we could stop downtown at Provisions to pick up food for our picnic — they make the best sandwiches."

"What's this about dear, what paddle?" Prudence asked.

"Nic and I are going to take the kayaks out to Coatue this afternoon. They're still in the shed, right? With the life jackets and all that?"

"Oh dear. No, actually they are not. I wish you'd said something earlier. I donated them to the Boys and Girls Club at the end of last summer — no one had used them in years."

"Well, that's not true, Mom. Dang it. Well, I'll give Sea Kayak a call, I'm sure we can rent. That'll be easier anyway than having to lug them down. Who wants to give us a lift? Or lend us a vehicle?" Cade said, waggling his eyebrows up and down, adorably, Nic thought.

John folded a corner of his paper down again looking at Cade over the top, "I can drop you downtown, I'm meeting the boys at the club for lunch."

"Cool. Thanks, Dad. Lexi, do you want to join? And where's Rick by the way?"

"Thanks, but I'm all set with the open water sports, and Rick actually had to fly a friend to Providence."

"Well, what are everyone's plans for dinner tonight?" Prue asked, "Should I expect you all for dinner or are you going your separate ways?"

Cade exchanged a look with Nic like he knew what she was thinking — that she wanted time away from the whole family. "You know what, Mom, don't worry about Nic and me, we'll figure something out. Just kinda want not to have a hard plan, y'know?"

Prudence looked into Nic's eyes a beat longer than necessary which gave her a quick chill. As she stood to clear their breakfast dishes and head into the kitchen, Cade followed, having kissed his mother's cheek telling her to enjoy the day. To Nic he said, "I'm actually glad the old kayaks are gone — this is an easier plan all around. Let me call and reserve a couple. We'll grab towels and the waterproof dry bag I know we still have and we'll be good to go."

∞

Stuffing the Provisions sandwiches in the dry bag with some waters, Cade and Nic walked the short distance from town to Sea Kayak. It felt good to be on foot without having to stress about parking. The sky had cleared to pale blue with a steady temperature of 72 degrees but it felt sticky. Nic was glad they'd be spending the day out on the water, away from thick crowds and thicker air.

They'd decided on two separate vessels instead of one tandem, Nic wanted her own rig and to be moving on the water under her own power. They were sit-on-top sea kayaks as opposed to the sit-in style with a cockpit that Nic was used to. She wondered if they were more tippy — but decided getting on and off had to be easier than climbing in and out. Cade's was red and Nic's was a neon green, both life jackets were bright yellow.

Nic felt the vigor of her strokes moving her across the harbor and the ocean spray on her face as she breathed in its briny bouquet. How thrillingly different it was to be on the water than on land. She couldn't stop smiling paddling behind Cade as she looked all around her. Sail boats heading out for adventure and dinghies waiting to be called to action while others bobbed on their moorings. She was glad she remembered her new Cisco Brewery cap and sunglasses with the blinding sun bouncing off white sails and low ripples.

Cade waited for her to get closer so he could point out the shores of Monomoy, Shimmo, Quaise, and Pocomo further up the harbor. They could see the sandy shoreline of Coatue across the way, each crescent curve out to Coskata. Nic's arms and core weren't used to the steady work of pulling and the occasional double paddle on one side to steer but Cade was good about disguising short breaks. Which she needed anyway to capture what she could of the beauty with her phone. The waterproof pocket of the life vest was the perfect spot for her phone but getting it in and out was a force, the more she thought about not dropping it in the water, the closer she came to doing exactly that. *Just be in the moment*, chimed in her head, but still she couldn't resist trying to capture what she was seeing and feeling — knowing already its futility.

They circled around the harbor passing Wauwinet and ending up with the bends of Coatue on their right. They'd seen a few paddleboarders and fellow kayakers out there but she and Cade were sticking closer to the shoreline, which was fine with her. She pretended they were original natives taking chances in unfamiliar waters, exploring new lands. A carbonated joy bubbled up inside her, she wanted to hold onto it.

Finally, Cade chose a sandy curve where they pulled their kayaks up on a little beach. It felt clumsy to stand after being bent and seated for so long, all she wanted to do was spread their towels and lay back on the golden sand. But first she had to take in the view of town across the harbor from where they stood.

"Wow," she said, pivoting slowly, "just wow."

"A little change in perspective, right? You're a pretty strong paddler, I'm impressed."

"Please," Nic said, wishing she could see the blue of Cade's eyes behind his Maui Jims, "I know exactly what I am, which is very average, and I'm fine with it, Aquaman." She kissed him lightly on the lips, then took the water bottle out of his hands for a long pull of cold water.

"Nicolina Wright, there is nothing average about you. And the fact that you don't see that is probably the hottest thing about you."

She reached for his hand to pull him down beside her to just lie back and try to picture themselves from the sky, on the left fluke of the tail of this whale-shaped island. They pulled their sweaty t-shirts off and Nic wriggled out of her shorts to feel the full pulse of the sun before they both ran into the water to cool off. Popping up out of the blue water with her hair slicked long behind her, Nic blinked the salty sting from her eyes. "I still can't get over how warm the water is here, I'm so used to Maine where all you can do is run in, dunk, convince yourself you are not experiencing a cardiac event, and run out. As kids we'd stay in! I don't know how we did it."

"This is still the harbor though, remember, it's sheltered, not exactly open ocean. After we eat, we'll walk to the other side and check it out."

Cade handed Nic her curried chicken salad sandwich from Provisions and a bag of Black Pepper Brant Point Nantucket Crisps then placed his own smoked ham and swiss and Madaket Onion crips on the towel before reaching in for another treat — he'd snuck two cans of Cisco Summer Rays beer into the picnic.

She looked at him for a long minute and reached a hand to rest on his arm, "you thought of absolutely everything." They sat side by side, drying off in the sun and light wind, mouths too full to talk, Nic's heart too full to describe.

Lying back after lunch, Cade told her what he knew of Coatue, that it was a wildlife refuge containing over 390 acres of barrier beach that sheltered Nantucket Harbor from the Sound. "It's actually home to lots of rare plants and birds and, can you see those dwarf cedars over there? Constantly being buffeted by the wind stunts them — and there are even patches of cacti species hiding in there somewhere."

"But what I really want to know is did you guys party over here as kids in like a little skiff or something? There have to be stories…"

"Funny you should ask," Cade began, "I mean I could tell you, but then I can never un-tell you… HA! Seriously, we weren't as bad as what you see these days on @chadtucket, beaching Daddy's million-dollar yacht, or literally getting impaled on the jetties, but we've made our own mistakes misreading the tides and the sandbars — you can imagine."

"I'm trying to… Nantucket-Cade is different from the guy I've come to know. In a good way. It's quite disarming actually." Nic said, smiling and rolling onto her side to drape an arm across his chest, resting her head there too.

"How do you mean, how am I usually?"

"Maybe it's just vacation-Cade — no work pressures and responsibilities, wildly carefree. You know what I mean."

"I do. Because I'm totally enjoying wildly carefree, dogless, childless, Nic!"

"What's happening to our sunshine? You can actually see it dimming to a watery yellow — is that fog racing across the water way out there or clouds?" Nic asked.

Cade opened his eyes then leaned up on both elbows. The air did suddenly seem to have a chill at the edge. "That's the island for you — if you don't like the weather on Nantucket, wait a minute. Hey, let's drag our rigs across that narrow bit to the other side so you can get a feel for it from the outside. We can launch from there, then paddle around the tip back into the harbor to return the boats. You up for that?"

"Is it as calm on the other side, outside of the harbor?"

"It should be, but let's go check it out before the weather really falls apart on us."

Nic had to admit it was mind-blowing standing on that bend of sand looking out into the wide open Atlantic. She noticed the water stayed shallow and the same teal color on that north shore for a ways before dropping off and deepening to a true navy blue. As slang and almost meaningless as the word "awesome" had become, she thought of its definition: *inspiring an overwhelming feeling of reverence, admiration, or fear.* Standing there was freaken awesome.

They packed up their few things and paddled east, hugging the shoreline on their right to see what they could see. It was pristine, tranquil and felt completely remote. The paddling felt easier than she expected and she couldn't stop grinning. Cade came up beside her and she saw her joy reflected in the tilt of his smile. "Like a hot knife through buttah," she said slicing her paddle evenly into the water, "thank you for this amazing day."

"Really transports you, I know, but don't thank me yet — we've still got some paddling to do to get back, you good?" he asked as he reversed their direction to paddle west to the tip and then south.

"Right behind you, Captain." Nic felt the harder pull of her paddle as soon as they turned around — no wonder it had been so easy the other way, now they were moving against the invisible current and the wind which had definitely picked up. Ugh, she couldn't stop and rest because the wind would push her backward and she'd be losing ground, paddling twice the distance. *Just keep an even pace*, she coached herself, *settle into a rhythm*. Which she did, while she kept her mind busy appreciating the coastline now on her left. She couldn't believe how tropical it looked in places, this little New England island, thirty miles off the coast of Cape Cod.

Her armpits were starting to chafe from the life vest against her salty skin. And almost suddenly it appeared like she was no longer hugging the shore as she had been. She swallowed a knot of fear, but it only fattened in her chest when she saw how far she was from both Cade and the tip of land separating her from the harbor and the open Atlantic. She tried to call out to him, but the wind thinned her voice and carried it off. The sky was now a low ceiling of gray and the sea had turned pewter with whitecaps kicking up.

She struggled to close the gap between her kayak and Cade's, who'd finally noticed her distance from him and had started after her. Her biceps and shoulders burned with the effort of trying to stay the course, and as hard as she was trying not to panic, her breaths had become shallow and distressed. At least she couldn't get swamped and capsize in a sea kayak, there was that. But she felt like an inflatable toy at the whim of the gusts, getting blown out to sea like a beachball. Was the current getting stronger too? Or was she just getting too tired — she was officially losing her shit. Totally exposed on a neon piece of plastic with land getting farther away — shark bait.

The salty stinging wind whipped at her face and mingled with her tears; she was too scared to be embarrassed. She prayed to her father to help her get back in — this just couldn't be happening. *God,* how she hated weakness in herself. She kept paddling, even if she only stayed in place. It looked like Cade was getting closer, but was he? She started to wish they'd rented a tandem kayak instead. But then she told herself to get her shit together and breathe; innnn then ouuuut... Oxygenate the muscles and the mind. Okay. Okay.

Cade was closing the gap, closer and closer, until he could grab her outstretched paddle. She let one blubber of relief escape — but only one. "I am so sorry Cade, I don't know what happened. One minute I'm humming along admiring the beach from this side — next thing I know it's so far away and you were a red speck on the water."

"It's okay Nic, don't sweat it now, okay?" He said, fear and adrenaline changing his voice, "it's my fault, I take full responsibility, I'm sorry — the wind shifted so suddenly, I should have known better, we should have stuck to inside the harbor." He had to almost shout over wind on the water.

"How do we get back? Let's focus on that, I'm so tired Cade, my arms are jelly." Her kayak was snug parallel against his and she held onto his seat strap for all she was worth. He rummaged in the drybag, digging to the bottom until he pulled out a neatly coiled rope. Not a lot but enough. She sagged with relief. But she scolded herself to pay attention — one more wave like the last one and she'd be tossed like a cork. Cade worked efficiently securing the rope from the T-handle on the stern of his kayak to the one on the bow of hers. She didn't know how this would work or how long it would take but she didn't care. She wasn't alone. She. Wasn't. Alone.

It wasn't her finest moment paddling back, she felt like an idiot being towed, intermittently banging into his boat. Once they were safely inside the harbor she untied her bow from his stern. While there was no current pulling her and dragging her out, the water was rougher than when they'd started. The sky had darkened and rain seemed imminent. Damn, she hadn't wanted to be rescued. She hadn't wanted to *need* rescuing. But there she was. As she paddled her kayak beside Cade she kept pace, feeling strong in spite of things, and just wanting to know why the hell being an independent, strong-ass woman could be such a trial. Sometimes. The damsel-in-destress thing was not her game. But neither was this pity party she was throwing herself. She needed to snap out of it. It's not like she felt judged by Cade — that wasn't how he rolled. Knowing him, he was ticking off the all the ways he'd failed her that afternoon.

Feeling better after her self-chat, she thought she'd be cute and sprint past Cade, launching up onto the beach a boat's length ahead of him. He let her. Rain pelted their skin but at least they were laughing. Her legs were even more unwieldy this time and she wondered how much she owed to adrenaline and what the payback would be tomorrow. She remembered to retrieve her phone from the pocket of the vest before returning it and was glad that she'd captured at least a few photos from Coatue while the sun reigned over the day. She noticed she'd missed a few texts, one from Poppy, the other two from Evy. Before she'd allow herself to feel alarm or anything at all she opened her daughter's message. Thankfully it was just an *everything's fine but I miss you, when are you coming home again* text. Snoopy was fine, Ben was fine, everybody was fine. Nic could tell her daughter was struggling with the loss of her Papa. You never knew when it would sneak up on you…one day you're handling it like a boss and the next thing you know you're just minding your own business, cutting bananas for your cereal, and then *plunk* — fat tears in your Frosted Mini-Wheats.

Cade reached for her hand asking if she wanted to go home right away — they could uber — or if maybe she wanted to get a drink at Rose & Crown. "It's just a half-mile up the road into town — super chill vibe, perfect for a day like this. And would you look at that — rain's already moving on."

They could actually see the black curtain moving across the water, and since it was still humid, she was drying off and warming up. "Yes please, that sounds perfect. Ooh, do they have chowder?"

"Look where you are! *Do they have chowder…* ha! Just kiddin, *sNickerdoodle*."

Standing on the sidewalk in front of Rose & Crown, Cade asked if she wanted to sit inside or out. They chose inside since the whole front opened like garage doors to the outside but they'd be undercover in case the weather did an about-face.

"Awe, look at this place, all these old quarterboards and signs... and that giant mermaid on the wall, I love her! This might be my new favorite place."

"Leave it to you to pick probably the least expensive, most OG place on the island. I do like your taste, lady."

"Well, I hope so, I picked you."

"Wait a minute there — who picked who?"

"Whom."

"Don't start with me, English teacher."

"I'll start and finish with you, buddy." She meant it jokingly, but as soon as the words were out of her mouth they sounded different. How did she mean them? She hadn't had time to consider much past today and tomorrow, never mind the future with only one man in it — *this* man, who she'd known only four months, with his regular-guy way but also exclusive lineage and prominent family. But her gut knew, her insides *knew* that this was the only man she wanted. But she wasn't ready for him to see that. Thank God for the arrival of Violet, their server, who would be *taking care of them*.

The chowder and beer hit the spot. Nic's body felt pleasantly fatigued and her brain had a soft landing for every thought. She liked watching the people walk by, so many kinds of people. Were they day-trippers or summer renters? Did they own a home there or did their family? Sometimes she was certain she could tell — by their clothes, their swagger, or how they spoke — but you just never knew. Everyone had a story.

"A *Nickel* for your thoughts?" Cade said, "Looking very pensive…"

The sound of his voice tore her attention from the passersby. "What? Oh, I don't know — just listening to snippets of conversation as people pass. We're really all the same aren't we? *What are we doing for dinner, did anyone take the dog out, what would your super-power be, what's the most annoying color, will this love last forever?*"

Laughter and relief spilled into his voice. "You forgot; *would you rather have no nose or no arms, how many chickens would it take to kill an elephant, and what sport would be the funniest to add a mandatory amount of alcohol to?*"

Laughter bubbled up from her toes, Cade was a keeper.

"In all seriousness," Cade said, "who really knows what the future has waiting for you. And if you could know, would you spoil it?"

"I know, I know, you're right. And I do try to keep my mom's advice in my heart: *trust in your journey, your life is unfolding exactly as it should.*"

"Whoa... I really dig that," Violet their server said, suddenly appearing, "can I, like, steal that?"

"Knock yourself out. Words to live by, right?" Nic said. As Cade settled the tab, Nic felt her phone ping with a text. It was from Poppy, which reminded her that she never opened her earlier text.

"Everything alright with the kids?" Cade asked, taking a last pull of his beer.

"Yes. This is actually from your niece," Nic said, squinting, she was blind without her readers that she didn't have with her. And in the interest of being present and not on her phone, she decided to catch up on the texts once they were home.

"You guys got pretty close while she was here, huh?"

"We did actually, she's an impressive young woman. I guess you could say we bonded over discovering that painting in Quidley's that first night and she's been doing some digging on her end with her MFA connections. There is just something evocative about that artist I can't articulate but I'm almost positive I've seen her work before. I had a sort of flashback the other day in this antique place Poppy and I went to where they had a Stella Fera painting hanging for sale. I was staring at it — then all of a sudden I was eleven years old in my parents' closet for hide-and-seek bumping up against a framed painting...it was *so* like this Stella Fera's style! It was like this shock of recognition."

"Okaayyy, so, knowing that your mom has actually been here to Nantucket, what's the connection? Did she buy the painting while she was here?"

"But the sicker on it said $4,500! So, I can't see that. Except it would have been a fraction of that then but still..."

Nic felt these new bits of information about her mom were like crystals being tossed up at a window, but then clattering back down to the sidewalk into even more pieces. She couldn't put it together.

While Nic finished her Whale's Tale Ale she tried to explain the pieces to Cade. "I'm not sure I can do them justice, the feeling, of all five senses being involved looking at her paintings, or into them. Immediately you're there, on a thin towel feeling every grain of sand, under a big canvas striped umbrella in your 1920's bathing costume, the salty wind blowing in off the water that you taste on your lips as it lifts your coiffed hair, threatening to take your hat, the surf booming then receding again... You are there with these young people that dress like old-timers, but who are so making a supper plan at the yacht club or at Johnny's Gran's lawn party out in Sconset at an enormous house on the bluff..."

The way Cade looked at her, she knew he got it. "That's what I'm talking about — you can smell that beach, feel that wind, can't you? You can hear those mustachioed buddies making jokes about who's a better sailor, who can't hold his liquor, and who has precisely no chance with Ruth *or* Barbara..."

"How do you do that?" Cade said.

"And your Uncle Tom has one of her paintings in his bedroom."

"Wait — what? Back up, you've lost me."

Nic told Cade about getting lost in Tom's house the morning of the brunch. "It was actually an authentic moment standing in front of it looking at it together with Tom before Poppy found me and joined us. Anyway, apparently it'd been in storage since their move and they'd just recently hung it. But he said something cryptic like *I've said too much already*, something about your long-lost Uncle Theo. And then Celia came in to drag him back out to the guests and that was that."

"That's a lot to unpack, let's free up this table and walk a little."

Chapter Seventeen

The late afternoon had turned sultry and felt like it had been two days instead of one. Their walk after Rose & Crown took them home to Pine Street, Nic's body was feeling the miles, aquatic and otherwise, and she couldn't wait to shower outside. "Dibs!" she called, grabbing her towel first.

"Of course," Cade said, "Take your time." He winked over his shoulder which she took as a combo-message of *I won't intrude, but give me a sign and I'm there.* How had she gotten so lucky, she asked herself again. She was always half-waiting for him to reveal some indefensible thing about himself, a deal-breaker, so she could let herself off the hook, let go — instead of liking him so much that her heart kept trying to peek at a future with him.

Tilting her head up to the sky she breathed in the blue of it. The rainforest showerhead poured heavy warm streams down over her and she could do little to prevent the cavalcade of disjointed thoughts that rained down too. Prue...was she honestly hoping for Cade and Reagan to reconcile? While Nic trusted that Cade didn't want that at all, she couldn't help but wonder where else and how often Reagan might show up in their lives. *It shouldn't matter*, she told herself. But like so many things, it was so much easier to admire that stance than to carry it out.

Lying on her bed while Cade took his turn outside in the shower, Nic inhaled the mouth-watering smells that rose up from the kitchen. Lexi was making her special shrimp, scallop and garlic angel hair pasta with snow peas and Baby Red Pear tomatoes. What a departure from reality — being cooked for, with no one to have to take care of — animal or human — it was a little uncomfortable, she had to admit.

She retrieved her reading glasses and finally attended to Poppy's texts. She hoped she'd be forgiven a tardy response.

Hey there Nic — call me if you can.

Ok I'm sure you're busy having fun — how's it going? The city is sweltering, I'm so jelly you're on Nantucket and I'm not! Anyway — my buddy Sharon at MFA did some poking around on the Stella Fera paintings — there is not a lot of info out there. She did a deep dive on other painters from her era, on Nantucket and otherwise, and so far the only thing of interest was that apparently the name Stella Fera was a nom de plume, as they say in literature, a pen name of sorts. The artist's real name was Sofia Antonia Fiore. Weird huh? Why would anyone do that? We'll keep digging — ttyl.

Nic bolted upright, a vein of lightening splitting her mind. Sofia Antonia Fiore was her mother's name.

She couldn't breathe. The air blowing in through the window had turned cool and her wet hair made her shiver. *What was going on* — her mother? Questions ricocheted in her brain paralyzing her.... A painter? On Nantucket? How? When? *Why* was this kept a secret? Did her father know? She had no one now to ask!

Her head pounded, questions piling up in her brain.

"You're as white as a sheet, Nic, did you see a ghost?" Cade said, coming into the room and scaring her to death. When she didn't respond he sat down beside her on the bed. "Talk to me —are the kids alright? Your crazy dog? Say something."

Nic sat, unmoving, staring, swallowing. "Yes, I mean, no. Kids fine, Snoop fine." She stopped, turning her eyes to his, her mouth opening and closing around empty air.

"Okay, you're freaking me out a little, and what's that weird thing your eyes are doing — I've never seen them this color, are your pupils taking over? Do you get migraines? It wasn't cold enough for you to have gotten hypothermia out there today..."

"That artist, that painter I've been obsessing over...Stella Fera... she's my *mother*. Cade, Stella Fera's real name was Sofia Fiore..."

Cade took Nicolina's ice-cold hands in his. He rubbed his thumbs over her knuckles holding her gaze. Words seemed to scramble up the ladder of his throat until he said finally, "Okay, okay...well, this is, this is unexpected, right? I mean, I mean, what do I mean — this is pretty big for you, yes...but cool though, right? Because you're an artist too and you've said you never understood where that talent came from, so this is huge, this is *good*, right?"

Nic drew her hands back from his and stared through him, offering an imperceptible nod. "I...I guess. I'm just trying to wrap my head around it, you know? I mean it's incredible, my own mom, this extraordinary artist, these exquisite images she rendered...she was like this whole other person...so many questions..."

Cade listened. Without trying to answer, he let her talk and ask and ask some more.

"My dad must have known because, because that painting I told you I saw as a kid was right there in their closet — he had to know it was there. What happened to it? All our trips to the Museum of Fine Arts, her almost oppressive encouragement of my drawing and painting, how did she hide that part of herself, *why* would she ever want to, Cade?"

"I don't know, Nic, I don't know...but maybe we can find out, maybe Poppy can find out more? Or we could...I don't know...talk to some art people here?"

"Okay, right, right, that does sound like something we can — WAIT! What about your uncle Tom? He must know something! Remember? I told you he kind of clammed up about his painting? And this brother, Theo!"

Cade took a big breath and let it out. "Okay, let's just relax, go downstairs and eat, and talk to Lexi, is that alright? She's good for leaving emotions at the door, being strictly analytical. And wine, we'll drink wine and, you know, come up with a plan."

Nic nodded and unfolded herself from the bed. "*Ow*, yup, gonna be sore as hell tomorrow." She stretched her arms over her head and side to side then slid into her cutoffs and ran a brush through her damp hair before heading downstairs behind Cade.

"Well, thanks for gracing us with your presence — am I keeping you from something?" Lexi said with her incurable sarcasm, shredding fresh parmesan, "You look weird, no offense, like your eyebrows are all wrong or something."

"Why ever would I be offended?" Nic said, smoothing her features and noting Lexi's empty cocktail. "How many deep are you? I have some catching up to do."

"Yes, yes you do. No, seriously who fucking died?" Lexi looked quickly up at Cade as soon as the words were out of her mouth, searching for signs that someone maybe, actually, died.

Sitting heavily on a stool at the island, Nic poured herself a big glass of pinot noir. Not her favorite but she knew it would be a pricey version and therefore not taste like mud. As Cade set out silverware and napkins, Nic filled Lexi in on the late, great, elusive Nantucket painter, Stella Fera, also known as her *mother*, Sofia Fiore. She could barely wrap her mouth around the words.

"What the absolute f—?" Lexi said, nearly sending a serving of shrimp, scallops and angel hair to the floor. "You mean that artist you and Poppy have been going apeshit over? How is that even possible? How do you *not* know your mother was a freaken artist? On *Nantucket*? I mean for fuck's sake, that's a little weird, right?"

"Jesus Lexi, take it easy," her brother scolded.

"Yes! It's nuts! I just want to know *why*?" The three of them served themselves, poured wine and sat at the marble island. "This is *so good*, Lexi," Nic said around a mouthful, "A treat I do not take for granted." How was it that creature comforts, like a mouth-watering meal and good company, had the power, in the moment, to release you from the weight of the world?

"Like I'm making this delicacy for a party of one? Rick's off flying someone somewhere and I've given up keeping track of my parents' social calendar. How the hell do they keep the pace? *Anyway*, so you said Poppy dropped this bomb on you?"

"Oh, she has no idea it was a bomb. Just an innocent text — a colleague did a deep dive on Stella Fera, apparently, discovering that name was a pseudonym... you know I still can't believe these words are coming out of my mouth and that who we're really talking about is my MOTHER." Nic took an extra-large gulp of wine. Red wine isn't really good for that. But all she wanted was a fat cushion for her thoughts. "Oh shit, I almost forgot — your own uncle has one hanging in his bedroom! Did I tell you that?" Turning to Cade a little sloppily, "Did we *tell* her that? And about your Uncle THEO?"

"If you did, I wasn't listening. Why the hell, were you in my uncle's bedroom?" Turning to Cade, "Is she alright? *Theo*? Really?"

Cade filled his sister in about the wedding brunch at Uncle Tom's and the Stella Fera hanging in the master.

"Come on Caaaddde," Nic slurred, "you're leaving out the best part." Then turning to Lexi, Nic continued, "He loves her work too, he said. Hard to come by, he said, that there's a stoorrryyy behind it, or something. Sshhhh, he said, *I've said too much already*, he said. Not *too* sus! I mean ohmygod, right?! And why doesn't anyone talk about THEO?"

"Okay, that's enough wine for *you*," Cade said, sliding her glass out of reach."

"Cut the shit, Cade," Lexi said sliding it back, "I like her like this. But seriously, what the hell does Tom know about art? And how have we not seen this painting? We spent so much time at their house in Madequecham surfing all those summers. AND I haven't heard Uncle Theo's name spoken in, oh, I don't know, *ever?*"

Nic put her head down on folded arms on the cold marble island.

"So her mother must have *lived* here then, not just a little vacation, right?" Lexi said to her brother, "and what the Christ does it have to do with Theo the estranged brother? I hate to admit it but I'm lost and your girlfriend here is—"

"Don't talk about me like I'm not here," Nic said, only, as a single word. "Idonknow...I. Don't. Know," Nic said, dragging her head upright to face Lexi.

"Are you *crying*? Cut the shit. So, your mother comes here to Nantucket, takes up painting — or maybe, probably, she was already an artist, duh. She clearly had this *style,* right? How, again, didn't you know this? No judgement, I mean..."

Nic stared through watery eyes, not knowing how to arrange the thought bubbles floating in her head, wishing only that her mom were here to ask. "She never painted with me. I never saw her pick up a brush — but she encouraged me with this endless devotion, not wanting me to *waste my God-given talent*. While, apparently, she did exactly that."

"Something must have happened then, something awful or something too painful for her to be reminded of maybe? Why else do you bury stuff, lock it away, literally and figuratively?" Lexi said, "Let's do some more poking around tomorrow. I'll be your Poppy. As long as there's a boozy lunch in there somewhere. And I don't see how we can avoid what Uncle Tom said, Mr. *I've said too much already* — what the fuck is that?"

"Okay, let's change the subject, ladies," Cade said, just as his parents were walking in the front door.

"Hello Mumsie," Lexi said.

"Darling, you know how I detest that moniker," Prudence said, "and what on earth are you people doing eating so late?"

"It's summer, Mother, no clock and no rules."

"You are no longer a child, Alexandra, let's keep that in mind, shall we?"

Nic mouthed *Alexandra*, having had no idea that was Lexi's actual name.

"Yes, Mother, and you know how I detest *that* moniker," Lexi said, taking an extra-large and rather gauche gulp of wine.

"It's your God-given name, darling."

"Whatever that means, Mother, *you* gave me the name because what you really wanted was an *Alexander*."

"Will you never cease to be so entirely exhausting..." It wasn't a question. "And please do make certain all the lights are out when you go to bed," Prue said.

"Wait, Mummy," Lexi said, pushing the envelope, "before you go, does the name Stella Fera mean anything to you? She's a painter. Or *was*, I should say, back in your day."

Prue's eyes were more gray than blue in that moment, moving through several changes of weather before they settled. And then there was John, who suddenly broke into a coughing fit that had him heading straight back to their master bedroom beyond the kitchen.

Seemingly grateful for the distraction, Prue filled a glass with water to take back to her husband and saying nothing more than,

"Doesn't ring any bells, darling. I'll see you in the morning, goodnight."

Cade, Nic, and Lexi were all just looking at each other when Rick came through the door. "Hey gang, it is so good to be home. What'd I miss? Anything good? And what smells so divine? More importantly — is there any left?" Rick was literally a breath of fresh air. He brought in with him the sweetly salted air of a summer by the sea tucking itself in for the night.

"It's been a *day* — you could say," Cade said.

Rick looked from his brother-in-law to the ladies to read if this meant in a good way or bad. "I'm gonna need a little more, Cade? Anybody?" Rick served himself what was left of the shrimp, scallop and angel hair dish as Lexi summed things up for him.

"Apparently, Nic got sucked out to sea in a kayak because Cade wasn't paying attention, the artist your daughter and Nic have been gushing over turns out to have used a fake name on her work, which by the way Tom and Celia are in possession of one, *and*, wait for it, the artist known as Stella Fera turns out to actually be Sofia Fiore, Nicolina's freaken MOTHER. Other than that, you didn't miss a thing — just another day in paradise."

"Jeebus Christmas," Rick said. He physically could not swear.

The group took their glasses and another bottle of wine out on the bluestone patio into the sultry night. Nic had switched to water and was trying on different perspectives. And also trying not to lose her shit. She felt further away from home than ever. Tryp came around the corner from the front having heard their chatter. He looked as slick as ever, making her wonder just what he'd been up to. Did Lexi and Rick wonder at all?

She missed her kids and her dog. She missed her parents and everything about her life that she'd taken for granted. She thought about how perhaps everyone has a moment that splits their life in two

— a moment that creates a "before" and "after." And she had a strong feeling she wasn't there even yet. Her fingers went to the "**S**" to rub at the smooth parts they'd come to know by heart.

Chapter Eighteen

NIC COULD FEEL THE gauzy pull of sleep but she could not relax into it. She finds herself in an ongoing dream; disjointed, illusory, scenarios that begin as a celebration of her parents. Her brother and sister are there with extended family, friends, and colleagues from their parents' lives. Some guests wear black tie while others are night swimming in a pool that is more of a lagoon, an oasis surrounded by tropical plantings and lit to a luminescent aqua. In the dream, Nic can't find the right dress to wear. After choosing, finally, she's rushing to get it on over her head but can't. People and a hum of activity surround her, the party is in full-swing without her, she's naked and exposed until the dress is on and smoothed down.

She's unsteady in heels, on rubbery legs she reaches for the bottle champagne on ice in a silver bucket. Squinting with a closer look she sees that it's her parents' special bottle from their wedding, they'd been saving it for their 50th anniversary. *Who did this?* Then she's tripping over the length of her dress hurrying to find her brother to ask him. People are laughing and drinking all around her. The air crackles with merriment and she notices her mother's dead sisters appearing one by one.

She trips and goes down slowly, laughing, trying to get her shoe unstuck from the hem of her long dress. But she holds her champagne aloft — not losing a drop — so proud of this feat, *hold my beer*! she jokes. There are three handsome men watching her, mockery in their eyes. They are impeccably dressed, too good-looking, as they shake their heads calling her drunk. *No*, she's telling them, laughing still, *it's the dress, the damn shoes.* HA, these men don't bother her, what should their disapproval mean to her? She sees that someone has poured champagne in little nip bottles and she's grabbing as many as she can hold to pass out for when her siblings and she make their toasts. But she keeps dropping them. The toasts have begun. Why is she trying so hard to grab all the nips in pretty cellophane bags?

When she finally arrives at the spot where Enzo and Mia are standing to greet the guests, their father is with them. Her siblings are looking down at their practiced speeches — she has not prepared one. She'll wing it, she thinks, no worries. The venue has become cavernous like an auditorium and there are too many people watching, waiting. But when it's her turn, a big velvet curtain lowers on her. She's laughing, bending to stay ahead of the descending curtain, but everyone is already gone.

Enzo's disappointment in her behavior is palpable. Her dog appears by her side with a gash on his foreleg. Enzo tosses a twenty-dollar bill at her telling her to go buy Neosporin and take care of the poor animal. The next thing she knows they're standing on a hill, a salt marsh, spongey like moss. They're looking up at a cathedral, admiring its ancient stonework when a Quaker woman calls over to them asking how they got there, that they shouldn't be there because there are sink holes. *Whoosh* — the woman disappears into the ground.

Enzo and Nic look at each other in silent agreement to get out of there — thinking that if they stay light on their feet and skim the surface quickly they won't get sucked in. Enzo starts running but then *whoosh*, he's gone. Then *woosh*, her dog is gone. But she can see the bulge that is him just under the surface still moving forward. Can he breathe? *Why didn't she take better care of him??* Then *whoosh*, she is gone.

Then she pops back up! But she is all alone.

∞

Nic never knew what to make of her unhinged dream-world. Enzo was better at the analysis. She guessed he would tell her that her drinking was definitely a thing, a recurring theme — he'd ask why it held such importance. He'd suggest also that she didn't think she was good enough, worthy — and that that was a sure way to disappear. Whoosh.

"But you came back," he'd say, "you popped back up when no one else managed that —which speaks to your power. You *can* survive," he'd say, "alone."

The coo of a mourning dove outside her window changed her focus. She was glad of it. Dawn was breaking, and instead of feeling refreshed from sleep she was spent. In no rush to get out of bed she reached for her phone to google mourning doves. Was there a message there? Wasn't there always a message?

To hear the forlorn yet soothing cooing of a mourning dove is believed to be a call to seek and find inner peace. Some people sense the cooing of the mourning dove is a direct message from God. Its symbolism is spiritual and powerful, a message of faith and hope to those suffering.

Well, Mr. Google, I could sure use some inner peace, she said to herself. She reached for her book, needing to *not* analyze her dreams, her drinking. So yesterday was excessive, and, well, this whole week so far, big deal. A work in progress, she was, adjusting to her sense of self in the world, and reconciling the disappearance of things and people she'd counted on as steadfast and true. *Whoosh.*

∞

She was glad Cade was an early riser because she was hungry and tired of lying in bed thinking about all her shit. It was a cool morning, the sun sat small and naked between the trees, unable to push itself fully through the cloud bank. She decided the patio was the best spot to wrap her hands around a warm mug of coffee and hatch a plan for the day. John had the same idea and was in his usual spot with his usual sheaf of newspapers.

"Morning Mr. Swain," she said, relieved there was no Mrs. Swain and choosing a seat adjacent to him. "What's the good word?"

"Very little in this world today, young lady, I'll tell you that. I'll be dead and buried before the market recovers, if indeed it ever does." Folding a corner of his *Wall Street Journal* down to peer at Nic over his glasses, he added, "What's the good word with you?"

A laugh bubbled up in her at his question and at the smile starting in his eyes. "Well, we are here on this beautiful island on this summer day, for starters."

"True, true. That should be quite enough then, shouldn't it." It was more a statement than a question. "It's too easy to lose perspective nowadays, you are quite right. Reading all this rubbish is the equivalent of searching for something to be miserable about, why do we do it. Habit, I suppose, very difficult to part with, human nature and all of that."

Nic wasn't sure he even needed her for the conversation but she was enjoying it nonetheless. She wondered if you got to an age where mostly what you did was look back — because looking ahead was more of a roadblock. And unknown. Unknowns were frightening, unpredictable. She thought how most people probably preferred predictable. *Too many p's she thought.*

"I think maybe it's a good idea to live in the moment as much as possible, you know? Not live like you're dying necessarily — just gratitude and living fully," Nic said, surprising herself a little. "Whew, I should take my own advice."

"Sound advice," John said, "but one needs also to be prepared for the future, not just flying by the seat of one's pants."

Nic wasn't sure if he was questioning her financial independence, some commentary about her dating his son, hitching her wagon to the Swains. Or was he just speaking in general. She took things too personally probably.

"I have a good job Mr. Swain, teaching high school English and Literature for almost twenty five years, a retirement plan, no flying by the seat of my pants."

"What's that young lady?" he asked, having apparently already moved on. She laughed at herself.

"Who's flying by their pants?" Cade chuckled, stepping out onto the patio with bare feet, spearing his hand through sleepy hair.

Lexi and Rick were right behind Cade with their mugs of coffee. "Morning Daddy," Lexi said, kissing him on the cheek, then turning to Nic, "and how are *you* this morning?"

"Crazy dreams, a hint of a headache. I know, I earned it, I'm fine," Nic said, noting the impish glint in Lexi's eyes, wondering what she planned to say to *Daddy* that might possibly blow the peaceful morning wide open.

"So, Daddy, you headed off to bed last night before you got to answer our question about the artist, Stella Fera, you know that painter who did those like old-fashioned, sepia toned images with people from the 1920's on the beach mostly, with boats or bikes? Do you know who I mean?"

John pretended to be engrossed in his paper, as if his daughter would let him get away with that. She knocked on his paper like a door, "helloooo?" He was pretty well cornered. Nic's stomach folded not knowing what to expect — and the fact that he seemed to know *something* he wasn't eager to share was giving her a stomachache.

"Yes, I know the paintings to which you are referring," John said brusquely, "what is it with the inquisition?" Lexi looked to Nic in surprise, as if to say, *we've barely asked him anything, what inquisition, what is he hiding*? "Seriously, Dad? We haven't tied you to your chair — just doing a little intel. Why so defensive?"

"Where's your mother anyway?" John said.

"How should I know, probably out walking with Louise," Lexi theorized, referring to Prue's walking and garden club friend. "Lou and Prue the dynamic duo. *Anyway* — did you and Mother ever own a Stella Fera?"

"No."

"Okaayyy, then did you know that your brother Tom has one? And that he got all weird about it when Nic and Poppy were asking him about it? It all seems so sketch — what's the deal, Daddio?"

"Alexandra, that is *enough*!" John said, jowls quivering in annoyance, "I honestly do not recall anything about either the paintings or the artist, am I making myself clear?"

Turning away from her father and facing Nic and Cade, Lexi whispered, "Breaking out the full name, and evidently doubling down on *recalling* nothing. Interesting..."

"I am not deaf, Alexandra, and where is that boy of yours? He's been making too much of a racket in the kitchen when he finally decides to come home at night. If you don't speak to him, I will."

"Yes, Father. Is Uncle Tom still on-island?"

"I am not my brother's keeper."

"Well *that* couldn't be more obvious! Since no one seems to know or care where your brother Theo is!" Lexi said.

John crushed his paper down in his lap. "I will not tolerate this *impertinence* young lady! You have no idea what you're talking about, this is foolishness!"

Nic's blood took on a slow boil and she spoke out without thinking, "It's not foolishness!" Nic surprised herself by shouting, "Stella Fera was my mother! Except her real name is, was, Sofia Fiore..." she untangled herself from her chair and nearly tripped making her exit.

Nic needed time alone, there was too much reverberating in her heart and mind. She knew she could walk into town, but where would that get her exactly? She knew Nantucket had a historical society — but was that an actual place? Or just an organization. According to Google, there was an address on Broad Street and then on Fair Street there was a Nantucket Historical Association Research Library. This was probably not within their scope at all, but you just never knew — she had to start somewhere. She grabbed an Orange Mango Nantucket Nectars and sat on a bench outside the Hub to collect her thoughts. What exactly was she after? If it was muddled to her, it wouldn't make much sense to anyone else.

So, her mother came to Nantucket sometime around 1968. Her parents were married in 1972, so at most she lived on-island for three years. *Is that possible*, she thought? She was having an excruciating time trying to understand why her mother would keep this from her, which was a complete waste of her energy and emotion. She couldn't rewrite the past to accommodate her precious stubborn understanding of it — she didn't want to. She was simply torn between keeping her mother as she knew her or accepting obscure wonderful new things about her. One felt safe and the other was making the hair rise up off her neck in the hot sun.

She marched into the NHA offices on Broad Street next to the whaling museum before she could talk herself out of it. An older woman, Beatrice Lewiston, her nametag said, who looked like she'd been around since Mary Starbuck's time, was certainly kind enough but of little help. Nic wasn't entirely certain she'd expressed herself clearly but neither the name Stella Fera nor the art world seemed to light her up in any substantial way. Nic's heart crinkled a little noticing Beatrice's coral lipstick bleeding into the creases around her mouth, and the way the pearl chain of her eyeglasses tremored a bit while she listened. Nic supposed she was more used to folks looking to for tickets to the historic properties, their hours of operation, and maps of the sites. And volunteering her time at that. Beatrice did, however, suggest a visit to the library, that the Atheneum was not to be missed — even if you weren't searching for a thing.

Back outside Nic attended to the missed texts she felt coming in. Of course Cade wanted to know where she'd gone. And while she appreciated the concern, she didn't want company yet.

There on the corner of India and Federal Streets was the Nantucket Atheneum, the island's library. With its corner pilasters and Ionic columns, its classic Greek Revival style architecture occupied a prominent place in the heart of downtown. It dominated the space with its regal and powerful aura. Before stepping inside its doors, Nic wanted to appreciate its grandeur, knowing that it had stood there for 176 years, and to pull up more of its history on her phone — which was too easy and always felt like cheating.

Nic learned that the Atheneum was founded in 1834, and that it was originally a private members-only institution, not becoming a free public library until 1900. Maria Mitchell became its first librarian at the age of eighteen and held the position for twenty years. (Before discovering a comet and eventually leaving to become the first professor of Astronomy at Vassar College!) The library had free access to over a million books and downloadables. Nic couldn't believe that since reopening after the Great Fire of 1846, the library has had only *six* main librarians in total. Could there be a truer reflection of the timeless essence of the island? She couldn't wait to step inside.

Its antique winding staircase grabbed her attention right away — and her favorite thing — the smell of books and time. Enormous paned windows let in the buttery light and there were unexpected hallways hiding here and there. Figureheads and statues from old whaling ships and old portraits and paintings hung from the walls and filled corners.

Like many of Nantucket's buildings she'd visited so far it felt more like a museum than a library.

She saw that even from its earliest history, the Atheneum had sponsored educational and cultural programs that included such speakers as Frederick Douglas, Ralph Waldo Emerson, Hendry David Thoreau, and women's rights advocates Lucretia Mott and Lucy Stone. Powerful stuff. Her queries seemed suddenly dwarfed, her fragile sense of self a weakness. But there she was and it couldn't hurt to take a peek at whatever information she could find about a random mid-twentieth-century island artist.

∞

While Nic spent almost two hours in the Atheneum pouring over the island's art and history, losing herself and track of time, she was no closer to learning anything more about Stella Fera. Her brain was bursting with facts and folklore that she had no place for.

Learning more about Mary Coffin Starbuck was like reading about an old friend. Nic wasn't much further along in her book so she was intrigued by this grander scale of the life of one of Nantucket's foremost daughters.

She was ultimately was known as "the great woman" or the "great Mary Starbuck" and was unique among women of her time in the late 1600's. She became known for achieving success in business, as bookkeeper to her husband's trading post, and was the more eloquent speaker in her marriage. She was more highly regarded than her husband, Nathaniel, which was accepted, and she was revered for her soundness of judgement and greater clarity of understanding.

Nic felt a surge of pride learning that Nantucket was ahead of its time with women treated as equals early on and in many ways. This had evolved naturally since their fathers, husbands and sons left on whaling trips that could last years at a time, leaving women responsible for the business conducted on the island. Nic took a moment to be in awe of their tenacity, their courage. They probably didn't have the time to waste wondering if they were *enough* — they were too busy getting shit done! She felt like an ass for the luxury of self-pity and the wallowing.

The day had grown warmer and the new summer sun blinded her as she jogged down the library steps. She decided to walk over to Rose & Crown and took a seat at the bar wasting no time ordering a pint of Whale's Tale and a plate of chicken wings with honey mustard. She sent a quick text off to Cade letting him know that she'd be home in an hour or so then put her phone away. It had been good keeping to herself without anyone to answer to.

"So what does your pendant stand for," the bartender asked her.

"I'm sorry?" Nic said, lost in thought, "Oh, it was my mother's first initial. Why?" The dude asking was end-of-summer blond even though it was only day one, which meant he was either a surfer or lifeguard by day and then a bartender.

"See the guy at the end of the bar," he said pointing to Nic's left, "he has a ring with the same exact "**S**" like stamped on it, you know kinda like a signet ring?"

She was as surprised he knew what a signet ring was as she was about the guy next to her having the same ring as her pendant. She wiped the honey mustard wing mess off her hands and looked to her left beyond the two empty seats. She couldn't see much from where she sat and her bartender friend was busy around the corner. Nic couldn't let the guy leave without getting a closer look.

What did it mean? Was it some generic S-stamped piece of silver that anyone could buy? But it was such a specific script, swirly and unique. What it actually reminded her of was her mother's swoopy handwriting, now that she thought about it. Not generic. She took another stealth-glance at the man trying to determine his age. Impossible. Sixties? Seventies? He was lean with a thatch of gray-blond hair and a ruddy complexion from days spent outside. He was keeping to himself, alternately eating and watching the Red Sox on the giant TV over the bar.

When the bartender returned she asked if he knew the guy's name. "Dennis St. Claire," he said, "he's a regular, maybe just for the summer though. Not sure, I blow out of here and head down to Costa Rica winters."

Of course you do, Nic thought. Then kicked herself, literally, for judging. "Okay, thanks."

"Want an introduction?" he said.

"Um, no thanks," she said, looking up at the game, trying to think of an intelligent baseball observation to start a conversation with Dennis St. Claire. It did not look like the Sox pitcher was doing well at all.

"Hey, isn't this the guy who threw a no-hitter just a couple weeks ago?" Nic asked in his direction.

He turned as if noticing her sitting there for the first time. She was more used to being checked out by any and all men. Women too if she were being honest. This felt more normal.

"It sure is," he said, turning toward Nic then back to the game, "different ballgame tonight."

"Do you think they still have a shot at the playoffs this year?" As soon as she said it, Nic knew it was a dumb question. There were 162 games in the regular season — it was way too soon to make that call.

"Not if this keeps up. I don't have much faith in their pitching rotation. The depth just isn't there." He sounded like Cade. Nic wanted to move seats to get closer but thought that might be weird. Screw it, she couldn't squander the opportunity. She stood to settle her tab, then noticing the perfectly timed hit and the crowd going nuts, she walked over to where Dennis was sitting. "See what I'm saying?" Dennis said, "Now he's gone and loaded the bases, no outs. Jesus Christ." He took a long drink from his beer which gave Nic the chance to look at the ring on his right hand.

Her belly dipped and her fingers went to her own **S** — an exact replica of this Dennis St. Claire's ring. He was ordering another beer when he caught Nic's expression. "It's only baseball kid, nothing to get worked up about. Oh, don't tell me you're one of those dames all gah-gah over the new catcher?" He pulled out the barstool next to his. She sat. As she let go of her pendant to pull herself in closer to the bar, he stared at it then back up into her eyes. "Where'd you get that?" he asked.

"I was about to ask you the same thing," she said.

It felt like he was staring into her eyes for a long time. But he said nothing, gave away nothing, and turned back to the game. It wasn't until the next round of commercials that he spoke again but without looking at her, "It belonged to a buddy of mind. A long time ago. Now you."

Nic took a beat to assemble her thoughts. Did she even know for certain that it had belonged to mother? "Well, I've been assuming it was my mother's. She's been gone almost nine years now, but I just lost my dad last month. This was in an old box."

"What was your mother's name?"

"Sofia Fiore." If Dennis St. Claire recognized the name, his face was an ice sculpture. "What was your friend's name, the one who gave you the ring? And why did he give it to you?"

Nic's attention was drawn to her phone vibrating with texts on the bar. Shit, Cade was ready to send out a search party, Lexi was texting her too. She had to go. Instead of answering her questions about his ring, Dennis told her she should answer her phone. And then he paid off his tab and stood to leave. She couldn't let that happen! Could she ask for his number, they had to finish this conversation, he knew *something*. She quickly shot Cade a text that she was heading back now. When she looked up, Dennis was gone. "Did he leave?" she asked the bartender, eyes wide with panic.

"Yup. No worries," he added, noting Nic's anxiety, "he's no stranger to this place, he'll be back."

But while I'm still *here*, Nic asked herself, fuming at letting him get away. She rushed out onto the sidewalk — how far could he have gone? Her time on-island was winding down — there was no way she could leave without closing the loops. Enzo would be smarter about the untangling, *why didn't she tell him about the letter*? Because his plate was heaped.

Losing their dad had impacted her gentle brother profoundly in moments — decisions to throw pieces of him in the trash, that were woven into their own childhood, were private agonies. The way Enzo had held their dad's old canvas shoe-shine kit, how his voice broke holding it, faded and stiff with age, *how can I just put this in the trash, Nic? This* meant *something to him — he took care to polish his shoes, brushing and shining them so he would look his best...* Little-boy tears rolling down his grown man's face as he turned the kit tenderly in his hands.

There it was again, grief, sneaking up, so concentrated she could swim in it. And nobody could get you through to the other side but yourself. But she had to tuck it in her back pocket for now. She had to keep focused on her mother. Not being able to ask either of her parents for answers made her feel blindfolded in a glass box.

Her phone pinged with another text — why couldn't Cade just back off? Her irritation with him rose chafing hard against her affection. But the text wasn't from Cade. It was Poppy.

Stella Fera was your MOTHER?

Well, that cat is out of the bag, she thought, sighing deeply. Of course she should have known that Lexi would tell Poppy. And what good is a cat in a bag anyway.

Apparently, Nic typed.

This is HUGE Nic what are you gonna do? I need to come back...

Reading Poppy's words made her release the breath she hadn't known she was holding and comfort settled on her shoulders like cashmere. Poppy was a problem solver, sharp and intuitive. She got things done with unrivaled energy — yes, Poppy was exactly what Nic needed.

Please. I need you, Nic texted back, feeling lighter than she had in weeks. As she walked back to the Swain's on Pine Street, her brain shifted into productive mode just knowing she'd have a sidekick, a partner, a second pair of eyes and ears and a fresh brain. She had Dennis St. Claire's name for God's sake — how hard could it be to find someone on such a small island? He was obviously a local, or one of the Summer People at least. They'd find him, buy him dinner or something, somewhere they could put the pieces together.

They'd prepare a list of pointed questions: What was the name of the friend who gave you the ring? Who was he to you? Or *is* — why assume he's dead? Was it a gift he had made for you or had it been his ring? Is the name Sofia Fiore familiar to you? Or Stella Fera? Do you or anyone you know own a Stella Fera painting? What does the "**S**" stand for on your ring — Saint Claire? Swain? Sofia? Stella?

Poppy was sure to have her own list of questions. Then a thought barged in stopping her in her tracks on the cobblestones of upper Main Street. What if Cade's parents had heard of this guy? Her heart picked up pace with her stride — but dragged again remembering their odd dismissive reaction to the whole Stella Fera thing. It was time to enlist Lexi — she was a badass and someone you definitely wanted going to bat for you. She probably, definitely, always got a little wood on the ball.

∞

"WHAT? Dennis St. Claire? Are you fucking kidding me?" Lexi said, glass paused on its way to her mouth, "How, where? Oh Jesus, Nic."

"Shhh, your parents are right inside!" The patio had become one of Nic's favorite spots. To breathe in the salt ocean, the wild roses and pine. To just be still. But reflection was becoming a saboteur of peace.

"Oh they can't hear shit," Lexi said, "so give me the deets, woman, how in the hell did you end up with this guy?"

"For starters, I was not *with* him. I told you, I was grabbing some wings and a beer at the bar at Rose & Crown..."

"Look at you — all hanging out at bars alone."

"*Anyway*, the bartender commented on my pendant, saying the guy at the end of the bar had a signet ring with the exact design and letter S."

"Jake knew what a signet ring was?"

"You know the bartender? Never mind — and that was my exact thought too— he was 100% surfer boy. I digress. I moved closer to this Dennis guy by faking interest in the Red Sox."

"Stealth. Continue," Lexi said, taking a big swallow of her cocktail.

"We talked about the pitching while I tried to get a closer look at the ring. I almost choked on my own spit when I saw that it was the exact, *exact* wax-seal type medallion, with the exact font. He finally asked where I got mine and I asked where he got his, yada, yada, and all I learned was that an old friend gave him the ring. Who was the friend, was he alive, what's the S for? No idea. I turned for like one minute to text your brother and, poof, gone. Un*fucking*believable is all I can say."

"Wait — did you say Dennis St. Claire? Shut UP, are you sure? I *know* that name, I wouldn't recognize the face but that name falls under the heading of things *not to be discussed*!"

"What the hell are you talking about Lexi, I'm tired and confused," Nic said, moving into the living room and dropping herself into a loveseat.

"There is actually another brother, my dad's brother, that left Nantucket when he was barely twenty five. Theo. I'm pretty sure this

Dennis guy and Theo were best buddies — I don't know how I know that..."

"Your uncle Tom mentioned Theo — wait, so St. Claire knows Theo? Or knew Theo?? I'm losing it... Was he like an outlaw or something?"

"I wish I could tell you more. But it's never talked about — whatever the hell happened back then, has been a verboten subject ever since. My dad would say Theo just had no interest in Nantucket — that he had some bad times here and other things he wanted to pursue. Apparently he travels a lot overseas for work and for pleasure. I honestly have no idea what goes on with the brothers, whether they see him, talk to him, or not."

"That's the saddest thing! And his parents, your grandparents, are long gone, right? Why wouldn't they have reconnected?"

"People get wrapped up in their own shit. I don't know. Like I said, it was never discussed, I never knew my uncle Theo — you don't miss what you never had. Which is how my father and his brothers probably started to feel. Doesn't every family have a black sheep?"

"Harsh, but I can see it," Nic said, "I mean there are plenty of my parents relatives that I've never met, I've actually never thought about it because it didn't matter to me, didn't affect me. Sounds terrible to say — and these are people who live in my own state mostly — all those old Italians. Guess I figured if my parents wanted us to know them, we would, end of story."

"Right? You can tell who matters by who makes your parents' cut for your wedding guest list."

"So, this is huge then — Dennis and the mysterious Theo were friends?" Nic sat rubbing her temples. "And the ring! If the ring was Theo's... could the S be for Swain?" Nic looked dazed at the path her brain was taking, staring into Lexi's eyes as her heart beat in her ears at puzzle pieces sliding together but repelling. "Does your dad have this ring, or the other uncles?"

"I've never seen it if he does. Where are you going with this? You lost me."

"If the S isn't for Sofia — or Stella for that matter — and Theo Swain had the exact seal on a ring, then it could be some family thing, like a crest but more a monogram? But it would seem that all the brothers would have one — like maybe it was something your grandfather had made for his sons or something, maybe?"

"That seems like a reach. And how for fuck's sake would your mother come into this whole thing?"

"I don't know...I'm thinking out loud here and my brain hurts. Why aren't Rick and Cade back yet? You said they were fishing."

"Yup, about four of them took a boat to fish for blues off Tuckernuck. They're probably three sheets to the wind at this point at Brotherhood. Cade hasn't texted?"

"He's probably punishing me for wandering around all day not telling him exactly where I was."

"Cade's not the punishing kind, physically can't hold a grudge. But you probably know that — he's just giving you your space. Which, seeing how he feels for you, is probably hard for him. So, how serious are you guys anyway? You haven't been together very long."

"What's your definition of long? Things move faster when you're all grown up, totally different perspective. You know what you want a lot sooner."

"And you want Cade?"

Nic wasn't used to this more serious side of Lexi, this big sister side. But it was nice. Nic couldn't believe she'd only met Lexi four days ago, and she was glad her first impression wasn't entirely accurate. They clicked in some weird way which surprised and pleased her. Did she want Cade — that question didn't cover the half of it.

"Your brother is pretty hard to resist, as a human being in general, never mind as a gorgeous, disarming, and completely excellent, selfless, man with eyes so blue I want to skinny-dip in them."

"So, I'll take that as a *yes*."

There was a ruckus out front, the guys and their gear, and big moods fueled by beer and a bluefish haul. It was perfect timing, Nic wasn't in the mood to have to attach words to her feelings about Cade. It seemed unfair to harness specific words to describe a thing that felt so big.

"Hellooo beautiful ladies," Rick said as they rounded the corner of the house, carrying a cooler filled with their catch.

"The fearless anglers doth return from a day at sea," Lexi said, "and you sure as shit better put that in the garage fridge or Prue will stroke out."

"Doth, huh? What's in your glass, sweet sister? Or have we gone back in time," Cade said, turning to Nic for a closer, sweeter hello. She could taste salt and sweet bourbon on his lips. She wanted to linger there and melt into him. She curled against him as he lowered himself next to her on the loveseat and felt the intensity of the day leave her body. He rubbed her back and shoulders as Rick recounted their day — the blues were running off Tuckernuck and they'd gotten lucky. Burgers and beers at Brotherhood to celebrate and there they were.

"You both better hit the shower before you go inside, Prudence will not appreciate the stench," Lexi said, as Rick nestled closer.

"Whatever are you talking about, wife?" Lexi shoved him away, half playing, half not.

"So, Cade, does the name Dennis St. Claire ring any bells for you?" Lexi said. Nic's whole body tensing at the mention of the name — why did Lexi have to break the spell of their fleeting peace?

"Sounds vaguely familiar, refresh my memory."

"I know we never talk about dad's brother Theo, like he basically doesn't exist, but that Dennis guy was supposedly Theo's best friend a million years ago. I don't know how I know that, other than to say I forget nothing and I've been a world class eavesdropper since birth. ANYWAY — I'm burying the lead! Nic met him at Rose & Crown today," Seeing Cade's eyebrows shoot up, Lexi backtracked, "Well, not as in *met up with him*, like it was *planned* — no, she was just thirsty and you know wanted wings and this guy was at the bar too, blah, blah, blah. So, Jake the bartender made a comment about her necklace, telling her the guy at the bar had the same thing on a ring. Coincidence? I think not. When she asked about it, all he said was that a buddy gave it to him a long time ago. Then he was gone. Thoughts?"

Cade sat still as a stone for a minute. Was he processing? Trying to remember? Picturing Nic at a bar with a guy? Drunkish? Or none of the above. Nic could feel her shoulders inching up again. Guessing had to be worse than knowing. No matter what the answers were.

Cade withdrew is arm from around Nic's shoulders to lean forward with elbows on his knees, head in hands. "I'm trying to make sense of these random pieces of information —how are they connected? It's beyond strange that we're now talking about a potential connection between Nic's mother and our own family…"

"Did Poppy tell you what day she's coming back, Lexi?" Nic asked.

"She tries to come down weekends," Rick said, "she's not planning on skipping out early, is she?"

"How is Poppy involved in all this anyway?" Cade asked, leaning back in his seat.

Nic sighed, lining up her thoughts. "It kind of all started with the painting we saw in the window of Quigley's. We were both drawn to it, the style, the nostalgic vibe, but personally I couldn't shake the familiarity of it. I think Poppy was more interested from an art history point of view. She hit up a connection from the Museum of Fine Arts and that's how we learned that the artist's name, Stella Fera, was actually a pseudonym for Sofia Fiore, my mother."

Nic could feel her pulse in the air. "And now this Dennis person, with his ring, being your estranged uncle's friend — how does my mother figure into it all?"

"This is a lot," Rick said, "and you're right, Poppy may be able to get some intel that we don't have access to."

Lexi yawned, "Ugh my brain hurts, I'm calling it."

"Right behind you," Rick said, then turning toward Nic, "Let me think on this — someone has to know this Dennis guy, or failing that, someone in this family has to have contact info for Theo Swain."

"I was thinking the same thing about Theo," Cade said, "and let's try to hit up Tom too, I mean he has one of those paintings, right? And he'd be easier to break than Dad. We'll take him out for drinks. Lots of drinks... *in vino veritas*."

"Perfect," Lexi said, "tomorrow's supposed to be cloudy and rainy — excellent drinking weather."

Chapter Nineteen

NIC COULD SMELL THE rain before she heard it's muffled drumming on the roof. She snuggled deeper under the covers against the cool air that blew in through the window. Fog beaded up on the screen and pressed in. She welcomed a cozy, sweatshirt day. She was getting too used to having only herself to think about, no grocery shopping or dog walking, but that dull ache under her ribs told her how much she missed her kids and Snoopy. Time was suspended here, she thought, caught as she was, between the past and present. Nantucket was perfect for that with so much of yesteryear timelessly preserved. It was easy to surrender to it — but still there was that pulling forward, to revelation and to moving beyond whatever that was.

Lying there while Cade snored softly, she felt the familiar heaviness in her breasts. No cramps though which she was grateful for. Finally, her period, not the best timing, but it seemed like forever since her last one.

So, had her mother been in some kind of romantic relationship here on Nantucket all those years ago? Was there a muse for her evocative paintings? Could Sofia possibly have known Cade's father's brother? Was he an artist? Conjuring her mother as a young woman, a girl really, of nineteen or twenty, was a stretch. Photos from that era were deceiving, with everyone looking conservative, mature beyond their years. It was hard to picture them as carousing young hormonally flimsy kids with the judgement to match. Your parents are your parents — hard to see them as anything but.

Lying on her back under the cloud of down while rain pattered on the window sill, Nic succumbed to tougher thoughts, comparing the image of her mom as a brave young woman following her dream and embarking on a new life on an island thirty miles out to sea, to the frightened vacant woman the day of her final oncologist appointment. Sofia had been sitting in their family room on the couch with her hands folded in her lap, Nic beside her, feeling younger and more vulnerable than her thirty-eight years.

Nic's Parents had called her to ask if she'd come over while the kids were in school, they wanted to talk to her. So it started out weird. Nic remembers stopping at the grocery store first — a delay tactic in retrospect — to get her mom's favorite treat, chocolate filled croissants. In a fog, Nic put things in her basket that her mom loved. Having this small mission kept her brain too busy to consider what her parents needed to tell her. She remembers studying the book aisle looking for her mother's favorites — the ones with a handsome cowboy on the cover. *Bodice Rippers,* her dad always teased.

The memory of her younger self carrying the croissants and book up her parents' walkway was visceral, her heart beating at the bottom of her throat. She'd let herself in the side door that day singing *hellooo* in a voice too high and shallow, rambling on about her little purchases. Anything to keep her parents from talking, from telling her unbearable, unspeakable things. She kept talking, talking in the way she did when she was compensating, trying to change a moment from what it was turning out to be.

It was fall, but the crimson and butter-yellow foliage under the cobalt sky belied the gray of her mother's face, her folded posture, how she stared at the television set that was off. Nic's chest heaved now as it did then, unable to put her father's words off any longer: That even after her mom's chemo had gotten rid of the cancer, it was back. And spreading with an insidious fury. Nic could no longer recall the list of organs her father named.

"What can we do?" Nic had asked dumbly, eyes pleading with her father for a solution. She would not hear her father say, "there is nothing we can do, sweetheart."

Her mother didn't speak, didn't meet Nic's eyes. She was already gone.

Sofia was dead inside of six weeks. Instead of the possible four months that had been proffered. There would be no Thanksgiving, no Christmas. Never again in that wonderful home that she — and her own children — had grown up, and in which every memory was wrapped.

Hot fat tears rolled from Nic's eyes down into her ears as she lay there, all these years later, the pain as searing as her father's words that day. She let them mingle with fresh tears for Gino — how she'd had the same foolish thought that he had to live longer because he'd bought so much laundry soap and so many rolls of paper towels. He had to live at least long enough to use them up. Why did the brain tell you such stupid, stupid things.

Chapter Twenty

Cade had succeeded in getting his uncle Tom to meet them at B-ACK Yard BBQ on Straight Wharf for a late lunch at two o'clock. Everyone had slept in for a change on the first rainy gray day in a while. Nic felt cried out but refreshed too. An outside shower in the light rain had been cleansing. All this *starting over* business, it was a honeyed torment. She had to get used to carrying her parents around in her heart now, in her dreams, hearing their advice as clearly as if they were still there to give it.

Nic was ravenous, being a human being was not for the faint of heart. A pulled pork sandwich with a side of street corn had her practically drooling with anticipation. She could go with a Whale's Tale Ale BUT the Jimi Hendrix cocktail looked bomb; Aviator Gin, lavender and lemon. Boom. The guys got Cisco Gripahs, Lexi went with her traditional Stevie Ray; Tito's, lemon, cucumber and Jalapeno. Uncle Tom was already two Bulleit Bourbons in, neat. Nic was wishing Poppy were here now — she was the right measure of youthful charm and gravitas.

Nic wondered how they'd billed this little gathering to their uncle. If he felt ganged up on, outnumbered, he didn't let on. The hope was to head down memory lane, shoot the shit of yesteryear, with hopes he'd have loose lips.

The place was alive with rainy day revelers, custom-made for the vacation sport of day drinking. It probably wasn't heading anywhere good after that, but you never knew. Nic was concentrating on listening to their dialogue, wondering how they'd manage to make it all look like reliving old times while also steering the conversation in the direction of the estranged brother, Theo, and Stella Fera. It seemed to Nic that just when they'd landed on a path to the young brothers and their summer shenanigans in their late teens and twenties, the conversation veered to a fishing story, or running away to Tuckernuck to freak out their parents, or someone's conquest out on the high seas and getting caught in a storm and their father's wrath. Tom cast himself as the Casanova of the family, with Lexi and Cade's dad coming in a close second. They couldn't help but beg for more stories — which only served to detract from talk of Theo.

Impatient and uninterested in who she pissed off, Lexi jumped in, "But come on, Uncle Tom, what about Theo — did he have a special girl? What could he possibly have done for your parents to basically have kicked him off the island? From how you've described him, he seems more conservative and not the trouble-making type. What gives?"

Tom was plenty lubricated by booze and in his happy place with a mound of ribs on his plate. Nic watched him closely, hoping his guard was down enough to keep speaking candidly.

"What is it with you guys today — this sudden curiosity about an uncle you never knew?"

Was the jig up, Nic thought? Ugh, Poppy would know what to say, how to downplay, deflect. Without thinking, Nic jumped in, "Well, you can blame me for that — I'm just curious about the impressive family Cade comes from."

"Impressive? How so?" Tom asked, going in for another rib dripping in barbeque sauce.

"Oh, I don't know — you have to admit, being a founding family of Nantucket is pretty extraordinary," Nic said, on the fence about bringing his Stella Fera painting into it. But that had a way of clamming people up. Which, she considered, was exactly why she had to broach the subject, now or never. She took the last gulp of her Jimi Hendrix for courage and bit the bullet, "That Stella Fera painting you have, I'm wondering — did your brother Theo know her by any chance?"

Drinks paused, forks stilled, and Thomas Swain looked at her with an oversized slab of cornbread on its way to his mouth. He then looked to Cade, as if to say, *can't you control your woman?*.

The silence lingered a beat too long. "Forgive me," Nic said, "I don't mean to pry, Mr. Swain, but it's just…" It was do or die, she thought, "it's just that it turns out, what I mean to say, is that I've recently discovered that Stella Fera was my mother."

The noise in the restaurant took on a deafening vibration as their booth went silent. Everyone looked to Tom, who quickly disguised the look of shock in his eyes, immediately busying himself with the task of wiping his sticky hands with the pile of napkins before rising and excusing himself to the men's room saying that hot water and soap would be the only thing that worked.

"Well, now what?" Lexi was impatient for answers. "Looks like you hit a nerve there Nic — but what do we take away from that for fuck's sake? Do we keep drilling? We're still exactly nowhere."

Before Tom rejoined them at the table, the group had weighed the possibility of asking him about Dennis St. Claire — they were in this far, what was there to lose? But what if he didn't come back?

Tom returned to the table and sat, tenting his hands as though he'd arrived at a decision.

"It was a long time ago," Tom began, "our father was rigid about what we boys spent our time doing in the summer, requiring gainful employment at the earliest age possible, with eyes ahead to the family business. Theo, however, had his own ideas, marched to his own drummer, an artist who decided he wanted to design jewelry, learn silversmithing. Our father was having none of it."

There was a long enough pause that Nic wondered if that was it, end of story; the black sheep of the family is basically told if you're not part of the solution, you're part of the problem, boom, you're out. If Tom was waiting for them to decide they were convinced that that was enough reason for Theo Swain to have basically been black-balled from the family and Nantucket, Nic wasn't having it. It wasn't resonating, there had to be more.

"What about Stella Fera?" Nic asked, "did she and you brother share some kind of artist's studio or something? Was he some sort of mentor to her?" The more she asked, the more questions came— and the more she was forced to picture this Theo and her mother living a bohemian artist's life. Glimpses pushed back in of her mother twirling with her on summer solstice, with bare feet, her hair loose. And that faraway look she would get staring into paintings at the museum. It made sense to her in a way she couldn't explain.

"Yes," was all Tom said.

"Yes what — they knew each other, yes, they were friends? Or more than friends?" Nic was aware she was pushing it, but it didn't stop her, "Did Theo know that her real name was Sofia Fiore? Why did she change it?"

Tom sighed heavily, looking exasperated and like he wouldn't last much longer under fire. "I don't know!" His deep voice grew louder. Then quieted, "I don't have all the answers to your questions. All I do know is that she was self-conscious about her Italian name and heritage and didn't want that to affect her success or her —"

"Her what?" Lexi chimed in, "her chance of possibly being accepted into the white, white WASP world of the Swains?"

Her mother and the Swains? Was this a possibility? Nic felt like someone had peeled back the top of her head and reached in with a mixer turning everything she thought she knew into whipped potatoes. Was Tom suggesting that Sofia and Theo were in a relationship? Her mother and her boyfriend's *uncle*?

When she felt like she her mouth could say the words, she spit them out before she could swallow them, "Do you mean that your brother and my mother were lovers?" she asked Tom.

Tom looked up at Nic over his drink, put the glass down and said, "It was a long time ago."

"That's *it*?" Lexi said, "that's all you got? I mean, first of all this is an insane coincidence, but also, so fucking what? I'm failing to see the big deal here, the scandal of an Italian American girl falling in love with a precious Nantucketer — I mean really? That's all it took for Grandmother to exile her own son? This cannot be the story."

The table fell silent. What was everyone thinking, Nic wondered. Were her worlds colliding? The smell of Barbeque permeated the space and was making her nauseous. She rose to excuse herself to the ladies' room, pressing both hands on the table to steady herself, was she going to actually puke? She should have just had a beer. *Would she make it to the toilet*?

Locking the stall door behind her she lowered herself to the bowl noticing that a slow dizziness had replaced the nausea. She sat with her head in her hands to stop the spinning and to lasso her thoughts. *Mom, why couldn't you tell me any of this,* she whispered to herself, *how much did Dad know*? Had they only scratched the surface? She needed fresh air, she needed to walk. She washed her hands and splashed her face with cold water before heading back to their booth. Tom had already left, he'd had no more information to give. Whether they believed him or not, that was all they were getting. Nic took Cade's hand telling him she needed to walk.

The rain had dissipated to mist before stopping altogether. The sky remained a low gray ceiling and the air was thick. They headed up South Beach Street to Easton, rounding out to Hulbert Avenue where some of the most beautiful Nantucket homes stood. Nic felt the disintegrating strangeness of a dream as they walked. Reaching for pieces of the puzzle she'd held off but that were coming together anyway. She thought how you know before you know, of course, how understanding walks right in.

She wanted to appreciate the landscape and grand homes at her own pace. As if from some great distance she looked for timeless details, memorizing the artful curve of an upstairs alcove, the cushions on a porch rocking chair, fat hydrangea blooms bobbing in the thick air poking out of white fences, and pink sprays of roses climbing a garden trellis.

Cobblestone Hill had her huffing and puffing which brought them to Lincoln Circle. "Are we near Steps Beach?" Nic asked Cade, with an animation that surprised her, lifting her voice like a child's. I've seen photos of that — I've been dying to see it in person."

"Well, this is your lucky day," Cade said, leading her to a sandy path by a big stone with *Welcome to Steps Beach* engraved in it. "A literal engraved invitation," he said, with one arm around her shoulders.

"It looks *exactly* like the photos, can we go down?" Her voice sounding childlike, eager, denial making her giddy.

"Of course," Cade said, starting down the long wooden steps. The sun was doing its best to push through the dense gray, turning the water in the distance an eerie beautiful teal color. The steps gave way to a winding sandy path through scrub and dunes and Nic could see private staircases winding parallel across the scrubby vegetation leading down to the small beach from their castle-cottages. Conch shells adorned the sand fence that wound through the dunes —the exact image from the cover of the guide book. Being on Nantucket was like living in a postcard.

It was quiet and it felt like they had the island to themselves. Nothing could have been further from the truth, she knew, with the summer crowd swelling to almost 60,000 people compared to the conservative 10,000 off-season. But people were still pursuing their indoor rainy-day things while Cade and she walked from Steps Beach all the way around to Brant Point Lighthouse. Nic couldn't pass a perfect scallop shell without picking it up, collecting one after another, nesting them in the palm of her hand. She imagined them leaning against the window on the sill in her kitchen, lit up by the sun spilling in.

It felt like they were walking through private property, walking the edges of the distinguished homes overlooking the Sound, but Cade promised the shoreline was public. Ferries and steamships came and went, their horns announcing arrivals and departures. Like the ebb and flow of the tide, its relentless draw and spill, rushing in, rolling out. Boats bobbed on their moorings, sails tucked tight, as people waved hello to incoming passengers from the rocks of the point, and goodbye.

Walking across the shifting sands, Nic thought about life on an island — everything you needed to survive had to come from somewhere else. Mostly. You couldn't grow everything you needed, there weren't enough trees to provide enough lumber — the original settlers could tell you that. In fact an island only existed by some whim of fate, given a chancy foothold at best, and who knew for how long. Living on an island was a wild thing, vulnerable and unpredictable — there had to be a lot of letting go. Letting go of the perspective you thought you had, the castle you built by the water, the name you wrote in the sand. The fog rolling in over what you thought was clear, the ground moving under your feet making you feel, well, less grounded. Forcing you to just sink in and *be*.

Why do we feel like we have to know everything, have all the answers? Nic wondered. Questions were more forgiving, open-ended. How important was it if things weren't as we'd thought? Folding and bending them to suit our comfort would only be a misplaced attempt at order.

Nic breathed in the briny air all around her, felt the sand squish between her toes — then laughed as she tried to walk in the footprints ahead of her. They didn't fit. Of course. They were too small, too close together, a difference stride altogether.

Nic thought about the pursuit of happiness everyone talked about — you didn't need to chase it at all. It was in the creamy white scallop shell holding a puddle of the sea, it was in the way the sun sprinkled diamonds on the waves, the very evanescence of it. The way every wave came in with its treasures and promises, then turned and slipped away. How every single joy had that tease in it, leaving in us a wake of longing....

∞

Cade and Nic walked in silence along the north shore, there was no need to fill the air with words, the island whispered its beauty and hinted at its own secrets as they covered the miles back into town. Nic thought how it was one thing to be shocked by a revelation, but it was another to let it change the course of your life. Maybe the new path *was* the course?

They followed South Beach Street into Town, a quick wind pushing them along. Nic peeled a strand of hair from her lips and pushed it behind her ear. "I have to believe I was meant to be here. And with you," she said. Then wondered how she was supposed to go about convincing herself that a moment was real and solid when it felt so flimsy in her hands.

"Of course you were," Cade said, giving the hand he was holding a small squeeze.

South Beach Street poured them onto the sidewalk outside Rose & Crown. Nic walked in without thinking, heading to the far end of the bar. It was as if they'd scheduled to meet Dennis St. Claire who was sitting in the same spot where she met him.

She climbed up on the barstool beside him, Cade next to her. Tamping down her racing nerves, Nic introduced them. She had no plan. She noticed Dennis studying Cade; every contour of his face, coloring, and expression.

"It's a small island," Cade began, "how have we never met before this?"

"I was about to ask myself the same thing," Dennis said, "travel in different circles I suppose. You must take after your mother's side of the family, I don't see Theo in you."

"Do you know my father? And his other brothers?" Cade asked, struggling for some frame of reference. "Or should I say *did* you know them? Forgive me, I'm confused about your sudden appearance, this new knowledge about an uncle I never knew."

"My *appearance*, as you call it, is neither sudden nor a secret. Ask our bartender here, Jake, hey my good man could we get a round when you've got a minute? What are you and the lady drinking, Master Swain?"

Nic would do whatever it took to keep the conversation going. She ordered a glass of wine and Cade a beer. Dennis and Cade had landed on the subject of boats, Dennis's business — that frosting — level before getting into it. Dennis seemed chatty. Perfect, Nic thought.

Dennis had owned his own fishing charter company for the last thirty years, *Cod Father Charters,* before that he'd worked for other outfits on Martha's Vineyard and Nantucket. *You're either a Vineyard person or a Nantucket person — you are never both*, he told them. Dennis had made his choice long ago, even though his best buddy, Theo, had left the island for good.

As she sipped her wine, forcing her mind to stay open, Nic listened to Dennis describing the three vessels he had in his fleet — they were familiar to Cade. It *was* a small island.

"Theo always was too tender a soul for this world," Dennis said. "He would no more hook a fish on a rod than he could have hunted and harpooned whales back in the day. The only captures he made were with a camera, his gentle hands made to create beauty and magic with silver. Like this ring, and that pendant around your neck."

Nic reached for it, the silver warm against her throat. "*Was*?" Nic asked, "Is Theo no longer living?" Her heart crumpled at the thought, for no other reason than it was losing someone who'd been important to her mother once upon a time.

"No, no, no," Dennis said, "Theo's alive and well. I suppose I talk about him in the past tense with regard to this island. He's been gone from here since he was barely more than a boy. Twenty-four years old he was when his parents laid down the law — telling him he would be cut off from the family financially and otherwise if he continued *carrying on with that girl who came from nothing and was a dago to boot.* Not my words! They blamed him for carrying on with art instead of the family business *where he belonged* and so forth." Dennis let his gaze fall away from Nic's, seemingly embarrassed — allowing the ugly words to come from his mouth that were not his own. "It was a different time then, prejudice was as ugly in the sixties as it is now, but you got away with it."

Nicolina's head was spinning again, trying to weigh the prejudice her parents grew up with against the backdrop of today. It was no less confusing these days — trying to understand and keep up with the myriad ways people identified themselves from a gender perspective — never mind heritage. Hate seemed to come in more packages.

The next thing she knew Dennis was closing the tab and ushering them out onto the sidewalk and over to Old North Wharf to where his personal boat was moored. Nic was glad to be on the move. And she hoped they'd stay docked instead of motoring out to open ocean —who knew how long Dennis had been drinking.

"No, no," Dennis assured her, they'd be staying put, "just change of scenery, privacy at the very least."

What else was Dennis going to unload on them? She couldn't really enjoy the fifty-cent tour of the vessel that was somewhere between a fishing boat and yacht. The head was all she was interested in finding — she was wearing white jean shorts and was *sure* her period had landed by now. It was a tight squeeze and her anxiety was on the rise. She was simultaneously relieved and confused — no blood. She was not in the headspace to do the math nor certainly to consider pregnancy at her age — stress had to be muddling things. There was way too much going on.

It had started to sprinkle again so the guys were sitting below deck. Which worked for her rather than being stared at by passersby — a floating diorama. Dennis had poured another two fingers of bourbon for himself but Cade had declined. Nic had a seltzer but her mouth was still cottony.

"You sure you don't want something stronger, darlin?" Dennis asked her. Nic looked from Dennis to Cade, then back to Dennis again.

"Do I? You're making me nervous. Please, Mr. St. Claire, just tell us what you know about my mother and Theo Swain." Nic's fingers traced the wet circle her glass had made on the teak table and her eyes darkened to a seaweed green. It was silent but for the water slapping the hull and distant laughter skipping on the wind.

"I've known Theo most of my life — from elementary school through high school. The Swains had a lot more money than the St. Claire's but you'd never know it by Theo, he was salt of the earth. Still is I imagine. My father was a fisherman, one of the town drunks — Theo's, a banker and board-member type. His folks were never too thrilled about our friendship but that didn't bother Theo. Neither one of us had many friends — maybe that's why we hit it off. He wasn't much for sports, fishing, or hunting, but he was a solid kid, curious and kind, spending his time either in the library or the art room."

Nic was hearing the words but impatient to know how any of it tied to Sofia. Her blood felt like syrup in her veins while her heart doubled down.

"I'd never seen him as happy as that summer he met your mother. They fell for each other hard and fast. As if each of them fulfilled the other somehow. He'd never been like that before. He was most often at odds with his family and what was expected of him, while she seemed adrift on her own sea of insecurity."

Nic had to remind herself that Dennis was speaking of her *mother*. The unreality of it floated in the air between them. Her mouth felt full of sand, the seltzer popped in her throat and left a stinging trail.

"They'd finagle shifts together at Beach Street Café and spend their free time at the beach, riding bikes, in a sweltering attic studio, or heading out to Coatue with me in my beater Starcraft Runabout."

It sounded awfully idyllic to Nic. Dennis looked lost in the memory.

"While Sofia painted, Theo experimented with silver and his soldering kits. He stamped the family **S** into two circles of silver, one for him and one for her — in hopes they'd one day share the same name. He would have given her everything. But I knew she would break his heart. And she did."

Nic started to interrupt, either in defense of Sofia or to blame Theo — Dennis raised a hand to stop her.

"But not the way you might think. Let me finish," Dennis took a deep swallow of bourbon.

"When Theo's mother and father told him that he was to end things with Sofia or be cut-off, he made a decision. He wanted nothing do with their money, and if these were their terms, he'd rather leave the island to be with the woman he loved. As Theo dreamed up plans to leave the island with Sofia to pursue their art and life together, Sofia came to me, crying, confiding that she couldn't let him do it, she would not sever Theo's relationship with his family. She said she always knew she didn't belong here, that these weren't her people — that this was her punishment for feelings she still carried for another. That while she loved Theo and all he had inspired in her, it now caused her only shame."

The night sounds of the wharf fell away as Dennis continued. "I was the only one they had to confide in — keeper of their secrets, caught in the middle. The note she left Theo went something like this: *Dearest*

Theo, I have to go. I could not live with knowing you'd surrendered your family for me. But I'll treasure every moment you've been in my life and what you've helped me see in myself. I'm leaving Nantucket with a greater gift than you will ever know, and leaving my art behind as sacrifice. I'm keeping the one I titled Once Upon a Dream. *Remember me with love in your heart, Sofia..*

Had Nic not considered this very possibility? That her mother had been in love with a man who was not her father? She'd managed to keep it tidily away, behind a closed door with her back up against it. Now that door had been shoved open and slammed down, off its hinges, in a cloud of dust.

"I kept my word. And more. That Sofia never knew I knew. That when I caught sight of her slight frame boarding the ferry that windy morning tying up my boat, I took in her delicate silhouette and the soft ripening of it. But I would never know for certain. Until meeting you, Nicolina. You are the image of Theo, with skin more golden than olive, fair hair, and eyes of sage green."

Nic's vision narrowed to a tiny pin of light and the deck seemed to go sideways under her. She fainted dead away, sliding from her cushioned bench seat beside Cade, to the deck of Dennis's boat.

Chapter Twenty-One

THE REVELATION THAT THIS new reality would make Nicolina Cade's *first cousin* did not have time to land as Cade cradled her in his lap.

Nic opened her eyes, darting from Cade to her surroundings, confused about where she is. "What...where...Cade, where are we, where are the kids?" she asked, pinching the place in between her eyebrows.

"She may have hit her head on the table on her way down," Dennis offered, from his knees next to Nic. "I'm sorry, I didn't think through what I was going to say — this is a bombshell, poor kid."

"Ya think?" Cade said, with no small amount of sarcasm, his fear thinly disguised as anger. "What *was* all that, St. Claire — are you *serious*? Where do you get off? How are we supposed to take your word for such outrageous claims? Especially if you're so conveniently the only one who knows all this? Jesus, I can't do this right now, she could have a concussion."

They helped Nic to the bench seat and got her to sip water while finding an uber to Cottage Hospital. "I'm fine, I don't need to go to the hospital, come on. I'm just dehydrated, and getting my period seriously, please. I'm so tired..." she kept protesting, but from some weak and dazed place. Cade wasn't taking chances. Nor did he think Nic had any recollection of what Dennis had just told them. He got her to her feet, she was unsteady climbing off the boat, but they managed getting off the pier and to the top of Harbor Square to wait for their ride.

Nic rested her head on Cade's shoulder on the short ride to the hospital. She kept closing her eyes but Cade made her stay awake — that being the only thing he remembered about concussions. Luckily an ER nurse recognized Cade as Prue's son and they were seen sooner rather than later. "Connections, huh, handsome?" Nic said, sounding more like a cartoon character of herself, "Nurse Nancy *is* very pretty..."

"Nope, not one of my connections. Sometimes it pays to have a mother who has her nose in everything, you know?"

"I *don't* know, but how nice for you," Nic said, "*and* dear Prudence. *Waaait* a minute — isn't that a Beatles song?" in a voice that said I've had three margaritas. .

Cade stepped to the side of the ER bed where a nurse was taking Nic's vitals and asking her what happened; did she know where she was, how she got there, what day it was, and who the current president was. Her stats looked fine and when she was asked why she thought she fainted, Nic simply told her it had been a long day, she'd been *drinking* — but not enough water — and that she thought she had her period but it was *way* late and... "Okay then," the nurse interrupted, is it possible you could be pregnant? Why don't we get some bloodwork done, and go from there, so we know for certain, how does that sound?"

Cade turned green at that last bit and the nurse asked how he was doing and if he needed a chair.

"Who me? I'm about two heartbeats away from an aneurism — but let's focus on Nic." Cade said, sitting woodenly while Nic's blood was drawn. When the nurse left and they were alone he pulled his chair closer to try and determine what she was thinking, what she remembered of the bomb Dennis dropped in her lap. He watched her face. Then it was as though seeing him sitting there jarred her memory. He watched realization morph her features, the pageant of emotions marching across her face.

Nic reached to grab his arm, "Cade — it can't be true! *Can it?* What Dennis *said* — did he say — did he really *say* that my mother got pregnant while she was here? And that my father *isn't* my real father? That *Theo Swain* is my *father*?! Is that what he said Cade?!" Gulping in mouthfuls of air while hot tears spilled, she went on. "Gino Tucci is my father!" *Was*! He's gone! My dad is *gone*...my mom is *gone* and I have no one to talk to about this, Cade, how can this be happening! This *can't* be happening..."

"Shh, I know, It's a lot," Cade said, gently sweeping the hair out of her eyes, "and honestly, Nic, we have no idea if any of this is true... Gino will always be your dad, no matter what, shh, it's okay, it's okay..."

Cade held her as her body shook with silent sobs, "What if I'm *pregnant*, Cade? I CAN'T BE PREGNANT! If we're first cousins? *Oh my God*, I can't...I can't believe this, any of this...it can't, it just can't be, I know I'll wake up any minute now..."

∞

When the nurse returned, pulling back the privacy curtain, a doctor came with her. Was there something even more wrong with her, she wondered, some awful cancer or other shitty thing?

"Mrs. Wright, my name is Dr. Jenson, how are we feeling?"

"Well, I don't know about *we* Dr., but I am not good, no, not good at all."

"And why is that?" he said looking down at his computer reviewing her file, "Your bloodwork is perfectly healthy, vitals are good. You're a strong forty-seven year old woman who's estrogen and progesterone levels are in flux which is to be expected. Your follicle-stimulating hormone is on the lower side which is normal for a woman entering perimenopause. Not unnatural, especially if your mother had a similar experience, there are far worse things."

"Wait — so I'm starting menopause early? I'm not *pregnant?*"

"I'm sorry, no, not pregnant."

"Don't be sorry — *Jesus*, you could have led with that, Doctor! Forgive me, I'm a mess right now, so confused, I just...this is all just a lot..." Nic put her head in her hands and cried. She blew her nose loudly and cried some more. She cried for the relief of not being pregnant, but also for menopause taking that away from her forever. She cried for the loss of her father, for the possibility that he never was her father, and she cried for the impossible possibility of being Cade's first cousin.

She asked to be alone. And when Cade, Doctor Jenson, and the nurse left her bedside drawing the curtain closed behind them, a pitted despair gripped her body. Like old stone that had met with a wrecking ball — she felt the ache of each piece as it clattered to the ground.

∞

Cade tucked her into bed back at the house on Pine Street once they returned from Cottage Hospital. The doctor had prescribed Valium to help her calm down enough to sleep, it was understood that, moving forward, no amount or type of drug would be the answer to her healing. She hadn't wanted the Valium, all she wanted were her children — to hug them and hold them and to know they were real. She'd let the doctor and Cade convince her she needed a solid night's sleep, at the very least, to be able to approach things with more clarity in the morning. But her brain was a magic-8ball, its bubbled blue responses teetering between "Better not tell you now" and "Outlook not so good."

While she slept, Cade sat at the kitchen island with Lexi and Rick. It was late and they were relieved that Prue and John had retired early. There would be no keeping these daunting revelations from them — some of which they had to already have known — but tonight was not the time.

"This is worse than an ABC After School Special for fuck's sake," Lexi said, swirling the ice in her tumbler, "How do we know if this is all true? I mean what reason would St. Claire have for making it up, but..."

"So, before all this I'd been thinking about getting Nic's kids over here for the weekend, you know, to surprise her. She's been really missing them — even more so now. Is that doable? Or even a good idea at this point?" Cade asked, turning from Lexi to Rick

"That actually sounds like a really great idea," Rick said.

"Umm, what if this shit just explodes and really goes south," Lexi said, "have you guys thought of *that*? Talk about a shitstorm — Sweet Satan's diaper!"

Cade sat combing his hands through his hair, "Problem is I don't have the kids' numbers or anything..."

"You don't have any of their social media contacts, *nothing*? What kind of twenty-first century boyfriend are you?" Lexi said, "what about the ex — aren't they staying with him?"

"Yes — but all I have is his name, but we should be able to track him down, right? Brad Wright, in Rowley.

"You mean Brad Wrong? Ha, I crack myself up. What does he do, company name, *anything*?" Lexi said.

"Umm I know he's in sales..."

"Well that narrows it down," Lexi said, "You know — sometimes I swear you have the IQ of Tickle Me Elmo."

"Not helpful, Lex," Rick said, "Okay, you do some intel on that, Cade, you should land on something with an internet search even if you only have Brad's name and where he lives, and hey, we could either get them over on a ferry OR I could fly them over — they'd love that, right?"

"Slow down cowboy," Lexi said, "Before you take a victory lap, think about it — they don't even *know* you."

Rick drummed his fingers on the marble island, "You're probably right, what dad in his right mind would just drop his kids at an airfield to get on a plane with a stranger…"

"Not that I'm agreeing to Brad Wright having a *right mind*," Cade said, "God, I'm losing my own mind. But yeah might be too much. Evelyn is a superstar, she'd be able to get them to the ferry in Hyannis no problem — but how do we bill this to her, to them? She's gonna want to know what's going on."

"Just tell her you want to surprise their mom — that she misses them, yada, yada. And to bring the dog."

Cade dropped his head in his hands, elbows on the island, defeat chasing him hard.

"Awe shit, bro, this sucks. I am so sorry," Lexi said seeing her brother slumped and sad. "Can she really be our first freaken cousin? I mean this is nuts! Wait a minute — why haven't we googled this shit…hold the phone, people." Lexi grabbed her phone, swiped, clicked, swipe, swipe, click, click. "Okay; *Can genetic testing determine if my cousin is actually my cousin?* Holy crap, listen to this: 'A curious adult asks: *I am wondering what kind of a test I could use to determine whether or not someone who I always thought was my cousin is actually my cousin. I am male and she was (supposedly) my father's brother's daughter; however I have overheard aunts and uncles hinting that she may not actually be my uncle's daughter. How could I determine the truth?'* Oh my actual GOD — did you hear that? It's our exact sitch."

Cade sat up straighter, "So what does it say?"

"Let's see, okay, a Dr, Barry Star says, hang on let me skim here… standard DNA tests, yada, yada, '*but if the two of you are related through brothers, you can't use a mitochondrial DNA (mtDNA) test. You'll need a test that will compare each of your DNAs at lots of different places scattered throughout all of your chromosomes.'*

"Whoa, whoa, whoa, back the chromosome train up Lex, I have no idea what you just read. What the hell is an mtDNA test?"

"Okay looks like mtDNA test traces a person's matrilineal or *mother-line* ancestry using the DNA in his or her mitochondria. Ugh, which is why that won't work in this case."

"Of course not, why would anything be simple at this point," Cade said. "Wait — what about that Ancestry.Com or 23andMe stuff?" Cade said.

"Already on it," Lexi said, clicking and scrolling. "Okay it says that either test will be able to tell with pretty high confidence if the two of you are related at or around the level of first cousins." Lexi continued to scroll, click and read, "But then it says here that '*Traditional paternity and relationship tests compare 15 or 20 different areas of DNA to try and figure out who is related to whom. This works fine for paternity when mother, father and child are tested and is even OK most of the time for father and child. But these tests that look at so little DNA are not nearly so good at determining relationships when you aren't looking at direct descendants like father and child. They can have trouble seeing if two people are brother and sister, let alone first cousins!*' Ugh, are we anywhere with this? Isn't science more black and white than this?"

"Listen," Rick said, "let's call it a night. I think we're pretty well fried right now and nothing's making sense."

Cade pressed his hands into the cold marble as he rose to stand. His hair stood on end from where he'd stabbed his hands through it over and over that night. He looked up at his sister and Rick, "Where do I go? Do I crawl in the bed next to her? I mean is that wrong?" His eyes were red and shining with unshed tears.

"Come here," Lexi said, wrapping him in a hug, "Of course you do. Stop this. Go to bed."

Rick and Lexi exchanged looks hearing the burden of Cade's footsteps echoing on the old wood stairs up to his room.

∞

In the dream, she couldn't get there. The boat was heaving violently in a storm, she had no footing, and every attempt to move was denied by the weight of fear and paralysis. Her blood was thick and slow and she felt her body strain with a scream that tore her throat but no sound came. They couldn't hear her. Her parents. But not her parents — they were supposed to be Gino and Sofia but they looked different. She had to save them, get lifejackets on them. It was summer, the water was warm enough — they could survive a shipwreck if help came soon enough. They had to *live*, their story wasn't finished yet. But then she couldn't see them, couldn't find them — "NO, no, no Nooooo!" There was a hand on her shoulder, shaking her, turning her, she wouldn't look, she shut her eyes tight.

"*Nic*, Nic, shh, it's okay, wake up, you're dreaming, I'm right here," Cade said in the dark, his voice frayed.

When she finally opened her eyes, she only stared up into the middle distance. It was the darkest part of the night and wind whistled through the screen knocking the accordion blinds against the sill. She gasped and thought for a beat that she was still on the sinking boat. The more she reached for pieces of the dream, the faster they broke apart and fell into the blackness. She reached for Cade, who stayed close to her, but silently, waiting for her to take the lead. "Are you okay, Nic, do you need some water?" he asked, but her eyes had already closed again. She rolled away from him onto her side. He pulled the covers up over her shoulder and laid back on his pillow, not touching her, space yawning between them.

"I love you," he heard her whisper — from sleep, from a valium haze, or from some dream space.

Sleep would not come to rescue Cade. He rose from the bed they shared before the dawn. Grabbing a t-shirt and shorts, he crept from the room and down the stairs. The patio off the kitchen faced east and the sky was already starting to pinken with newness. He wasn't out there with his coffee for ten minutes before he was joined by both of his parents.

"Darling, what, for goodness sake, has gotten you up at this hour, couldn't sleep?" Prue said.

"Nope."

"Cade, darling, you are far too sophisticated to be using such lackadaisical slang, it's unseemly. Now what's the matter, dear, you can tell your mother."

Birds began to trill their news of the day, the quiet slowly vanishing. "Did it ever occur to you Prudence," John began, "that he just might have come out here at this hour for a little peace and quiet? It's a bit early for even you to start —"

"Stop. Both of you, please." Cade said, in an uncharacteristic tone of impatience and turmoil. "What do either or both of you know about Dad's brother Theo? And Stella Fera? Please spare me the expression of shock, and for once in your life, be honest with me. Do you think you can *do that*?"

"Well, I *never*," Prue began, pinching the top of her summer robe closed at the throat, with eyebrows shooting up under the silver swoop of her perfect bob, "what on *earth*—"

"Prudence, stop!" John said, from his chair, "Just how much longer do you plan on carrying on with this charade? It is quite enough already — especially since it is honestly none of your business! And never has been. I can't believe I've let you talk me into this, this code of silence all these years, and for what? To what end, for God's sake?"

"Fine! Well then, John, dearest, I shall leave it to you to tell your son about your derelict brother and that hussy — oh PSHAW — what on earth does it matter now? It was a lifetime ago, Cade, darling, and has absolutely no bearing on your life or your sister's — why ever would we have burdened you with the whole ancient sordid affair? I simply don't understand."

"And how would you know that, Mother? How would you know what affects me and what doesn't? It seems all you've ever cared about is how things affect *you,* how things might make *you* look."

"Oh, good Lord, whatever are you talking about, dear? I am at quite a loss here."

"That's *rich*, Mother, really, even coming from you," Lexi said, stepping out onto the patio suddenly, in her tank top and pajama shorts. "Good Christ, it is way too early for this shit."

"Alexandra! You know how I despise that kind of language."

"Despise away, Mother. So, are you two going to enlighten us or what? Do you have *any* idea what kind of shitstorm has been brewing since the last time we saw you?"

"Obviously I cannot begin to imagine, but I will tell you I do not appreciate such insolence from my own children!"

"Oh, *we're* insolent?" Lexi said, "Really, Mother, please enlighten me as to what level of arrogance is necessary for someone to basically exile flesh and blood from a family because the person he loved wasn't the right *nationality*, didn't come from people the right shade of white, with the proper lineage and deep enough pockets to match? Oh don't look at me like that, I know it was Grandmother who laid down the law — and not even your mother, but Dad's, but you were complicit, you were *with* Dad then, weren't you — you knew all this went down!"

"Cade," John said, "where is all this coming from now? What does any of this have to do with you, or the *present* at all?"

"I'll tell you, dear old Dad—" Lexi began,

"No, *you* will keep your mouth *shut* for once in your life, Alexandra," John said.

Cade was silent, until he could remain so no longer. "Dad, we've met a man named Dennis St. Claire, your brother Theo's best friend."

"I remember who he is, son, go on."

"He told us all about Theo and the woman he loved and wanted to be with, Sofia. Sofia Fiore. And how Theo's parents, *your* parents, gave him an ultimatum! That if he continued to carry on with her, and his art, he would be cut off. Only he never wanted anything to do with the family money. But he lost her anyway. Sofia ended up leaving *him*, leaving the island, so he could preserve the life he had, his family. She was gone without a trace before he could stop her. She left this island almost fifty years ago, selflessly, leaving no way for Theo to ever be able to find her.

"Now, hold on a minute there. That was not her name. She was that painter, Stella Fera that you all have been asking about — who is this Sofia Fiore?"

"She used a less ethnic name for her artwork, something a little more French — for the very reason of *not* being discriminated against, Dad, her real name was Sofia Fiore. Theo never knew that she was carrying his child when she left the island — that she would give birth to Nicolina six months later."

Chapter Twenty-Two

WHAT COULD BE DONE to rectify the past? Not a single thing. Prue and John were struck with matching expressions of shock and disbelief, aghast at this stunning impossibility. Cade stood to go. The enormous elephant in the room unveiled, immovable.

"Where you goin, bro?" Lexi asked, following Cade through the kitchen, "Cade, stop!" she said, then louder when he didn't. She followed him out the front door. "Talk to me."

Cade kept walking, down the shell driveway and down the street. "What is there left to say Lexi? This is like some hideous nightmare I can't wake up from — how can I lose her, Lex? She's the most authentic and incredible woman I've ever known, how in the hell am I supposed to just stop loving her? Just let her walk out of my life? I need to get out of here, ride some waves, I can take Rick's Defender, right?"

"Sure, if you want your ass handed to you. Yup, I know — nicest guy on the planet — but do not mess with his rig. I'll wake him up and he'll go with you. You really shouldn't be out there shredding the gnar alone in your condition." They reversed direction back to the house, at a faster clip now that Cade had a plan.

"Will you hang around? You know, for when she wakes up? I have no idea how to help her, or if she'll want anything to do with me."

"Are you fucking kidding me, Cade? What's the gigantic blind spot men have about women? Especially the women who adore them?"

"Lexi — we are freaken *first cousins* — we cannot be together! What about that don't you get? There is just no way around this. Jesus *Christ*, did you forget the part about her *pregnancy* test last night? Can you even imagine that shitstorm if THAT had happened?"

"I cannot. But it didn't, so we don't have to! And let's not get all *boo-hoo it's over* until there's some fat lady singing and we get some blood tests, DNA, chromosome shit — whatever we gotta do. Alright? Hysteria doesn't look good on you. Just chill. Until further notice anyway."

"Yeah. Sure. No problem! Wake up your lazy husband, I need to get in the water."

"It's barely 6:30 a.m. dude. Rick may be a lot of things, but lazy ain't one of them."

"Whatever. I'm leaving in five, with him or without him."

∞

Once the guys had gone Lexi opened Nic's door as slowly as humanly possible, to check on her without disturbing her. She repeated this every hour until ten o'clock, when at last there was movement.

"Hey," Nic said, rolling over to face Lexi.

"Well, Isn't this a nice change of events — me wide awake and chipper and you looking like a stool sample," Lexi said.

"What time is it? Where am I? *Do I know you?*" At Lexi's stricken expression Nic said flatly, "I'm kidding. Jesus. Get me, making jokes when my life is in the toilet — the Porta-potty kind — with steaming stinking piles of crap rising up to meet me."

"Stop. And yeah I get it, things at the present do resemble a concerning amount of waste. A literal shitstorm. But we don't know for sure!"

Nic flopped herself back on the bed to stare at the ceiling. Her whole body was aching and sore — how could emotional trauma be this physically brutal. "So much for the calming effects of valium, the supposed *reduction of psychic tension*. Terrible night, awful dreams... losing my parents all over again. Only both at once. Then it wasn't even them. I don't even know."

Lexi sat on the edge of the bed. "How about I set you up in that big old tub across the hall — we can do an aromatherapy bath bomb or some detox soak bath salt shit that's supposed to be good for you? I've read they contain like these organic herbs that are supposed to increase brain activity the same way drugs like ecstasy do."

"For real?"

"Yup — you can even have an out-of-body experience, feel delirious or whatever, and the effects can last up to four hours! Believe me, I know whereof I speak."

"Oh yeah? And where-else-of do you speak — you're an ecstasy pro now? I thought vodka was your master."

"Shut up and get your ass out of bed. I'll start the water — how hot do you like it?"

"Scalding."

"On it."

∞

Rick and Cade straddled their longboards out in the dawn patrol lineup. The swell had started out slow but was building. Cade heard

Rick breathing heavy and said, "maybe we're getting too old for this, I'm beat."

"Come on — never! Looks like a decent set coming in. But how did it get so crowded out here, man," Rick said.

"All these kids. Remember how secluded it used to feel in the old days?" Cade said.

"Okay, Gramps, I'm taking this one — we can call it quits if you want." Rick paddled like a madman to catch the next wave, leaving Cade there in his contemplation.

Cade knew early morning was the best time to surf, before the lifeguards showed up to kick everyone out at every possibility of a shark fin sighting. That was getting old. Or maybe just he was. They took a few more in before conceding fatigue, lying their bodies on the hot sand for a bit before heading back.

"Have you gotten a hold of the kids yet?" Rick asked, face up toward the sun.

"I did actually — had plenty of time *not* sleeping to do some sleuthing on Brad's company to reach him. He was pretty cool about giving me Evelyn's cell number — I got the feeling he'd be psyched to have them out of his hair for the weekend. The dog too, I hope that doesn't backfire."

"Hey, why don't we coordinate with Poppy? Since she's headed back here for the weekend anyway — she'd be the perfect person to meet them at the boat in Hyannis."

Cade leaned up on his elbows to face Rick, "that's brilliant, why didn't I think of that? Let's line it up now, get them all here as early tomorrow as possible. I'll reach out to Ev and you call Poppy, okay? Evy and Pop will get along great I have a feeling."

"On it," Rick said, getting out his phone.

∞

The bath was almost too hot, Nic thought, numbing. She was in between not wanting to feel anything at all and letting the whole mess bleed through completely. *Immersion therapy*. She couldn't unlearn these potential truths about her parentage — was there *any* hope of falsity?

She sank deeper into the water, her face dropped into her soapy hands as hot tears mingled with the bath water. Her face contorted, a mask of grief, a different despair than she'd ever known. How could she give up this man...this remarkable human being who'd landed in her life like a stunning meteor, changing forever what being loved felt like? And then the enormity of what it felt like to love like that. Her shoulders shook, poking at the nerve-deep pain she'd been trying to soothe. How could life be so hatefully unfair?

The water chilled, as though she herself were ice, tainting the warmth she'd meant to disappear into. Or under. She got it, she understood how people made that permanent decision to end a temporary problem. And wasn't it *all* temporary? Every single damn thing, good or bad, it passed. It always passed. Or dulled at least. Wasn't that the promise? The great passage of time, the ultimate healer? "Well, *fuck* that, fuck everything," her voice bounced off the water and fell down the walls.

She needed to leave — this beautiful home on this incredible island. She didn't belong here.

But, didn't she just? "My God," she said to the empty room, "who even *am I*?" All she wanted was to go home to her children, to her life the way it was. Even back to the familiar grief of losing her father — *that* she could make sense of, that was the natural order of things.

How would she reconcile *this*?

She pulled the plug on her bath, feeling none of the promised effects of the salts and suds. Absently she toweled off her body, noting the gooseflesh and pruned fingers, but feeling none of it. In the room she'd shared with Cade she threw on a t-shirt and shorts then dug her suitcase out of the closet filling it with her things without folding or order. She wanted only to keep moving, no stopping to think, just go, go, before Cade and Rick returned. What could be said or done at this point, she needed to put the ocean between them at least. For now. *Forever?*

What were the chances of getting out of there without being seen, she wondered, thinking only enough to order an uber and of leaving no trace. She was single-minded in this mission, right or wrong — she'd have more time than she wanted to think about it all later — to boil it down, to fold it away.

It wasn't until she was on a bench in the ticket office of the Steamship Authority on Steamboat Wharf that she felt herself breathe. She couldn't get a seat on the high-speed ferry until 5:30. Then she would board that boat and leave it all behind her.

Mom? Is this what if felt like for you all those years ago?

∞

With Nic set up in her bath Lexi got in a run for herself. No time for a Peloton class at the club, plus she'd promised Cade she'd keep an eye on Nic. She grabbed a shower outside before heading upstairs to see how Nic was doing. As she was filling a tall glass with ice and water, she saw that the guys were back, rinsing their wetsuits at the hose.

"You survived — I suppose that's a good thing," she called out through the open door.

"Oh, we did more than survive, we were killin it out there," Rick said.

"Doubtful but, hey, I just put some coffee on, I'm heading up to check on Nic. It's kinda quiet up there, let's hope her head's still above water."

"Don't even say things like that, Lexi," Cade said, "and we've got the perfect plan in motion." They filled Lexi in on Poppy, Ev, and Ben coming tomorrow on the first fast ferry.

"Impressive. You guys work fast, excellent. And this is a surprise, correct?" She said, before leaving the kitchen and taking the stairs two at a time. The bathroom was empty, tub drained, everything in order. "Good sign," she said to herself, turning to knock on the bedroom door. It was ajar so she slowly pushed it open, noting the space looked more bare than it should for two people. There wasn't a single thing of Nic's anywhere — she threw open the closet door to find her suspicions confirmed. Only Cade's things. "Shit, shit, *shit*," she said to the empty room.

Thundering down the narrow stairway, hands reaching out to the walls to brace herself from taking a header, Lexi stumbled into the kitchen where the guys were looking at her like she'd left her head upstairs. "Gone."

Cade set his coffee mug down, "what do you mean she's *gone*?"

"*Sorry* — she didn't drown herself in the tub if that's what you were thinking, she's just not here. Not gone for a walk — all her stuff is gone from your room, *that* gone."

Rick reached for his keys, "Steamboat Wharf or Straight Wharf? You guys came in on the HyLine but she might try for an earlier ferry out of the Steamship dock, right? So she'd try to change her ticket to get on an earlier boat, am I right?"

"I don't know! Probably — she can't just leave! We should split up, Lexi, you jump out and check the Hy-Line, Rick and I will head to the Steamship. *Shit*. I cannot believe this is happening."

"Right, good plan," Lexi said as the Defender crawled through the summer throng of traffic, with her hand on the door handle ready to jump out. "Jesus I could walk there faster — I'm hopping out here," she said as she did just that at the top of Main Street. "Text me if you find her!" were her parting words as she jogged through the ambling tourists.

Rick took the left onto Center Street then right onto Broad. "Steamship must have just docked with this flood of cars and trucks off-loading — she might try to get on that car ferry if she couldn't get on the Iyanough, do you think?"

"I don't know what to think, Rick, this is all insane — she can't just be *leaving*, can she? Making this big exit out of what we've started to build? Is that what's happening?"

"Could you blame her, Cade? This is not at all what she bargained for when you invited her to Nantucket. Who would believe all this?"

Cade swiped to read a text coming in from his sister, "No sign of her at Hy-Line."

Rick circled the Steamship lot, stopping in front of the ticket office. "If she's not sitting in there waiting for the next boat, do not freak out. We'll try the airport.

∞

Nic couldn't sit still. The steamship ticket office was a swarm of activity — people trying to exchange tickets, trying to switch from slow boat to fast ferry, and then those deciding to get off the island early with some approaching storm. She could only people-watch for so long, her skin was crawling. What choice did she have but to sit and wait? She couldn't walk around hauling her bags. But if she sat there much longer, she'd be found for sure — this would be among the first places Cade would look for her. She could absolutely not handle that. She was raw, incapable of clear thought, in no headspace to make decisions. She needed air, she needed to move her body.

With some quick research on her phone, she found a luggage storage place on Candle Street — totally doable at ten dollars per bad and just a five minute walk from where she was. *Was it worth it*? Ugh, she'd be spotted for certain, walking through town. She asked the woman sitting next to her if she'd mind keeping an eye on her bags while she went to the ladies' room. She couldn't sit still for one more minute.

Cade held his breath and pushed open the Steamship ticket office door. His eyes scanned the people at the counter, the people in line, and then those sitting in the small space. No Nic. Had he really thought it would be that easy? He pushed the door open to leave and walked over to the covered area with families waiting to board the car ferry. No luck. From behind the wheel of his truck, Rick watched Cade strike out and already had it in gear before Cade shut his door. Without a word they angled out of Steamboat Wharf in the direction of the airport.

"Thank you," Nic said to the woman watching her bags, "let me know if I can return the favor." Reclaiming her seat by the window, she gasped to see Rick's Defender pulling away from its spot in front of the ticket building with Cade in the passenger seat.

Her heart writhed, spirals of agony in her chest. Profound sorrow clashed with her longing, the futility of it. Her legs made no move to run after the truck, paralysis rooted her. She lowered herself to sit, her body as wooden as the bench. What was her plan once they docked in Hyannis? She couldn't exactly uber all the way home. She hadn't reached out to her kids yet — having no clue what to say. She should try Poppy. *She couldn't impose like that*! What was she thinking? What was she *doing*? She just wanted to close her eyes, not think of anything, especially her future. Getting through the day would be enough.

Leaning on her duffel, head in hand, she succumbed to exhaustion.

∞

Cade jumped out of Rick's truck as soon as they pulled up to the airport. An unimposing cedar-shingled building smaller than some homes. It would take him less than five minutes to sweep through the entire airport and its restaurant, Crosswinds. She was nowhere.

Back in the passenger seat of Rick's truck Cade's face told the story. Rick asked anyway. "Did you speak to anyone? I know passenger manifests are not public information but maybe I could make a call?"

"Thanks man, but I just don't see her getting on a little plane — she's not the biggest fan of flying to begin with — I'm pretty sure this is a dead end." Cade scraped his hands through his hair which stood on end, stiff with salt from surfing. "I hate feeling so powerless. God, this sucks." His phone pinged from the console and he grabbed it so fast he fumbled it and it slipped into the Bermuda-Triangle-zone between the console and seat. "Godammit!"

"Hey, take it easy. We'll find her, we'll straighten this out."

"It's from Poppy," Cade said, retrieving his phone, "they may not be getting in as early as planned. Rain and fifty mile-per-hour winds predicted — boats may stop running. She'll keep us posted."

"A blessing maybe?" Rick said, "Gives us more time to find Nic — Jeebus, that would be awful if she was still missing when the kids arrived. Or back home already — where *is* she? Do you think she could be getting a drink or a bite somewhere?"

"No. But what do I know? She couldn't have gotten off already, right?" Cade asked, panic firing his eyes to a midnight blue. "I mean we've been to both docks, the airport — she *has* to still be on-island, what are we missing? Would she stash her bags and walk somewhere? Fall asleep on the beach?"

"Stupid question but — have you tried her phone?" Rick said.

"Straight to voicemail. Ghosting me or her phone's dead, who knows. Anything from Lex?"

Rick looked down at his phone again. "Nope. Oh, wait — what's this?" He said looking back at his phone."

"Hey, I'm getting something too — well this is weird, it's from my dad," Cade said, swiping open the text.

"Mine too — what's going on?" Rick said. "And looks like Lexi's in the thread too. *I need to speak with the three of you and Nicolina as soon as possible. I saw my attorney this afternoon and have learned things I have heretofore not been privy to, pertaining to my father and things that transpired before any of you were born. I'd like to share with you what I've learned.*

"Wow," Cade said, "sounds heavy. And my father never texts, much less create a text group. Now where the hell is Lexi — he won't tell us a thing unless we're all there. Except Nic. Can't do much about that, dammit, this is some next-level twilight zone."

As they headed into town from the airport Rick got another incoming text. He handed over his phone for Cade to read while he drove.

"It's Lexi — she wants us to pick her up at the steamship ticket office. Looks like she's exhausted her search too, *great.*"

Lexi had given up waiting for Rick and Cade and had started to walk. The sun was still hot and she was sweating. Cade saw her approaching just as they were about to take the right off Easy Street. She hurried to jump in the back and they swung around to get back on Broad Street. "Cryptic text from Dad, eh?" she said.

"Yup."

"Nic's outta here," Lexi said.

"Tell us something we don't know."

"No, I don't mean missing, I mean she is in the middle of the Atlantic about now. I saw her on the Iyanough as it was pulling away, I'm sure it was the back of her blond head with a messy bun and wearing that hoodie you bought her."

"You just described half the Nantucket population," Cade said, looking at his watch wondering how it was already after three o'clock.

"I yelled her name. I was running to the edge of the dock, as far as I could beside the boat, and she turned and I saw her face, those pistachio-green eyes, hard to miss and so damn full of sadness."

"Shit!" Cade said, "Dammit all to hell — why did I think that somehow, some way she was still *here* somewhere? So that's it — it's over? And how pissed do you think she'll be that I've pretty much abducted her kids and her dog now too?"

Lexi didn't say a thing.

They pulled into the driveway of their parents' house. "Let's get this all over with — whatever Dad has to say, it can't be worse than what we already know," Cade said.

"Ha! Jokes," Lexi said.

Chapter Twenty-Three

JOHN AND PRUDENCE WERE seated in the living room beside each other on the same couch. "Well, now this is already weird," Lexi said.

"Never mind your impertinence, Alexandra," her father said, "sit down and keep your mouth closed. If you can manage that. Where is Nicolina?"

Lexi rolled her eyes and fell back onto the loveseat like a disgruntled teenager across from her parents. Cade sat beside his sister and Rick took a seat in fat chair of faded rose chintz beside them. "She's gone. And I'm thinking there should be alcohol for this conversation," Lexi said.

"Alexandra!" John and Prudence said at the same time.

"What do you mean gone, she's left the island?" Prudence said.

"Yes, Mother, on a fast ferry back to *America*, although I'm sure not fast enough to hightail it out of this shitstorm."

"There *is* a storm due — I'm surprised the boats are still running, quite frankly," Prue said.

John, visibly uncomfortable and in a rush to unburden himself of whatever news he was holding onto, continued, "As I mentioned to you all, I've been to see my attorney, Arthur Barnard, today. His office has been handling this estate since my father's father. I acquired answers to questions I didn't know needed asking, if you follow. All this talk about my estranged brother, Theo, has brought certain revelations to the light, things I hadn't known were buried."

Cade moved to the edge of his seat with his elbows on his knees, hands clasped, fingers absently rubbing his knuckles.

"Cade looks like he's about to puke, Father, let's have it already," Lexi said.

"*Really*, darling, must you be so crass, good *lord*," Prudence said, "please let your father speak. This hasn't been easy for him you know."

"Hasn't been easy for *him*? Are you kidding me? This is what you get for keeping family secrets — continuing the façade, all the fake bullshit in the name of saving face, the right face that is," Lexi said, staring into the indignant faces of her parents. "Too far. I know, *sorry*. I'll stop talking."

"That's a relief," John said, "Now, as I was saying, the law offices of Arthur Barnard have represented the family for generations. And as you know, the Barnard family history on this island is as long-rooted and established as the Swain's."

"What does that even matter, Dad? Jesus, get over your *proprietorship* from days of yore. Alright, *alright*, I'm shutting up!"

"As I was saying, I approached Arthur with questions about Theo and any potential financial settlement that may have existed within my father's Last Will & Testament. And as the saying goes, you look, you find." Seeing that Lexi was about to interrupt again, John raised his wide hand to stop her and continued. "Yes it is true that my brother Theo was, *exiled*, if you will, from the Swain family, but it is far more complicated than that."

"Sounds simple enough to me," Lexi said.

"*Alexandra*, for the love of God and all that is holy, will you shut your mouth and let me finish! Evidently the name on Theo's original birth certificate was Theodore Upton. His parents perished in a shipwreck in a storm on their way here to Nantucket, thereby orphaning their seven month-old son, Theo. The Uptons were from my mother's side of the family and were coming to start their life on the island. Apparently, as the boat was going under, Theo was handed off to a young family who managed to keep him alive until they were rescued.

"WHAT? Wait, so you're saying that Theo isn't your biological brother?" Lexi said, "Jesus Christ you could have led with that! Oh my fucking GOD this means Nic and Cade are not blood-related at *all*!"

"Your mouth is atrocious Alexandra, haven't you an ounce of pride?" John said, "but yes, that is correct.

John continued, "Having no other living relatives in the country other than my grandmother and therefore my mother, my parents took him in to raise him as their own. Since he was only seven months old with no memory of his parents, my parents changed Theo's name officially to Theo Swain. My parents had quite a brood anyway, living here year-round with their friends and colleagues merely summering here. No one was ever the wiser. Now I know what you're thinking — how could they do that, never telling the boy, etcetera, etcetera, but things were different back then. Not the painful and unnecessary need for *transparency* and full disclosure of today and all of that sort of thing."

Lexi held her tongue, but everyone had to be thinking the same thing — how in the bloody hell could you keep something like that a secret? The chaos, the fallout, the lawlessness.

Cade's body unfolded as he leaned heavily back on the couch with a powerful exhale, eyes to the ceiling. "Thank God, thank God, thank God," was all he could manage.

"Now, dears, we will leave you to it, and to finding Nicolina to clear things up with her, poor thing, what an unfortunate calamity.

Believing she's in love with her very cousin. And on the very heals of her losing her father." Prue drew in a sharp, quick breath, "Well, now, oh dear, this doesn't mitigate the fact that Gino is not her father after all now is he? Oh, this won't be completely good news for her then will it..." Prudence said, in an unusual display of empathy, wringing her weathered, bejeweled hands.

There it was, that serving of celebratory news but with a side of unthinkable.

∞

Nic watched the island recede and any hope of blue skies with it. The sky ahead, it seemed, was bent on mimicking the roiling steely gray of her heart and mind. The sea responded. *Surreal* didn't begin to cover it. And despite recent events, she had this sudden overpowering sense that she was headed in the wrong direction. It scudded across the surface of her mind that if she could jump ship and swim back she would. She felt gutted. And her kids, her remaining source of solace and permanence felt beyond reach.

What did she expect? They were adults. On their way to their own lives — that wouldn't always include her. Was the planet spinning out from under her? On the portside of the stern she grabbed the railing to steady herself. The weather and her internal storm were colluding to undo her. She sat outside wanting the simplicity of the elements. And found herself thinking about the classics she'd assigned over the years in English Literature like *Wuthering Heights, Romeo and Juliet, Jane Eyre* — how teenagers craved romance, stories of once-in-a-lifetime love — but how those were all quite frankly tragedies. All ending with despair and death — portraying big love as a force that obliterates you! That didn't seem right, but it was irresistible because the romance is so enormous and true. Nic thought about her parents, the fairytale love she'd believed they'd had, and they *did* have that...they made their story, their tapestry — wove it right around the gaps and bumps, concealing the sacrifices. Like Mary Coffin Starbuck and Nathaniel. She thought of the word *epic* and its true meanings: *long or great in size or scope, a long poem; heroic, majestic, impressively great.*

It wasn't' Nic's place to cast judgement on Sofia's or Gino's decisions, even though it seemed an unbearable weight on her now. Of course Nic was the trouble Sofia alluded to in the letter, the reason she needed Gino's help. And that made Nic lucky in countless ways after all. But what had Gino had to sacrifice? And Sofia?

And losing Cade, just the idea of him, and all he brought to her life, that was a splintering collapse all its own.

Rain started to pelt down out of nowhere. Moving inside from the deck she saw the panic around her. "What's going on?" she asked the woman seated just inside the door.

"Big storm. Coming in faster than predicted — looks like we're turning back."

"What? Does that actually happen, we're halfway to the mainland? Oh my God — it's June — what kind of storm are we talking about?" Nic said.

"Apparently some rogue Nor'easter ripping up the coast — a fast one, some twelve-hour cyclonic, monsoonish thing. Bloody climate change, right?" The woman said, "but this is a first for me — the boat turning around."

Nic hustled to find an empty seat inside along with everyone else who'd come in from the decks catching the last of the sun. Things were unfolding fast, yet she felt like she was going backwards. Which, in fact, they were — heading back to Nantucket.

Her phone pinged. She swiped excitedly, certain it was Evy or Ben — but it was Cade. Her phone almost fell from her hands, heart suddenly stuck in her throat. Everything felt stuck, neither here nor there — like she was, in the middle of the ocean, with a storm chasing her back to a place she both belonged and didn't.

Can I call you? Please, we need to talk. Xo

Did he know she'd left the island?

And did anything good, *ever*, in the history of the world, follow the sentence, *we need to talk*? She couldn't talk to him here, now. Her phone was on its last bar and of course her charger was the one thing she'd forgotten, she could picture it still plugged in by the bed at the Swain's home on Pine Street. She looked back at Cade's text and her phone went black.

The wind had turned cold and she was grateful for the hoodie that Cade had bought her. With her windblown hair piled on top of her head, in cutoffs and a sweatshirt, it struck her that she probably looked more like a kid than the forty-seven year old woman she was — sparking a whole new blitz of gene pool speculation. The facts were too painful at the moment; she preferred theories.

She had so much more baggage now than she came with.

∞

Lexi, Cade, and Rick had moved into the kitchen to find something to make for an early dinner — the rote tasks that humans revolved around to maintain a semblance of normalcy and self-preservation. "So, we *cannot* let the revelation of Nic's paternity completely obliterate the fact that you two are not related and can *be* together! Right?" Lexi said, turning to her brother. "I mean what a waste to let those two things cancel each other out. You and Nic belong together, anyone can see that."

"Agreed," Rick added, "Nic will need time, of course, to assimilate all of this. But I think ultimately she'll understand that it shouldn't preclude you two being together. And since both or her parents are no longer living, it won't, I mean, it can't really affect their relationship, am I right?"

Cade speared his hands through his salty stiff hair for the umpteenth time. "I don't know what to think. She's so smart but also sensitive, with a soft heart, you know? And she's been through a hell of a lot — just losing her dad last month, never mind all of this. *Dammit*, I just wish I could talk to her. She's not returning my text asking her to call me."

The front door opened and sprang shut and in walked Tryp. "Dudes, you won't believe this — the steamship fast ferry actually turned around in the middle of the ocean and is on its way back here!"

"First of all," Rick began, "we are not your *dudes,* and secondly, what are you talking about, Tryp?"

"Check it out," Tryp said, pulling up *Nantucket Current* on his phone to show them, "some whack storm crushing the cape — we were watching live footage at work down on the pier of boats in Hyannis getting like absolutely *annihilated* in their slips — it was fricken *awesome* dudes. Oops — *sorry*, I mean uncle and parental units. SO sick."

"That has to be the boat Nic was on, *is* on, right?" Lexi said, "*Shit*, I'm grabbing Dad's keys Cade, let's you and I head to the dock."

Cade slid his feet into the flip-flops by the door and out to his father's 1985 Jeep Wagoneer. hunter green with wood paneling and one of their father's favorite possessions. "Why don't you let me drive," Cade said to his sister, "you're looking a little wired."

"Ha! Better than whatever the hell you got goin on," she said with her hand circling the air in front of Cade's face, "Just get in — we do not have time to dicker. Wait, did I just fucking say *dicker*? Who even am I right now. Jesus fuck, let's go."

"Yeah, you're definitely down a pint — it's way past booze o'clock for you," Cade said.

Lexi smacked his thigh as hard as she could while still maintaining control of the Wagoneer on the cobbles heading down Main. "Do not distract me, the last thing we need is for me to mow down a tourist. So what's your plan, Tarzan, just gonna whisk her off the boat and throw her over your shoulder? Like she doesn't now have a completely different father — one who is actually still *living*?"

"Christ, I don't know — I just want to *see* her, talk to her! I hope we get there in time before she hides again. Remember, she still thinks we're related — she still thinks she's been sleeping with her first cousin! And she has absolutely no idea her kids and dog are arriving here tomorrow — if that is still happening — it's a lot, Lex!"

"No shit, Sherlock. But Poppy. We have *Poppy*, who, by some grace of God, is like a freaken angel and who can make anything all right — or at least make it seem like it *will* be. So we just have to get through tonight. I mean we have good news for her! Yeah, the new-dad thing is a bitch, can't imagine how I'd deal with that, but it's not the end of the world. And it's not like she can confront her parents — won't have to deal with that awkward convo or the whole path to forgiveness and all that, right? This is a done deal, that she'll have to either choose to accept and move on OR fall completely apart, cry over not knowing who she *really is*, her true heritage, where she truly comes from and all that happy horseshit. Personally, I think she's way too smart for the latter."

"I don't know...I think you're simplifying, Lex," Cade said, "she's definitely going to need time to accept all this. And seriously, what do we really have? A string of assumptions that only lead us to *believe* Theo is her birth father — we have zero proof! That's what I can't get past — no definitive science here at all. Yet."

∞

Steamboat Wharf was in chaos, with the rumored storm tearing up the cape and the Iyanough having actually done an about-face in the middle of the Atlantic to deliver its passengers and crew back to safety. Families crowding the wharf to meet the boat, people frantic speculating what might have happened if the ferry had plowed through into sixty-mile-per-hour winds and thrashing ten-foot swells.

"Let me out here," Cade said, jumping out of the Wagoneer and into the fray.

Chapter Twenty-Four

ROUNDING **BRANT POINT BACK** into the harbor was a movie in rewind, with the collapsing strangeness of a dream. Nothing felt familiar to Nic and the very people she'd reach out to for comfort and a reality check were unavailable to her. She was stranded on an island.

She felt the boat connect with the dock and the buzz of conversation crescendo. As if from outside her body she watched passengers push toward the exits. What was the rush, where were they going? The still-happy sky was fading to a bruised purple under the low sun but the only storm here was the crowd, trying to secure lodging, book passage off as soon as possible, decide on their next meal. Meanwhile Nic stood still in the eye of it as the bottom of her world continued to fall away.

In the moments she was caught off-guard she found herself wishing for Cade. He'd become her person in so many ways, as fluid as a golden river at sunrise. He'd become her first thought — she'd have to undo that, she thought with an anvil coming down on her heart. *It isn't fucking fair*! She screamed in her head. Then she heard her mother's voice, "who ever said life was fair?" Nic always hated when she'd say that! Her mother... *how could she do this to her*?!

She couldn't think about all that now, she needed a plan. But first she needed to press her way into the luggage cart throng, find number seven, and retrieve her bag. Was it cart number seven? Thirty one was also ringing a bell...ugh. She tried standing on tip-toes to look over the mosh of people poking around for their suitcases and duffels. Impatience is an ugly business. There it was, her shiny red Patagonia Black Hole duffel, couldn't miss it. *Hot ember* was its official color, a gift from her brother Enzo, and a small smile tugged at her mouth with the sight of this piece of home and her safe happy life. Before.

She was finally close enough to reach in to grab the bag when another hand got to it first. It was a man's hand, strong, tanned, with a worn leather bracelet encircling his wrist. Nic recognized it as though it were her own. Cade. Without thinking she turned to face him and threw her arms around his neck. He returned her hug, bag in hand, wordlessly maneuvering them away from the crush of harried people until he had space to drop the duffel and hold her in both arms.

Time and this unexpected new reality evaporated in his arms. But that levitation couldn't last. In the same moment that she knew she didn't want to be with any other man ever again, a jagged blade tore through her knowing she could never be with her first cousin. The loss was absolute. Her arms dropped to her sides, tears streamed.

"Get in you two!" Lexi shouted from her spot in the traffic exodus, "let's get the flock outta here!"

Cade moved Nic along with his hand on her back as though she were a child incapable of understanding or moving in the right direction. He ushered them both into the back seat, shoving the bags to the way back.

"Do I *look* like a taxi driver to you?" Lexi said from the front seat, "Don't answer that." But she may as well have been talking to herself.

∞

"Nic, look at me, Nicolina."

At his unusual use of her full name she met his gaze, but said nothing.

"Listen to me. We are not cousins. Do you understand me? We are not blood related, Nic. I *tried* to call you..."

Her green eyes doubled in size. "What...how...who have you talked to, how do you know this?" she asked, grabbing Cade's t-shirt, her breaths doubling over each other.

As Lexi maneuvered the Wagoneer through the crowd, Cade explained to Nic about his father's visit to the attorney's office, how Theo was taken in as a baby by John's parents, that he was NOT his father's blood-brother. "You see? You and I share *no* blood, no DNA!"

But a double-edged sword hung between them; at once the best news she could hear, but also facing that she had this other father that wasn't the one she'd loved her whole life. Her heart decided for her and she put one up on a shelf for later. She let the moment crackle for all it was worth and she crawled into Cade's lap with arms tight around him, burying her face in that space where his neck met his shoulder, the smell of him rising up out of the collar. Her anguish melted into relief and gratitude and a soft longing that felt warm and reachable. This news was a gift beyond what she'd dared hope for — the power of it flattening out the spikes.

She felt her body lean into his with a clear knowing that she was in exactly the right place. A sense of freedom coupled with belonging pooled in her body and her brain.

"Don't cry," Cade said, tipping her face to his, her cheeks slick with tears. "Whatever you need to do, to ask, wherever you need to go — for answers, clarity, whatever — I'll be right beside you, you know that right? I'm never, ever letting you go again."

Nic wiped her face on his t-shirt, and looked straight into his eyes. The sky was a crimson and violet fire behind them. Words skittered in her head — wanting to apologize for taking off without a word, how lucky she felt that he didn't give up on her and would be there for her no matter what. And that she loved him beyond any measure she knew.

But those were just words, wholly inadequate in that moment. So she kissed him. Soft and deep and long. And for the second time that day Lexi didn't say a thing.

Chapter Twenty-Five

SUN SPILLED IN THROUGH the window over the bed and the sky could not have been a clearer blue. Nic wanted to stretch but she didn't want to let air in between her and Cade — she might be permanently curved in the shape of a spoon. Cade stirred turning in Nic's arms to face her, kissing the tip of her nose. "I don't think you moved a muscle all night."

"I don't think I did either — I might be stuck wrapped around you, buddy."

"Just try to peel yourself away," he said smiling, "and did I tell you I have a surprise for you today?"

Nic reclaimed her arm from around Cade and tried slowly to lean up on her elbow to face him. "No — how did you manage that with everything going on? I wasn't even supposed to be here?"

"You were always supposed to be here. But you surely haven't made it easy."

"Don't call me Shirley," Nic said, her face shining with mischief and the pure absence of despair.

"Ha, ha, ha, you're a funny girl, Nicolina Wright. Let's get dressed and I'll take you there." Watching the light fade from her eyes at the mention of her full name, Cade recovered quickly. "I can see where that mind of yours is headed. You're thinking about your maiden name...and Theo's name — Swain but originally Upton — and you're wondering what in the world *your* real name is, or supposed to be. Am I right?" But before she could respond, and before he could tell her that he had the perfect answer to the question of her last name, his phone pinged from the nightstand. It was Poppy, on the fast ferry with Evy, Ben, and Snoopy — arriving at ten thirty.

"Excellent," he said, with a smile crinkling his eyes, "We are on schedule — get dressed!"

"Who was that texting? Schedule? Give me a hint..."

"Nope," he said, pulling on a fresh Cisco Brewery t-shirt over his head and grabbing a pair of faded khaki shorts, "I'll meet you downstairs in the kitchen."

∞

John had only been too happy to loan Cade the Wagoneer after the inconceivable turmoil his family secrets had caused. That girl deserved whatever happiness she had coming to her, he'd told Cade, whatever he could do, he was glad to. Even if that meant housing her two kids and dog for the weekend. They would have walked but for needing a way to transport everyone and their stuff back to Pine Street. They found a decent spot in the Stop & Shop lot, parked, and started to walk toward Straight Wharf.

"Well, don't you look just like the cat that ate the canary, Cade Swain, I cannot imagine what you have up your sleeve. But I'll admit, I'm super excited! Are we close?"

"We have cut it very close, as a matter of fact," he said as the boat horn of the docking Hy-Line blasted its arrival to Nantucket. "Now, you'll just have to be patient for a few minutes, okay? And no more questions."

"Wait a minute, I know! It's Poppy — she decided to come back for the weekend!" Nic said, clapping her hands like a little girl, the sun lighting her hair to the brightest gold, and Cade's own sunny expression beaming back at him from the lenses of her Ray Bans.

"Awe, come on, you're not supposed to guess the surprise," he said, sweeping her into a hug to keep her looking at him instead of who was walking down the ramp toward them.

She turned suddenly in the direction of a dog barking — like every dog mom who instinctively knows the sound of her own. Snoopy! Pulling Evy so hard she was practically a kite flying behind him. And Poppy and Ben — she couldn't believe her flooding eyes.

Hands up to her face, Nic looked from her family to Cade, then back to her little family again, while Snoopy bounced up and down on his back legs like a spring to hug his momma. Nic held her children one at a time and for a long time while Poppy and Cade retrieved the bags.

In a spot in the shade by a bench backed by hydrangeas, Nic took in their small entourage. "My whole heart — here in one little corner of the world."

∞

Since it was still early for lunch, they decided to put their bags in the Wagoneer and take a walk out to Brant Point. Nic thought it would be a fun perspective for the kids to see how they'd come in on the Hy-Line and a long enough walk to exercise Snoopy and for the rest of them to get the kinks out from their long drive to Hyannis that morning and then another hour on the boat. Snoopy could hardly contain himself, springing up on all fours and spinning around at the simple joy of being with his mom again. Nic saw that his leash skills had declined in the last week, if that was even possible. No heeling in sight, but weaving wildly and cutting her off and anyone else in his path. He'd have her hog-tied without a care, face first on the brick sidewalk, and she couldn't love him more. "Who is *so* naughty?" Nic said untangling his leash from her ankles, but all Snoopy would hear is, "Aren't you the *best* boy!"

Myriad emotions rushed in and Nic was glad they were on the move — it seemed to alleviate the heft of so many feelings chasing each other. Their collective excitement was palpable, a living thing that launched them on their way up North Beach Street to Easton Street to Brant Point Lighthouse, gleaming with its brand new paint.

"The most *icoNic* symbol of welcome here on Nantucket," Cade said, "The first thing you look for when you arrive, and the last thing you wave to when you leave."

"I see what you did there," Nic said with a laugh and a wink.

Evy broke into a jog as soon as they hit sand, and over to the big stones surrounding the lighthouse. She climbed as close as she could, trying to wrap her arms around it. That was how Nic felt, like hugging the whole thing, — its history, charm, its lore — despite, or maybe because of all it had come to mean to her. She was conceived there after all...

How much longer could she keep it from them? She wanted this uncomplicated joy first. Even conservative Ben had a smile playing at the corners of his mouth. She *knew* it, knew they would love it too.

"Look, Mom!" Ben said, holding up an amber scallop shell to the sun, you don't see these in Maine."

"That was my first thought too, Benj, so different, right? We're used to boring old clam shells, muscle shells, and more clam shells! I know you're going to want to collect every one you pick up, but resist!"

"But each one is so different — ooh, look at this tiny perfect one..."

Nic watched her nineteen-year-old son, bending his lanky form to get a closer look — had he grown in a week? He was looking more man than boy, but with still some filling out to do yet. His dark hair had grown past his collar and it looked good on him she thought — more like her brother than her ex-husband. She was glad for that. Evy's long chestnut hair was blowing free in the soft wind and Nic saw it catch the gold of the high sun in the pieces that framed her face.

Nantucket loved dogs — which was at least in the top three reasons to adore the place. Snoopy galloped like a pony thinking he might catch a seagull, or meet a new human anyway. Poppy held her sandals by their straps with her face to the sun, luxuriating in the sand between her toes and the warm water of the Sound. Cade stood, with as big a smile splitting his face as Nic had ever seen. And her mom's words came to mind again; *you have to trust that your path, your life is unfolding exactly as it should.*

∞

They walked to or, The Whale, (Moby-Dick; or, The Whale) a restaurant up on Main Street with outside dining in a secret-garden patio out back under shady trees with strings of bistro lights overhead. Again Nic watched and listened to her children to catch their first impressions of walking upon the ancient cobblestones and taking in the historic brick buildings that lined Main Street. Cade couldn't have arranged any gift more precious.

Behind oversized menus Cade talked them through the best choices while Snoopy slept under their table in its shade.

"How do you decide which beach to go to around here," Ben asked, "isn't the island surrounded with like 55 miles of beach?"

"Something like that," Cade said, "and it all depends on what you want to do. If paddleboarding is your thing, or kayaking, you'd want somewhere on the north shore — the calmer waters of Nantucket Sound — so Dionis, or Fortieth Pole. If surfing is what you're after, you hit the south shore."

Nic watched Ben's eyes grow wide at the mention of surfing — he'd been talking about wanting to learn this summer but didn't know anyone who surfed. Cade pulled out his phone to check his surf apps. "Let's see, looks like there could be some swell coming in later this afternoon, we could head out to Cisco Beach if you're up for it?"

"Are you kidding me? Hell yes! I never knew you surfed, Cade," Ben said.

Cade laughed, "Well, I don't as much anymore — kind of a wuss about Maine and New Hampshire water temps, but here, it's awesome. How about you Evy, you in?"

Nic saw a fleeting apprehension in her daughter's eyes, but knew she was a gamer and would try anything once. "Um, yeah, I guess! We'll see though, ha!"

"Excellent," Cade said, "we've got at least a couple of long boards Rick and I just took out so I know they're in good shape — maybe another in the shed that just needs fresh wax, we'll check it out after lunch. I think Poppy's brother, Tryp is off work today so he can join us — he's the same age as you, Ben, this'll be great."

Nic sat back and listened to their little group making excited plans. They were all laughing at something and it sounded like champagne. God, being a human being was an emotional maelstrom — you ended up spending as much time picking out your favorite horse on the carousel as you did trying to get off. She was anxious to talk to Poppy alone and was glad she'd agreed to hitting the beach with them. They'd bring Snoopy and go for a walk while the kids were in the water.

Chapter Twenty-Six

A WEEK AGO NIC might have been nervous about having her whole clan descend upon Prudence and John, but perspective was everything. How silly that seemed when so many bigger things were out there to shake you up and throw you down. Was she seeing Prue in a different light? Or was the older woman simply no longer heavy with secrets. Either way, Prue seemed alight with love and generous because of it — delighted to have Ben and Evelyn in her home and pleased to show them to the empty room upstairs, with two twin beds that would be perfect for them and Snoopy.

When she returned downstairs Nic went over to Prue before she could talk herself out of it to give her a gentle hug, "thank you."

"Oh now, Nicolina, don't be silly, it's nothing at all and John and I are glad to have them. All of you. It is lovely to have a full house. Most especially this handsome young man," she said, bending to smooth Snoopy's black ears, who by some miracle was sitting calmly accepting Prue's uncharacteristic tenderness.

"I promise he won't be any trouble," Nic said, anxious to allay any fears about her uninhibited dog in Prue's beautiful house.

"Of *course* he'll get into trouble — just look at that face — but it'll be just fine," Prue said, in an endearing doggy-baby-talk voice. Nic was picturing Prue as a young mother and recalling the story of her waiting up all night for their errant dog to find his way back home. And she smiled at Prue with a heart that had no edges.

When everyone was back downstairs, John and Prue were pleased to share the news that they had finagled a dinner reservation at the Wauwinet that evening for the ten of them.

"HOW in the free world did you manage that, Mother?" Lexi asked, "It's a freaken Saturday in June on Nantucket?"

"Oh now, dear, you know I have my sway here and there. Besides, we *did* have an existing reservation for eight of us that I'd booked back when I knew we'd all be here for your cousin's wedding — I fully counted on Cade having a plus-one. And now, well, the more, the merrier."

"Who are you and what have you done with my mother?" Lexi said.

"Charming, Alexandra. Now, Benjamin and Evelyn, shall we drive or would you prefer to ride the launch over?"

Ben and Evelyn looked at each other and Nic knew they were wordlessly confirming to each other with their eyes, *hell yes, the boat please*!

Nic was feeling uncomfortable at the edges with all the sudden generosity, but also powerless to stop the train. She'd also been trying to nail down an opportunity for time alone with her children to talk to them about everything. Sooner than later.

"This all sounds so lovely, Prue, but extravagant and quite expensive I'm sure," Nic said.

"Oh, you let John and me worry about that. It is the ideal evening for dining outdoors overlooking scenic Nantucket Bay on the awning-covered deck at Topper's. You will not be disappointed."

"Oh, believe me, I was not even for a minute thinking we would be! It sounds quite special and we are so grateful to you both, it is exceedingly kind — *everything* you've done for us. I don't know how we'll repay you," Nic said, worried she was running out of time to talk with her children. But it was as though Prue had read her mind.

"Say no more. Now go spend some time with your children before we catch the Wauwinet Lady at the White Elephant's dock."

Nic honestly had no idea how it would impact them, their own sense of identity, she didn't quite have a handle on what it had done to her own sense of self. Evelyn and Nic leaned back on the queen bed in her room with Snoopy between them while Ben pulled over the chair from the corner. Nic felt worse than being about to give an oral report in high school. Her mouth was the Sahara and her pulse pounded in her ears. How was she supposed to begin such a story?

From the beginning, she decided. How she'd slowly put pieces together starting with the letter in the box from her father's house and the pendant around her neck.

∞

If Nic had bet that Ben would have been the more emotionally practical one, she'd have lost. He took it harder than his sister. Maybe because Evelyn was two years older, or more of a romantic with a softness for a compelling saga that helped her take things in stride — with more surprise and wonder than sadness.

"Gino will always be your dad, Mom," she said, "and our Papa. Nothing can change that — not biology, not secrets." Nic couldn't believe how rational Evy was being, how what she said actually made a lot of sense. Ben, on the other hand, had his elbows on his knees and his face buried in his hands. Nic patted the spot on the bed next to her. He climbed up like a little kid who just needed his mom.

"I know it's a lot to take in," Nic said rubbing his back and letting him cry silently. "Like your sister said, it doesn't change anything for you guys, right? Or for me really."

"Except that you have a biological father out there somewhere, Mom," Evy interrupted, "aren't you even curious? Or maybe a little bit excited?" Evy asked.

"Oh, God, this is too weird," Ben said, "what if he has other kids? And you have *siblings* you don't know about? Or we have other cousins? OR some hideous derelict gene or something?"

Nic felt the air around them change, felt it grow heavy and specific. "I love you guys so much. And we have been so loved by Sofia and Gino, your Noni and Papa. Please don't ever forget that. Nothing else matters.

"It was *so* incredibly nice of Cade to think of bringing us here, I mean he had to talk to *Dad* to get my number — AWKWARD," Evy said, "Total keeper. And thank GOD he's not your cousin — holy shit, Mom!" Evy said, "How did you deal with all this?"

"Gross — do not go there, I can't." Ben said

"There's still so much to think about, Mom, I mean Noni was an artist? And she spent a summer here on this cool island? I can't even picture it all..." Evy said.

"I'm still trying to wrap my head around it, believe me. We have as long as it takes, you know. But for now, we do *not* have that much time before our very special Topper's dinner with Cade's family — I can't get over their generosity — please, please be sure you thank them."

"We're not twelve, Mom, we got it," Evy said, curling a salty strand of hair around her finger. Hey, can I take a swim in that clawfoot tub? That looks amaze."

"Yes, but don't dawdle! And, you, my ripe son, can hit the outside shower. Never mind that look, you will love it, trust me."

∞

The boat ride over on the Wauwinet Lady was magical, with the sun tipping the wake in rose gold. John and Prue were up front with Captain Rob and Lexi and Rick. Lexi wasn't the biggest seafaring vessel fan, but she kept her eyes on the horizon and the straw of her tumbler in her mouth. Tryp and Ben had become fast friends with no shortage of subjects to talk about — revolving mostly around Tryp's pier job of stocking yachts with booze and provisions and of course the endless parade of hot tourist girls. Poppy and Nic were quiet, tilting their faces to the sinking sun while Cade sat back taking it all in. He was smiling at her. A bowl-you-over-smile. This close to being too smooth for its own good. But redeeming itself because it also seemed another way — nervous, grateful, accidently smooth.

With the summer wind lifting her hair as they motored to Wauwinet Nic's spirits rose to match. And while she tried to remain in the present moment, she couldn't help but imagine the island and its people of centuries ago — how a place once barely hospitable had evolved into one of the most desirable destinations in the world. She wished she could have visited here with her mother, but she knew also that it was never meant to be that way. But there was so much more she wanted to know about the parts she never knew — that young woman in love with this place, her art, and with a man who wasn't the father she did know.

And if she were being honest with herself, she wanted to know about that man. In time. The man with whom she shared half of her DNA, who might wink like she did when she laughed, or flip the pillow all night like she did to get the cool side, and have the same green eyes. A flurry of anticipation rose up, almost impatience to know Theo Swain. And she let it vibrate inside her like a tuning fork.

She breathed deeply, the sweet ocean air filling her lungs and her imagination. She would paint it someday, from the pictures she'd carry home in her heart, like her mother, but different.

Chapter Twenty-Seven

THE REST OF THE weekend slipped like sand through her fingers, but with radiance and the melody of summer drenching every hour. Nic's heart felt plumped in the company of her children, all bonded in their gratefulness. While Ben was psyched to get more surfing in with Tryp and Cade, Nic was eager to take Evy to finally see the Oldest House on Sunset Hill with Poppy as their knowledgeable tour guide.

"Here we are," Poppy said as they reached 16 Sunset Hill, looking up at the relatively small home. "Now before you comment, I know it doesn't have the ancient crumbling down appearance you may have been expecting. And that's because in 1987 it was struck by lightning, which caused some major damage. It needed extensive repairs and partial reconstruction of the roof and chimney. But let's not get ahead of ourselves. And trust me, once we're inside you'll get that seriously antique vibe."

Nic wanted to just stand there and look at it a minute and remember what she'd read about Mary Coffin Starbuck, the island's first settlers, the feud between the proprietor families, and sixteen-year-old Mary

Gardner for whom this house was built. And there she was, standing before it, its air of chaste isolation on its solitary hilltop — on an island teeming with trophy houses and Hamptonites, it took her breath away. With just a few gnarly lilacs edging the stony drive and a bare yard all around, the stark and solemn house seemed a sacred thing.

"Okay, now try and stay with me," Poppy began, "also known as the Jethro Coffin House, The Oldest House was built in 1686 and is believed to be the oldest residence on Nantucket still on its original site. It was built as a wedding gift for Jethro Coffin and Mary Gardner and it represents—"

"The unity of two of the island's oldest families," Nic said, finishing Poppy's sentence.

"Wow, someone's done their research," Poppy said.

"Nerd," Evy said.

"You're exactly right, Nic, and stop me if you've heard this one before," Poppy laughed, "So, Jethro was the grandson of one of the island's original proprietors, Tristram Coffin, and Mary was the daughter of John Gardner, one of the leaders of the so-called Half-Share Revolt, in which the island's tradesmen rallied against the wealthier full-share proprietors. And although the relationship between Gardner and Coffin was never super-close, the marriage of Mary and Jethro helped unite the families and heal old wounds. Built on Gardner land using Coffin lumber, this house is a physical manifestation of that unity."

"I love that," Evy said.

"I've always loved that story too," Poppy said, "Now, before we go in let me just long-story-short it for you. By the late nineteenth century, the house was abandoned and had fallen into disrepair. Then there was a Coffin family reunion held on the island in 1881 which sparked some renewed interest in the property. The Nantucket Historical Association acquired the house in 1923, and four years later, the Society for the Preservation of New England Antiquities started a serious renovation in an attempt to return the house to its historic awesomeness. The Oldest House was designated a National Historic Landmark in 1968. So, ladies, today, this house stands as a monument to the lives of the island's earliest English settlers and, as you will see, offers a glimpse of daily life on Nantucket in the seventeenth century."

"Whew," Nic said, "our very own art historian on-site."

"So, while it may not look like it, this was an impressive house for its time, with its two stories in height and long sloping roof in the back, which is probably an original feature," Poppy explained as they went inside. The low doorways reminded Nic how much smaller people were back then — her brother would have to bend in half to fit. Massive fireplaces were the dominant features of the rooms on each floor. The front room was called the great hall, and was the center of the family's domestic life, especially in the winter. Nic could walk straight into the fireplace it was so big. She tried to picture Mary and Jethro and their growing family and wondered how they were ever truly warm in winter.

From there they went into the parlor, the lean-to kitchen which was in the back sloped part of the house, and the borning room where small antique cradles set the scene. Up the narrow and inconceivably steep staircase, two bedrooms were on the second floor with an attic above. Nic could imagine, back then, that from that height on the hill the Coffins and their children could see for miles. A bare simplicity compared to the extravagance of the view now.

Back outside in the warm sunshine Nic took a longer look at the simple Quaker house. "That's quite a chimney," she said, looking up at the brick tour de force that was embellished with an inverted U in relief. "What's the story there, Pop?"

"Pick your story," Poppy said, "Some think it celebrates the uniting by marriage the two warring families — the Gardners and the

Coffins. Some think it's a lucky horseshoe, inverted for the dumping of evil household spirits, and call the place *Horseshoe House*."

"It sure is hard to wrap your head around the modesty of Quaker life compared with the riot of excess of today — embarrassing, isn't it?" Evelyn said.

"Perspective is everything," Nic said, "I can't even imagine what things will look like when you two girls have families..."

"Yikes — a convo for another day for sure," Poppy said, "who's hungry?"

∞

Poppy wanted to make sure Nic and Ev experienced lunch outside at Slip 14 before they started packing up for their boat home. Old South Wharf was a true memory lane, with small fish and scallop shanties — turned galleries and tiny bougie shops — as the only remaining wharf structures like those that occupied the wharves in the first half of the nineteenth century. "Imagine it back in the day when this little island was the whaling capital of the world," Poppy said, "a working wharf, smelly and anything but cute."

"When did it all change?" Evy asked, "I mean when did Nantucket become this total summer destination?"

"Well, after so much loss between the Great Fire, the Gold Rush, and the Civil War in the mid to late nineteenth century, Nantucket had to reinvent itself, you know? It became this sort of living museum of quaintness and the simple life."

"I wish it had stayed more like that," Nic said, peeking in between the shops to where massive yachts swayed in their slips. "Look at the size of some of these boats..."

"I know," Poppy said, "but don't focus on that. Picture artists and dreamers coming here in the early 1900's and forming their own art colony, converting the shacks into small studios — later becoming

Nantucket's first art galleries! Look around you, that vibe is still flourishing here today."

Their table in the covered outside dining area of Slip 14 was the perfect spot, with peeks of the stately yachts along the pier and the crunching footsteps of summer people on the blinding shell lane. Nic felt a simple happiness rise up at just sitting there in that place on a Monet-sky summer day. They ordered fun drinks to toast the afternoon and the buoyancy of summer. Poppy got the *Berry SEXY Cocktail*: Triple Eight vodka, berries, raspberry puree, with a champagne floater. Evelyn chose the *ShineBox* which was Gale Force gin, white grape juice, fresh grapes, and a splash of Sprite. And for Nic it was a *Life's a Peeaach* with Bacardi Peach Red and Nantucket Nectar's ice tea.

Nectar, Nic thought, the life-giving drink of the gods. Listening to Poppy and Evy commiserate over the rigors of the dating world for women in their twenties Nic's muddled mind pulled her back to young Gino's letters to Sofia. The agony of her dad's defeat and sense of failure, of being sweepingly not good enough for her mother. How making such huge and shortsighted decisions changed the course of his life, Sofia's life. And certainly Nicolina's own sense of being and history.

"Mom? Did we lose you? And you just turned some kinda pale..."

"No, I'm here — sorry — sometimes it all knocks the breath out of you, you know? When will it stop feeling like that? Losing my dad has been hard enough — but, oof, I can't even say the words. Because he is, *was* my dad, no matter what. I just have to reconcile all this other stuff, find a place to keep it." She stirred the ice in what was left of her drink, avoiding eye contact. It was still too close to the surface. The tenderness in the way they'd look at her would make her cry. The summer breeze lifted her hair off her neck, carrying the sultry sea on it. It was lovely. "So hard to leave!" she said, wiping a tear before it fell.

"You'll come back!" Poppy said, "Both of you — all of you! This is only the beginning."

Nic was filled with both wanting to believe that and a deep knowing that it was true.

∞

They stood at the port-side railing of the fast ferry with the other passengers leaving the island, Snoopy with his paws up on it. It was nearing the hour of the island's magic light, a gilded glow that the sinking sun cast over everything. As they rounded Brant Point Lighthouse they each jingled their pennies in hand, readying them to be tossed over at just the right moment. Lore had it that if you did that, you're guaranteed to return. Leaving nothing to chance, Nic tossed all the coins from her purse. Cade put his hand on her shoulder and tugged her close as they watched the lighthouse shrink and the island recede from view.

Chapter Twenty-Eight

WAKING UP ALONE IN her own bed back home was jarring. Too quiet and later than she thought, the birds had long since concluded their dawn chorus. Snoopy, sensing her wakefulness, made a running head start from the doorway, flying up onto her body. "OOF, you crazy dog, you have no sense of personal space do you?" Her words were wasted on him as he went to work waking her all the way up with his specialty wet-willy kisses. Impossible to scold this teddy-bear dog who only knew how to love.

Nic was temporarily paralyzed with what to do with the day and with all the days coming. The last time she'd woken up in that bed, in that house, she'd known exactly who she was. And while intellectually she understood that nothing had changed that, her unquiet mind had her questioning every nuance of her being. And that wasn't going away.

She reached for her phone psyching herself up for missed messages. The first text was from Evy saying she'd fed Snoopy and let him out before work — that she didn't want to wake her. There were rows of X's and O's from Cade saying it would be an eternity until dinner and should he should hit Bertucci's for takeout on his way home. The last text was from her brother — oh, how she needed to see Enzo. As close as they were, she'd told him nothing of what she'd learned about their mother and father. Had it been a week since they'd spoken or two lifetimes?

∞

She invited Enzo to Tuscan Sea Grill in Newburyport for lunch. How in the world was she going to start the story? She'd bring the letter. And she hadn't taken off the pendant. It was going to be a long day.

As usual, her punctual brother had beaten her to the restaurant and had secured them the best spot on the wide covered deck at the edge of the water heaving with moored boats. It wasn't Nantucket, but Newburyport had its own charm and history. Enzo stood when she entered and brought her in tight for a hug.

"It's so good to see you, Nic, you look beautiful. Different is some way I can't name, but that tan makes your eyes shine like jewels. I've never been, but there must be something special about the Nantucket sunshine."

"Oh stop. You look good too, Enz, and I can't tell you how relieved I was to hear that Layla's scans are clear."

"For now, yes. We'll take it! But as you know…"

"I do — cancer is a stealthy, duplicitous beast. But let's just stay in this bubble of positivity for as long as possible, okay?"

"Deal."

"I know! You two should do a Nantucket weekend, maybe in September while it's still so warm there — I hear it's the best month to go. You'd love all the bike paths — you could travel the entire island with just your bicycles, right up your alley." Nic smoothed out the lap of her dress as she sat across from her handsome brother, trying to attend to his words while inside her nerves felt plucked like violin strings out of tune. They skipped along topics of conversations like flat stones on the water — one story leading to another. Kids, jobs, health, and the perils of being human. The wine went down easy. *Flowers,* the only Napa chardonnay on the menu, Nic's favorite — a delicate balance of citrus, pure fruit and light oak. It was expensive but worth it for its subtle notes of sugar cookie and vanilla. Nic felt it go to her head from the first sips.

She caught herself drifting in and out of his story — intent only on how she'd lay hers out for him. That she was technically only his half-sister — she hated that description. She was whole. And had to keep reminding herself of that — no matter how much it all blew the roof off her brain.

"Your turn, sis. What's all this about that you couldn't text me — *molto misterioso,* Nicolina. You and Cade are still good, right?"

Feeling the pulse in her throat and her view blur with unshed tears, she rolled the stem of her wine glass between her thumb and forefinger, back and forth, back and forth. When she finally looked up at Enzo, he covered her hand with his own without words or diverting his gaze. And waited.

Nic withdrew her hand and reached into her bag for the letter from Pandora's box. She slid it across the table to her brother. "Wait," she said, stopping him from opening it, "this won't make much sense without the backstory from letters that came before this one. Oh God, there is actually a lot I haven't caught you up on...like how did I never know that Dad was rejected from the Navy? Did you know this?"

Enzo's eyes grew round as marbles. "What are you talking about, Nic? Dad was definitely in the Navy — remember that big trunk we unearthed? With all his stenciled gear? Those sailor hats of his that mom put on us every time we were at the beach? His best friend?!"

"Right, yes, I know that — but apparently he failed some initial entrance-aptitude exam or something — and he wrote to Mom telling her what a total loser he felt like, that she shouldn't waste her time with the likes of him — that he wasn't good enough for her! They broke up, Enzo."

Servers moved in and out seamlessly as the story unfurled. Coffee succeeded the wine, boaters motored into and out of their slips across the day, and as shadows grew longer Nic told the tale of Stella Fera and Theo Swain — the secret of a lifetime unspooled in an afternoon.

Listening open-mouthed to his sister, Enzo alternately moved his chair away from the table for room to breathe and coming in closer again, rubbing at his artful two-day scruff.

"It's a lot," Nic said, "take your time."

"How...did they...how was...an actual artist, a *painter*? Why didn't they...when... Jesus, Nic, how the hell are you dealing with all this — I can't believe you've kept it to yourself. You could have called me you know — should have called me — and I would have been on the first boat! My God, Nic, to find all that out alone..."

It was Nic's turn to reach out for her brother's hand, to comfort him if she could. That was always easier, wasn't it, helping someone else through a thing. "I wasn't alone — I had Cade and his sister, her husband Rick, who is the nicest human, and their daughter who was a Godsend — I wasn't alone. Until I chose that — and we know how that ended. The universe spun me right back around to the island. And I am so glad it did."

"You couldn't have unloaded all this during the alcoholic beverage portion of the afternoon?" He was only half-kidding.

"Order something! I think they've given up on turning over this table anytime soon."

With his head in his hands, Enzo looked down at his feet where he'd leaned the package he'd brought against the table leg. "Shit, I almost forgot — this was in a box of old frames from Dad's attic— it has your name on it."

Nic looked at the flat, smallish square wrapped in brittle brown paper Enzo had placed on the table. Seeing *Nicolina* written in her mother's script took her breath. Tears made dark dots on the paper as she stroked Sofia's handwriting. Before she could ask herself if she was ready for whatever was inside, she tore the cracked paper away.

It was a six inch by six inch stretched canvas, a sepia-toned Stella Fera original, her mother's trademark **SF** painted in the lower righthand corner. She touched her fingers to feel the relief of her mother's brushstrokes from so many years ago — the image of a young couple sitting under a striped umbrella, facing the ocean, backs to the viewer, sharing a secret that melded their bodies into one. It was called *Once Upon a Dream*. The single painting Sofia had kept. The one Nic had seen in her mother's closet that hide and seek day.

A note slipped from behind the painting, also in her mother's familiar swirled script.

My Nicolina,

If you are reading this, my dear sweet girl, your father and I are both gone, and this painting has found its way to you. I can't know where your heart has led you, or what things you have learned along the way. Just know that you are, and have always been, loved.

I painted this, once upon a time, when you were growing not only under my heart, but in it, on the fabled island of Nantucket, where destinies are both fulfilled and reversed with the tide. It's beauty and history are unparalleled — I hope you experience its magic for yourself one day, and that it teaches you the boundlessness of love — that the more love you give, the more love you will get to keep.

Bella, ti amo con tutto il mio cuore. I love you with my whole heart.

Xoxo, Tua Mamma.

"It's Mom's voice," Nic said, looking up at her brother with eyes pooling, "it's like she's here at this table with us." Nic's throat tightened around the words. They sat very still, and let their tears come, Nic trying to imagine Gino's towering immeasurable devotion to his Sofia.

"What will you do now, my dear sister? And when will you tell our wayward Mia?"

That at least made her laugh. "That depends on her being on or off the grid, right? And can't you just hear her— *Well that shouldn't come as any huge surprise, look at you with your halo hair, green eyes and gold skin — while the rest of us turn a gross olive in winter and dark hair* **everywhere**."

"Ha! You're probably right, black and white that one. Practical with her emotions, conservative with circumstance. And she'll tell you that Dad will always be your father, that nothing can change that, just like we'll always be your brother and sister. And she'll be right."

"I know. And that being family has little to do with biology, like being close has little to do with geography. So, what will I do now you ask? I think I want to talk to Theo, Enz, maybe meet him if he's amenable. He doesn't know I exist though, so there's that."

"Well, good for you, Nic, that is very brave and very grown up."

"I suppose we do have to grow up now, for real."

"Yeah, I know, it's just that being parentless — I can't tell if that makes me feel more like a scared kid or old with sorrow and the wisdom that comes with it."

"Life lessons. Around every corner lately, in every drawer. I'm so glad I have you," Nic told her brother.

"We're lucky to have each other. Now let's get outta here and walk the waterfront. I'd like to hear more about Cade — do you think you'd ever get married again?"

"Whoa, whoa, whoa," Nic said, walking beside her brother along the boardwalk, their bodies in motion, the warm summer wind playing at the edges of her skirt. "you know I've always said I don't feel the need to do that again."

"I know. But that was before Cade — he changes things, doesn't it?"

"You know what — you'll be the first to know, how's that? But for now — I'm looking forward to calmer seas, you know? The big surf has had its way with me this summer, chewed me up and spit me out, and it's not even July."

"Well — you know what they say, bigger the risk, bigger the reward."

Punching his arm playfully she said, "Oh yeah? What about *the higher they climb, the harder they fall?*"

"Oh boy. How about getting some ice-cream? That's what Dad would do. Jeeze he had two gelatos a day in Italy that summer, remember that?

"Who doesn't remember that?" Nic laughed, "He was either too hot or too tired of walking — all those gelatos broke up the day!"

Nicolina and Enzo wound their way over to Market Square into Dolce Freddo Gelato, memories of their dad scrambling for purchase. They ordered one lemon and one tiramisu in waffle cones and brought them outside to sit and look out over the square.

In Nic's mind it was the Piazza del Duomo in Florence, Italy that Tuscan summer. The city sun was relentless, the history enormous. Finding a slice of shade and a cool treat to bask in the antique beauty became part of their routine. The Duomo rose up to the sky — magnificent and one of the greatest masterpieces of the Italian

Renaissance. Nic remembered the kids wilting with relief and joy whenever Papa said it was gelato time. They'd crowded around the small wrought-iron tables and bistro chairs in one piazza or another, licking their frozen treats trying to make sense of things that were so many centuries old. Gino Tucci, finally, living his dream, in the home-country of his every ancestor with all of his *grand-a-children*. His break-out Italian accent got them every time.

    The miles they'd covered from the medieval village of San Gimignano, the Piazza del Campo in the center of Siena, to the island of Sicily, Napoli, and the Amalfi Coast — countless memories made and gelatos consumed in Italy's sun baked the air.

    Nic turned to Enzo. She could tell the same movie reels were playing in his mind, every day carrying its weight in gold. Then Nic burst out laughing, "*How* did we get Dad on that bike in Florence?" Nic said.

    "And what were we *thinking*?" Enzo said grinning, pressing a napkin into Nic's hand to wipe her tears. "He was a good sport, Nic, He never complained, the way his body betrayed him in the end, turning every step into Everest…"

    She cried from some mix of sadness and happiness, whose proportions she could never quite sort out.

    She noticed her lemon gelato dripping down the sides of the waffle cone and over her fingers. She tipped it to her brother's.

    Salut a Papa…

∞

Epilogue

It took Nic a few months before she found the nerve to use Theo's contact information and reach out. As it happened, he had been waiting for her. Dennis finally tracked him down in Florence where he taught courses in marble sculpture. He reminded him of the spectacular story of that Nantucket summer and the ending he never knew. Theo wanted nothing more than to meet Nicolina. He had a daughter! It was beyond his dreams.

Hearing Dennis say how much Nicolina resembled him was both a blessing and a curse for Theo. His ego would soar to look into the eyes of a beautiful woman born of his flesh and blood, a pride above anything he'd accomplished. But then if she had taken after his dear Sofia, it would be like getting to see her again.

Nic and Theo communicated via email until he was back in the United States, when they planned to meet for the first time. They'd become familiar and easy with each other through their digital letters — learning that they were both teachers, history enthusiasts, had a thing for Monty Python, were allergic to maraschino cherries, and agreeing that cilantro tasted like soap.

∞

They met in the Boston Public Garden in the spring, by the swan boats. Nic had meant to be there first, to watch for him walking toward her. But she'd forgotten to take the kayak rack off her car and it wouldn't fit in the public garage. Street parking was a dance and a half. She was late, so he was the one watching her walk toward him.

He stood up from his bench when he spotted her, a smile lighting his face. She quickened her pace seeing him standing there, knowing anything she'd played in her mind hadn't prepared her for this, this person who shared her features. When she reached him they looked into each other's eyes for hardly any time before Theo enfolded her in a hug, with just the right amount of pressure and for the exact right amount of time. As though he'd always been a dad and knew just how to be. Nic felt like if she stepped out of her body she would break into blossom.

They talked about their Nantucket plans for August, the big wedding. How Theo was back in the fold of his brothers and their families, and that he owed that to her. There was no owing, she'd said.

They sat in the lemony sunlight, dappled from the shade of an ancient Beech tree and listened to the green whisper of leaves in the puffs of breeze. College students sprawled on the green and moms walked by pushing strollers with sticky kids holding balloons. Single strangers bopped along to their private music thinking about tomorrow while grandparents held hands, leaning into each other, remembering yesterday.

Nic thought how spring fever did that to people, bonded them in their joy.

∞

"So, you'll be a Swain after all," Theo said.

"Will you give me away?" Nic said.

Theo's lips met in a smile that said, *yes,* while his sparkling green eyes said, *never.*

The End

Acknowledgments

As an indie author my list of thank yous looks a lot different. There aren't whole teams of agents, editors, and publishers who've helped me bring my book to life. But it takes a village nonetheless. A very small village of the family and friends who love me enough to let me do my thing and who pick up the slack. Composing, rewriting, polishing, and publishing novels while maintaining my job as a Pre-K Paraprofessional has been no small feat.

Thank you to Ema Barnes for your editorial assessment and ideas — I hope I've done them justice. Thank you to Sarah Lahay for your formatting excellence and quiet patience with my interminable edits, and for a stellar cover in collaboration with the gorgeous photography of Anthony DeNitto.

Thank you Deb McManus for being the first reader I trusted with my manuscript — I'm so lucky to have you. And to Allison Soucy for being there every single day, for the ups and the downs, and your ever-present company in a glass (or three!) of wine.

Endless thanks to you, Billy Burliss, my husband, for taking over the grocery shopping — especially when you remember the cat litter, birdseed, and chicken jerky for the dog — for making our dinners while I'm still at my computer under two or three animals, and for wrangling fresh sheets on our bed every week. Forgive me for not always listening when you're talking, I hear you and love you.

Special thanks to my brother, Michael, for the countless miles we've covered on our walks, for the hours of conversation, curiosity, laughter and tears. My life is so much bigger with you in it. While our other brothers seem far at times, we know they're always there. Our parents' hearts would be brimming.

My children! To Cody, Madison, and Ryder; a rising pilot, Functional Training/Nutrition extraordinaire, and Environmental Scientist — my pride is boundless! And, oh, how we have inspired each other to make our dreams real! I love each of you beyond measure.

About the Author

Doreen Burliss, author of *We'll Always Have Nantucket*, and former lifestyle columnist and newspaper correspondent, lives in a small woodsy town north of Boston with her husband, two fat cats and a dog. They have three grown children who, alas, have all flown the coop. *That Nantucket Summer* is her second novel.

PHOTO BY: ALYSSA BAYLEY